SOUTH WITH SCOTT

Printed in Great Britain

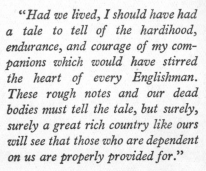

"Had we lived, I should have had a tale to tell of the hardihood, endurance, and courage of my companions which would have stirred the heart of every Englishman. These rough notes and our dead bodies must tell the tale, but surely, surely a great rich country like ours will see that those who are dependent on us are properly provided for."

[Signed] R. Scott.

General Editor : JOHN R. CROSSLAND

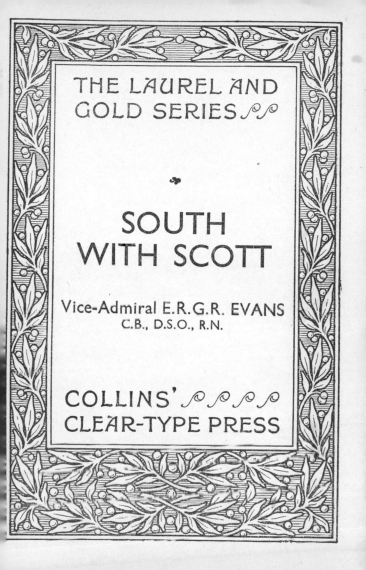

THE LAUREL AND
GOLD SERIES

SOUTH
WITH SCOTT

Vice-Admiral E. R. G. R. EVANS
C.B., D.S.O., R.N.

COLLINS'
CLEAR-TYPE PRESS

PREFACE

THE object of this book is to keep alive the interest of English-speaking people in the story of Scott and his little band of sailor-adventurers, scientific explorers, and companions. It is written more particularly for Britain's younger generations.

I have to acknowledge with gratitude the assistance of Miss Zeala Wakeford Cox of Shanghai and Paymaster Lieutenant-Commander Bernard Carter of H.M.S. *Carlisle*.

Without their help, I doubt if the book would have found its way into print.

EDWARD R. G. R. EVANS.

HONG-KONG
   February, 27, 1921.

BRITISH ANTARCTIC EXPEDITION, 1910.

PERSONNEL

Shore Parties.

ROBERT FALCON SCOTT Captain, C.V.O., R.N. (The "Owner," "The Boss").

EDWARD R. G. R. EVANS Lieut. R.N. (" Teddy").

VICTOR L. A. CAMPBELL Lieut. R.N. (" The Wicked Mate").

HENRY R. BOWERS Lieut. R.I.M. (" Birdie").

LAWRENCE E. G. OATES Captain 6th Inns. Dragoons (" Titus," " Soldier").

G. MURRAY LEVICK Surgeon R.N.

EDWARD L. ATKINSON Surgeon R.N., Parasitologist (" Atch ").

Scientific Staff.

EDWARD ADRIAN WILSON B.A., M.B. (Cantab.), Chief of the Scientific Staff, and Zoologist (" Uncle Bill").

GEORGE C. SIMPSON D.Sc., Meteorologist (" Sunny Jim ").

T. GRIFFITH TAYLOR B.A., B.Sc., B. E., Geologist (Griff ").

EDWARD W. NELSON Biologist (" Marie ").

FRANK DEBENHAM B.A., B.Sc., Geologist (' Deb.')

CHARLES S. WRIGHT B.A., Physicist.

RAYMOND E. PRIESTLEY Geologist.

HERBERT G. PONTING F.R.G.S., Camera Artist.

PERSONNEL

CECIL H. MEARES	In charge of dogs.
BERNARD C. DAY	Motor Engineer.
APSLEY CHERRY-GARRARD	B.A., Asst. Zoologist ("Cherry").
TRYGGVE GRAN	Sub.-Lieut. Norwegian N.R., B.A., Ski Expert.

Men.

W. LASHLY	C. Stoker, R.N.
W. W. ARCHER	Chief Steward, late R.N.
THOMAS CLISSOLD	Cook, late R.N.
EDGAR EVANS	Petty Officer, R.N.
ROBERT FORDE	Petty Officer, R.N.
THOMAS CREAN	Petty Officer, R.N.
THOMAS S. WILLIAMSON	Petty Officer, R.N.
PATRICK KEOHANE	Petty Officer, R.N.
GEORGE P. ABBOTT	Petty Officer, R.N.
FRANK V. BROWNING	Petty Officer, 2nd Class, R.N.
HARRY DICKASON	Able Seaman, R.N.
F. J. HOOPER	Steward, late R.N.
ANTON OMELCHENKO	Groom.
DIMITRI GEROF	Dog Driver.

Ship's Party

HARRY L. L. PENNELL	Lieutenant, R.N.
HENRY E. DE P. RENNICK	Lieutenant. R.N.
WILFRED M. BRUCE	Lieutenant, R.N.R.
FRANCIS R. H. DRAKE	Assistant Paymaster, R.N. (Retired), Secretary and Meteorologist in ship.
DENNIS G. LILLIE	M.A., Biologist in ship.
JAMES R. DENNISTOUN	In charge of Mules in ship.
ALFRED B. CHEETHAM	R.N.R., Boatswain.

PERSONNEL

WILLIAM WILLIAMS	Chief Engine Room Artificer, R.N., Engineer.
WILLIAM A. HORTON	Engine Room Artificer, 3rd Class, R.N., 2nd Engineer.
FRANCIS E. C. DAVIES	Leading Shipwright, R.N.
FREDERICK PARSONS	Petty Officer, R.N.
WILLIAM L. HEALD	Late Petty Officer, R. N.
ARTHUR S. BAILEY	Petty Officer, 2nd Class, R.N.
ALBERT BALSON	Leading Seaman, R.N.
JOSEPH LEESE	Able Seaman, R.N.
JOHN HUGH MATHER	Petty Officer, R.N.V.R.
ROBERT OLIPHANT	Able Seaman.
THOMAS F. McLEOD	Able Seaman.
MORTIMER McCARTHY	Able Seaman.
WILLIAM KNOWLES	Able Seaman.
CHARLES WILLIAMS	Able Seaman.
JAMES SKELTON	Able Seaman.
WILLIAM McDONALD	Able Seaman.
JAMES PATON	Able Seaman.
ROBERT BRISSENDEN	Leading Stoker, R.N.
EDWARD A. McKENZIE	Leading Stoker, R.N.
WILLIAM BURTON	Leading Stoker, R.N.
BERNARD J. STONE	Leading Stoker, R.N.
ANGUS McDONALD	Fireman.
THOMAS McGILLON	Fireman.
CHARLES LAMMAS	Fireman.
W. H. NEALE	Steward.

CONTENTS

CHAPTER I

SOUTH POLAR EXPEDITION—OUTFIT AND AIMS

IT is nine years since the last supporting party bid farewell to Captain Scott and his four brave companions, whose names are still fresh in the memory of those who were interested in Captain Scott's last Polar Expedition. The Great War has come and gone and the majority of us wish to forget it, but the story of Scott undoubtedly appeals still to a great number of people. It is a good story, and my only hope is that I can retell it well enough to make my volume worth while reading after so much has already been published concerning the work of the British Antarctic Expedition of 1910.

The main object of our expedition was to reach the South Pole and secure for the British nation the honour of that achievement, but the attainment of the Pole was far from being the only object in view, for Scott intended to extend his former discoveries and bring back a rich harvest of scientific results. Certainly no expedition ever left our shores with a more ambitious scientific programme, nor was any enterprise of this description ever undertaken by a more enthusiastic and determined personnel. We should never have collected our expeditionary funds merely from the scientific point of view; in fact, many of our largest supporters cared not one iota

13

for science, but the idea of the Polar adventure captured their interest. On the other hand, a number of our supporters affected a contempt for the Polar dash and only interested themselves in the question of advanced scientific study in the Antarctic. As the expedition progressed, however, the most unenthusiastic member of the company developed the serious taste, and in no case did we ever hear from the scientific staff complaints that the Naval members failed to help them in their work with a zeal that was quite unexpected. This applies more particularly to the seamen and stokers.

Captain Scott originally intended to make his winter quarters in King Edward VII. Land, but altered the arrangement after the fullest discussion with his scientific friends and advisers, and planned that a small party of six should examine this part of the Antarctic and follow the coast southward from its junction with the Great Ice Barrier, penetrating as far south as they were able, surveying geographically and geologically. This part of the programme was never carried out, owing to the ice conditions thereabouts preventing a landing either on the Barrier or in King Edward VII. Land itself.

The main western party Scott planned to command himself, the base to be at Cape Crozier or in McMurdo Sound, near the site of the *Discovery's* old winter quarters at Cape Armitage, the exact position to be governed by the ice conditions on arrival.

Dogs, ponies, motor sledges and man-hauling parties on ski were to perform the Polar journey by a system of relays or supporting parties. Scott's

old comrade, Dr. E. A. Wilson of Cheltenham, was
selected as chief of the scientific staff and to act as
artist to the expedition. Three geologists were
chosen and two biologists, to continue the study of
marine fauna and carry out research work in depths
up to 500 fathoms. The expeditionary ship was to
be fitted for taking deep-sea soundings and magnetic
observations, and the meteorological programme
included the exploration of the upper air currents
and the investigation of the electrical conditions of
the atmosphere. We were fortunate in securing as
meteorologist the eminent physicist, Dr. G. Simpson,
who is now head of the Meteorological Office in
London. Dr. Simpson was to have charge of the
self-recording magnetic instruments ashore at the
main base.

Study of ice structure and glaciation was undertaken by Mr. C. S. Wright, who was also assistant
physicist. The magnetic work of the ship was
entrusted to Lieut. Harry Pennell, R.N., an officer
of more than ordinary scientific attainments and a
distinguished navigator. Lieut. Henry Rennick was
given control of the hydrographical survey work
and deep-sea sounding. Two surgeons were lent
by the Royal Navy for the study of bacteriology
and parasitology in addition to their medical
duties, and Mr. Herbert G. Ponting was chosen
as camera artist and cinematographer to the
Expedition.

To my mind the outfit and preparations were the
hardest part of our work, for we were not assured
of funds until the day of our departure. This did
not lighten Scott's burden. The plans of the British
Antarctic Expedition of 1910 were first published
on September 13, 1909, but although Scott's appeal

to the nation was heartily endorsed by the Press, it was not until the spring of 1910 that we had collected the first £10,000. Personally, I was despatched to South Wales and the west of England to raise funds from my Welsh and west country friends. Scott, himself, when he could be spared from the Admiralty, worked Newcastle, Liverpool, and the North, whilst both of us did what we could in London to obtain the money necessary to purchase and equip the ship. It was an anxious time for Scott and his supporters, but after the first £10,000 had been raised the Government grant of £20,000 followed and the Expedition came properly into being. Several individuals subscribed £1000 each, and Government grants were subsequently made by the Australian Commonwealth, the Dominion of New Zealand and South Africa. Capt. L. E. G. Oates and Mr. Apsley Cherry-Garrard were included in the donors of £1000, but they gave more than this, for these gallant gentlemen gave their services and one of them his life. An unexpected and extremely welcome contribution came from Mr. Samuel Hordern of Sydney in the shape of £2500, at a time when we needed it most. Many firms gave in cash as well as in kind. Indeed, were it not for the generosity of such firms it is doubtful whether we could have started. The services of Paymaster Lieut. Drake, R.N., were obtained as secretary to the Expedition. Offices were taken and furnished in Victoria Street, S.W., and Sir Edgar Speyer kindly consented to act as Hon. Treasurer--without hesitation I may say we owe more to Sir Edgar than ever we can repay.

We were somewhat limited in our choice of a

ship, suitable for the work contemplated. The best vessel of all was of course the *Discovery*, which had been specially constructed for the National Antarctic Expedition in 1900, but she had been acquired by the Hudson Bay Company, and although the late Lord Strathcona, then High Commissioner for Canada, was approached, he could not see his way to obtaining her for us in view of her important employment as supply ship for the Hudson Bay Trading Stations. There remained the *Aurora*, *Morning*, *Björn*, *Terra Nova*, Shackleton's stout little *Nimrod*, and one or two other old whaling craft. The *Björn*, a beautiful wooden whaler, would have served our purpose excellently, but, alas! she was too small for the enterprise and we had to fall back on the *Terra Nova*, an older ship but a much larger craft. The *Terra Nova* had one great defect—she was not economic in the matter of coal consumption. She was the largest and strongest of the old Scotch whalers, had proved herself in the Antarctic pack-ice and acquitted herself magnificently in the Northern ice-fields in whaling and sealing voyages extending over a period of twenty years. In spite of her age she had considerable power for a vessel of that type.

After a preliminary survey in Newfoundland, which satisfied us as to her seaworthiness in all respects, the *Terra Nova* was purchased for the Expedition by Messrs. David Bruce & Sons for the sum of £12,500. It seems a high price, but this meant nothing more than her being chartered to us for £2000 a year, since her owners were ready to pay a good price for the ship if we returned her in reasonably good condition at the conclusion of the Expedition.

Captain Scott handed her over to me to fit out, whilst he busied himself more with the scientific programme and the question of finance. We had her barque-rigged and altered according to the requirements of the expedition. A large, well-insulated ice-house was erected on the upper deck which held 150 carcases of frozen mutton, and, owing to the position of the cold chamber, free as it was from the vicinity of iron, we mounted here our standard compass and Lloyd Creek pedestal for magnetic work. Our range-finder was also mounted on the ice-house. A new stove was put in the galley, a lamp room and paraffin store built, and store-rooms, instrument, and chronometer rooms were added. A tremendous alteration was made in the living spaces both for officers and men. Twenty-four bunks were fitted around the saloon accommodation, whilst for the seamen and warrant officers hammock space or bunks were provided. It was proposed to take six warrant officers, including carpenter, ice-master, boatswain, and chief steward. Quite good laboratories were constructed on the poop, while two large magazines and a clothing-store were built up between decks, and these particular spaces were zinc-lined to keep them damp-free. The ship required alteration rather than repair, and there were only one or two places where timber had rotted and these were soon found and reinforced.

I shall never forget the day I first visited the *Terra Nova* in the West India Docks : she looked so small and out of place surrounded by great liners and cargo-carrying ships, but I loved her from the day I saw her, because she was my first command. Poor little ship, she looked so dirty and uncared for and yet her name will be remembered for ever in the story of the sea, which one can hardly say in the case of the stately liners which dwarfed her in the docks. I often blushed when admirals came down to see our ship, she was so very dirty. To begin with, her hold contained large blubber tanks, the stench of whale oil and seal blubber being overpowering, and the remarks of those who insisted on going all over the ship need not be here set down. However, the blubber tanks were withdrawn, the hold spaces got the thorough cleansing and whitewashing that they so badly needed. The bilges were washed out, the ship disinfected fore and aft, and a gang of men employed for some time to sweeten her up. Then came the fitting out, which was much more pleasant work.

Scott originally intended to leave England with most of the members of the Expedition on August 1, 1910, but he realised that an early start from New Zealand would mean a better chance for the big depot-laying journey he had planned to undertake before the first Antarctic winter set in. Accordingly the sailing date was anticipated, thanks to the united efforts of all concerned with the fitting out, and we made June 1 our day of departure, which meant a good deal of overtime everywhere.

The ship had to be provisioned and stored for her long voyage, having in view the fact that there were no ship-chandlers in the Polar regions, but those of us who had "sailed the way before" had a slight inkling that we might meet more ships, and *others* who would lend us a helping hand in the matter of Naval stores.

Captain Scott allowed me a sum with which to equip the *Terra Nova ;* it seemed little enough to me but it made quite a hole in our funds. There were boatswain's stores to be purchased, wire hawsers, canvas for sail-making, fireworks for signalling, whale boats and whaling gear, flags, logs, paint, tar, carpenter's stores, blacksmith's outfit, lubricating oils, engineer's stores, and a multitude of necessities to be thought of, selected, and not paid for if we could help it. The verb " to wangle " had not then appeared in the English language, so we just " obtained."

The expedition had many friends, and it was not unusual to find Petty Officers and men from the R.N.V.R. working on board and helping us on Saturday afternoons and occasionally even on Sundays. They gave their services for nothing, and the only way in which we could repay them was to select two chief Petty Officers from their number, disrate them, and take them Poleward as ordinary seamen.

It was not until the spring of 1910 that we could afford to engage any officers or men for the ship, so that most of the work of rigging her was done by dock-side workers under a good old master rigger named Malley. Landsmen would have stared wide-eyed and open-mouthed at Malley's men with their diminutive dolly-winch had they watched our new masts and yards being got into place.

Six weeks before sailing day Lieut. Campbell took over the duties of Chief Officer in the *Terra Nova*, Pennell and Rennick also joined, and Lieut. Bowers came home from the Indian Marine to begin his duties as Stores Officer by falling down the main hatch on to the pig iron ballast. I did not witness this accident, and when Campbell reported the matter I am reported to have said, " What a silly ass ! " This may have been true, for coming all the way from Bombay to join us and then immediately falling down the hatch did seem a bit careless. However, when Campbell added that Bowers had not hurt himself my enthusiasm returned and I said, " What a splendid fellow ! " Bowers fell nineteen feet without injuring himself in the slightest. This was only one of his narrow escapes and he proved himself to be about the toughest man amongst us.

Quite a lot could be written of the volunteers for service with Scott in this his last Antarctic venture. There were nearly 8000 of them to select from, and many eligible men were turned down simply because they were frozen out by those who had previous Antarctic experience. We tried to select fairly, and certainly picked a representative crowd. It was not an all-British Expedition because we included amongst us a young Norwegian ski-runner and two Russians ; a dog driver and a groom. The Norwegian has since distinguished himself in the Royal Air Force—he was severely wounded in the war whilst fighting for the British and their Allies, but his pluck and Anglophile sentiments cost him his commission in the Norwegian Flying Corps.

Dr. Wilson assisted Captain Scott in selecting the scientific staff, while the choice of the officers and crew was mainly left to myself as Commander-elect of the *Terra Nova*.

Most Polar expeditions sail under the Burgee of some yacht club or other. We were ambitious to fly the White Ensign, and to enable this to be done the Royal Yacht Squadron adopted us. Scott was elected a member, and it cost him £100, which the Expedition could ill afford. However, with the *Terra Nova* registered as a yacht we were able to evade those Board of Trade officials who declared that she was not a well-found merchant ship within the meaning of the Act. Having avoided the scrutiny of the efficient and official, we painted out our Plimsoll mark with tongue in cheek and eyelid drooped, and, this done, took our stores aboard and packed them pretty tight. The Crown Preserve Co. sent us a quantity of patent fuel which stowed beautifully as a flooring to the lower hold, and all our provision cases were thus kept well up out of the bilge water which was bound to scend to and fro if we made any quantity of water, as old wooden ships usually do. The day before sailing the Royal Geographical Society entertained Scott and his party at luncheon in the King's Hall, Holborn Restaurant. About 300 Fellows of the Society were present to do us honour. The President, Major Leonard Darwin, proposed success to the Expedition, and in the course of his speech wished us God-speed. He congratulated Captain Scott on having such a well-found expedition and, apart from dwelling on the scientific and geographical side of the venture, the President said that Captain Scott was going to prove once again that the manhood of our nation was not dead and that the characteristics of our ancestors who won our great Empire still flourished amongst us.

After our leader had replied to this speech Sir Clements Markham, father of modern British exploration, proposed the toast of the officers and staff in the most touching terms. Poor Sir Clements is no more, but it was he who first selected Captain Scott for Polar work, and he, indeed, who was responsible for many others than those present at lunch joining Antarctic expeditions, myself included.

CHAPTER II

VOYAGE OF THE "TERRA NOVA"

SAILING day came at last, and on June 1, 1910, when I proudly showed Scott his ship, he very kindly ordered the hands aft and thanked them for what they had done.

The yards were square, the hatches on with spick-and-span white hatch covers, a broad white ribbon brightened the black side, and gold leaf bedizened the quarter badges besides gilding the rope scroll on the stern. The ship had been well painted up, a neat harbour furl put on the sails, and if the steamers and lofty sailing vessels in the basin could have spoken, their message would surely have been, "Well done, little 'un."

What a change from the smudgy little lamp-black craft of last November—so much for paint and polish. All the same it was the *Terra Nova's* Indian summer. A close search by the technically expert would have revealed scars of age in the little lady, furrows worn in her sides by grinding ice floes, patches in the sails, strengthening pieces in the cross-trees and sad-looking deadeyes and lanyards which plainly told of a bygone age.

But the merchant seamen who watched from the dock side were kind and said nothing. The old admirals who had come down to visit the ship were used to these things, or perhaps they did not twig it. After all, what did it matter, it was sailing day, we were all as proud as peacocks of our little ship, and from that day forward we pulled together and played the game, or tried to.

Lady Bridgeman, wife of the first Sea Lord, and Lady Markham hoisted the White Ensign and the Burgee of the Royal Yacht Squadron an hour or so before sailing. At 4.45 p.m. the visitors were warned off the ship, and a quarter of an hour later we slipped from our wharf in the South-West India Docks and proceeded into the river and thence to Greenhithe, where we anchored off my old training ship, the *Worcester*, and gave the cadets a chance to look over the ship. On the 3rd June we arrived at Spithead, where we were boarded by Captain Chetwynd, Superintendent of Compasses at the Admiralty, who swung the ship and adjusted our compasses. Captain Scott joined us on the 4th and paid a visit with his " yacht " to the R.Y.S. at Cowes. On the 6th we completed a series of magnetic observations in the Solent, after which many officers were entertained by Captain Mark Kerr in the ill-fated *Invincible*. We were royally looked after, but I am ashamed to say we cleared most of his canvas and boatswain's stores out of the ship. Perhaps a new 3½-inch hawser found its way to the *Terra Nova ;* anyway, if the *Invincible's* stores came on board the exploring vessel she made good use of them and saved them their Jutland fate. We left the Solent in high feather on the following day.

The *Sea Horse* took us in tow to the Needles, from whence H.M.S. *Cumberland*, Cadets' Training Ship, towed us to Weymouth Bay. This was poor Scott's last Naval review. He had landed at Portsmouth and busied himself with the Expedition's affairs and rejoined us at Weymouth in time to steam through the Home Fleet assembled in Portland Harbour. We steamed out of the ' hole in the wall ' at the western end of Portland Breakwater and rounded Portland Bill at sunset on our way to Cardiff, where we were to be received by my own Welsh friends and endowed with all good things. We were welcomed by the citizens of the great Welsh seaport with enthusiasm. Free docking, free coal, defects made good for nothing, an office and staff placed at our disposal, in fact everything was done with an open-hearted generosity. We took another 300 tons of patent fuel on board and nearly 100 tons of Insole's best Welsh steaming coal, together with the bulk of our lubricating oils. When complete with fuel we met with our first setback, for the little ship settled deeply in the water and the seams, which had up till now been well above the water-line, leaked in a way that augured a gloomy future for the crew in the nature of pumping. With steam up this did not mean anything much, but under sail alone, unless we could locate the leaky seams, it meant half an hour to an hour's pumping every watch. We found a very leaky spot in the fore peak, which was mostly made good by cementing.

On the 15th June we left the United Kingdom after a rattling good time in Cardiff. Many shore boats and small craft accompanied us down the Bristol Channel as far as Breaksea Light Vessel. We hoisted the Cardiff flag at the fore and the Welsh flag at the mizen—some wag pointed to the flag and asked why we had not a leek under it, and I felt bound to reply that we had a leak in the fore peak !

It was a wonderful send-off and we cheered ourselves hoarse. Captain Scott left with our most intimate friends in the pilot boat and we proceeded a little sadly on our way.

After passing Lundy Island we experienced a head wind and the gentle summer swell of the Atlantic. In spite of her deeply-laden condition the *Terra Nova* breasted each wave in splendid form, lifting her toy bowsprit proudly in the air till she reminded me, with her deck cargo, of a little mother with her child upon her back.

Our first port of call was Madeira, where it was proposed to bunker, and we made good passage to the island under steam and sail for the most part. We stayed a couple of days coaling and taking magnetic observations at Funchal, then ran out into the north-east Trades, let fires out, and became a sailing ship.

Whilst lazily gazing at fertile Madeira from our anchorage we little dreamt that within two months the distinguished Norseman, Roald Amundsen, would be unfolding his plans to his companions on board the *Fram* in this very anchorage, plans which changed the whole published object of his expedition, plans which culminated in the triumph of the Norwegian flag over our own little Union Jack, and plans which caused our people a fearful disappointment—for Amundsen's ultimate success meant our failure to achieve the main object of our Expedition : to plant the British Flag first at the South Pole.

Under sail ! Quite a number of the scientists and crew had never been to sea in a sailing ship before, but a fair wind and a collection of keen and smiling young men moving about the decks were particularly refreshing to me after the year of fund collecting and preparation.

We learnt to know a great deal about one another on the outward voyage to New Zealand, where we were to embark our dogs and ponies. The most surprising personality was Bowers, considering all things.

Officers, scientists, and the watch worked side by side trimming coals and restoring the 'tween decks as cases were shaken and equipment assembled. The scientific staff were soon efficient at handling, reefing, and steering. Every one lent a hand at whatever work was going. Victor Campbell was christened the " Wicked Mate," and he shepherded and fathered the afterguard delightfully.

Wilson and I shared the Captain's cabin, and when there was nothing afoot he made lovely sea sketches and water colour drawings to keep his hand in. Certainly Uncle Bill[1] had copy enough in those days of sunlit seas and glorious sunrises. He was up always an hour before the sun and missed very little that was worth recording with his artistic touch. Wilson took Cherry-Garrard under his wing and brought him up as it were in the shadow of his own unselfish character. We had no adventures to record until the last week in July beyond the catching of flying-fish, singing chanties at the pump, and Lillie getting measles. We isolated him in the dark room, which, despite its name, was one of the lightest and freshest rooms in the ship. Atkinson took charge of the patient and Lillie could not have been in the hands of a better or more cheery medico.

[1] Dr. Wilson's nickname.

Not all of the members of the Expedition had embarked in England, although the majority came out in the ship to save expense.

Captain Scott had remained behind to squeeze out more subscriptions and to complete arrangements with the Central News, which he was making in order to give the world's newspapers the story of the Expedition for simultaneous publication as reports came back to civilisation in the *Terra Nova*. He also had finally to settle magazine and cinematograph contracts which were to help pay for the Expedition, and lastly, our leader, with Drake and Wyatt, the business manager, were to pay bills we had incurred by countless items of equipment, large and small, which went to fill up our lengthy stores lists. Thankless work enough—we in the ship were much better off with no cares now beyond the handling of our toy ship and her safe conduct to Lyttelton. Cecil Meares and Lieut. Bruce were on their way through Siberia collecting dogs and ponies. Ponting was purchasing the photographic and cinematographic outfit, Griffith Taylor, Debenham, and Priestley, our three geologists, and Day, the motor engineer, were to join us in New Zealand, and Captain Scott with Drake at Capetown.

In order to get another series of magnetic observations and to give the staff relief from the monotony of the voyage as well as an opportunity for doing a little special work, we stopped at the uninhabited island of South Trinidad for a couple of days, arriving on July 26.

Trinidad Island looked magnificent with its towering peaks as we approached it by moonlight. We dropped anchor shortly after dawn, the ship

was handed over to the Wicked Mate and Boatswain, who set up the rigging and delighted themselves with a seamanlike refit. Campbell had a
party over the side scrubbing the weeds off, and
many of the ship's company attempted to harpoon
the small sharks which came close round in shoals
and provided considerable amusement. These fish
were too small to be dangerous. After breakfast
all the scientists and most of the officers landed
and were organised by Uncle Bill into small parties
to collect birds' eggs, flowers, specimens, to
photograph and to sketch. A good lunch was taken
ashore, and we looked more like a gunroom picnic
party than a scientific expedition when we left
the ship in flannels and all manner of weird cos-
tumes. Wilson, Pennell, and Cherry-Garrard shot
a number of birds, mostly terns and gannets, and
climbed practically to the top of the island, where
they could see the Martin Vaz islets on the horizon.
Wilson secured some Trinidad petrels, both white
breasted and black breasted, and discovered that
the former is the young bird and the latter the
adult of the same species. He found them in the
same nests. We collected many terns' eggs ; the
tern has no nest but lays its eggs on a smooth
rock. Also one or two frigate birds were caught.
Nelson worked along the beach, finding sea-urchins,
anemones, and worms, which he taught the sailors
the names of—polycheats and sepunculids, I think
he called them. He caught various fishes, including
sea-perches, garfish, coralfish, and an eel, a small
octopus and a quantity of sponges. Trigger-fish
were so abundant that many of them were speared
from the ship with the greatest of ease, and Rennick
harpooned a couple from a boat with an ordinary

dinner fork. Lillie, who had recovered from measles, was all about, and his party went for flowering plants and lichens. He climbed to the summit of the island—2000 ft.—and gave it as his opinion that the dead trees strewn all round the base of the island had been carried down with the volcanic debris from higher altitudes. It was also his suggestion that the island had only recently risen, the trees which originally grew on the top of the island having died from unsuitable climate in the higher condition. Gran went up with Lillie and took photographs. " Birdie " Bowers and Wright were employed collecting insects, and, with those added by the rest of us, the day's collection included all kinds of ants, cockroaches, grasshoppers, mayflies, a centipede, fifteen different species of spider, locusts, a cricket, woodlice, a parasite fly, a beetle, and a moth. We failed to get any of the dragonflies seen, and, to the great sorrow of the crews who landed with us, missed capturing a most beautiful chestnut-coloured mouse with a fur tail. Land crabs, a dirty yellow in colour, were found everywhere, the farther one went inland the bigger were the crabs. The blue shore crabs were only to be seen near the sea or along the coast and water courses. Several of these were brought off to the ship for Dr. Atkinson to play with, and he found nematodes in them, and parasites in the birds and fish.

During the afternoon a swell began to roll in the bay and those on board the ship hoisted the warning signal and fired a sound rocket to recall the scattered parties. By 4.30 we had reassembled on the rocks where we had landed in the forenoon, but the rollers being fifteen feet high, it was obviously unwise to send off cameras and perishable gear, and since it was equally inadvisable to leave the whole party ashore without food and sufficient clothing and the prospect of an inhospitable island home for days, we all swam off one by one, the boat's crew working a grassline bent to a lifebuoy. The boat to which we swam was riding to a big anchor a hundred feet from the shore, just outside the surf. There were a few sharks round the whaler, but they were shy and left us alone. Rennick worked round the boat in a small Norwegian pram and scared them away. Many trigger fish swallowed the thick vegetable oil which the boat's crew ladled into the sea to keep the surf down, and I think this probably attracted the sharks, though it was not very nice to swim through. None of us were any the worse for our romp ashore, but the long day and the hot sun tired us all out. Nearly all the afterguard slept on the upper deck that night, and, but for the dismal roar of the swell breaking on the rocks and the heavy rolling of the *Terra Nova*, we spent quite a comfortable night. Dr. Atkinson and Brewster had been left ashore with the gear, but they got no sleep because all night the terns flew round crying and protesting against their intrusion. The wail of these birds sounds like the deep note of a banjo. The two men mostly feared the land crabs, but to their surprise they were left in peace.

Next day about 9 a.m. I went in with Rennick, Bowers, Oates, Gran, and two seamen to the landing place, taking a whaler and pram equipped with grass hawser, breeches buoy, rocket line, and everything necessary to bring off the gear. We had a rough time getting the stuff away undamaged by the sea, but the pram was a wonderful sea-boat and we took it in turns to work her through the surf until everything was away.

At the last, when nearly everything had been salved and got to the whaler, the collections in tin boxes, wooden cases and baskets, and the two men, Atkinson and Brewster, were on board, a large wave threw the pram right up on the rocks, capsizing her and damaging her badly. Her two occupants jumped out just before a second wave swept the boat over and over. Then a third huge roller came up and washed the pram out to sea, where she was recovered by means of a grapnel thrown from the whaler. The two on the rocks had to face the surf again but were good swimmers, and with their recovery our little adventure ended. It was a pity we had bad weather, because I intended to give the crew a run on the island when Campbell had finished with them.

We remained another day under the lee of Trinidad Island owing to a hard blow from the south-east —a dead head wind for us—because I felt it would be useless to put to sea and punch into it. We were anchored one mile S. 4° E (magnetic) from the Ninepin Rock, well sheltered from the prevailing wind. We left Trinidad at noon on the 28th, well prepared for the bad weather expected on approaching the Cape of Good Hope.

Whilst clearing the land we had an excellent view of South West Bay and saw a fine lot of rollers breaking on the beach. I was glad we kept there that day, as, in my opinion, our anchorage was really the only fair one off the island. By noon on the 29th we had left South Trinidad out of sight, the wind had freshened again and we could almost lay our course under sail for the Cape.

B

This next stage of the voyage was merely a story of hard winds and heavy rolls. The ship leaked less as she used up the coal and patent fuel. All the same we spent many hours at the pump, but, since much of the pumping was done by the afterguard—as were called the officers and scientists —we developed and hardened our muscles finely. In the daytime the afterguard were never idle ; there is always plenty to do in a sailing ship, and when not attending to their special duties the scientists were kept working at everything that helped the show along. Whilst on deck they were strictly disciplined and subordinate and respectful to the ship's executive officers, while in the wardroom they fought these same officers in a friendly way for every harsh word and every job they had had imposed on them.

Campbell was a fine seaman ; he was respected and admired by such people as Oates and Atkinson, who willingly pocketed their pride and allowed themselves to be hustled round equally with the youngest seaman on board. The Wicked Mate generally had all the afterguard under the hose before breakfast, as washing water was scarce and the allowance meagre on such a protracted voyage.

In the hotter weather we nearly all slept on deck, the space on top of the ice-house and in the boats being favourite billets. There was no privacy in the ship and only the officers of watches and lookout men were ever left with their thoughts. One or two of the younger members confessed to being homesick, for the voyage was long and it was not at all certain that we should all win back to " England, home, and beauty."

Those who were not sailor men soon acquired the habit of the sea, growing accustomed to meeting fair and foul weather with an equally good face, rejoicing with us sailor men at a fair wind and full sail and standing by top-gallant and topsail halyards when the prospects were more leaden coloured and the barometer falling. We numbered about forty now, which meant heaps of beef to haul on ropes and plenty of trimmers to shift the coal from the hold to the bunkers. One or two were always stoking side by side with the firemen, and in this fashion officers, seamen, and scientific staff cemented a greater friendship and respect for one another.

On August 7, after drinking to absent friends, Oates, Atkinson, and Gran, "the three midshipmen" were confirmed in their rank and a ship's biscuit broken on the head of each in accordance with gunroom practice, and after this day, during good and bad weather, these three kept regular watch with the seamen, going aloft, steering, and taking all the usual duties in their turn.

From the start Pennell, who was to relieve me in command of the ship on her arrival at the Antarctic base, showed an astounding knowledge of birds, and Wilson took the keenest interest in teaching him about bird-life in the Great Southern ocean and giving him a preliminary idea of the bird types to be met with in Antarctica.

Reflecting back to these days one sees how well we all knitted into the places we were to fill, because a long sea-voyage searches out hidden qualities and defects, not that there were many of the latter, still one man developed lung trouble and another had a strained heart. One of these, to our great regret, was forced to leave the expedition before the ship went south, while the other had to be ruled out of the shore party—an awful disappointment to them both.

We reached Simon's Town on August 15, and here the Naval authorities gave us every assistance, lent us working parties and made good our long defect list. We were disappointed on arriving to find that Captain Scott was away in Pretoria, but he succeeded in obtaining a grant of £500 from the South African Government and raised another £500 by private subscription. When Captain Scott came amongst us again he wrote of the *Terra Nova* party that we were all very pleased with the ship and very pleased with ourselves, describing our state of happiness and overflowing enthusiasm exactly.

Those who could be spared were given leave here ; some of us went up-country for a few days and had a chance to enjoy South African scenery. Oates, Atkinson, and Bowers went to Wynberg and temporarily forgot the sea. Oates's one idea was a horse, and he spent his holiday as much on horseback as he possibly could. In a letter he expressed great admiration for the plucky manner in which Atkinson rode to hounds one day at Wynberg. These two were great friends, but it would be hard to imagine two more naturally silent men, and one wonders how evident pleasure can be obtained with a speechless companion.

Scott now changed with Wilson, who went by mail steamer to Australia in order to organise and finally engage the Australian members of our staff.

Our leader was without doubt delighted to make the longer voyage with us in the *Terra Nova* and to get away from the hum of commerce and the small talk of the many people who were pleased to meet him—until the hat was handed round—that awful fund—collecting.

CHAPTER III

ASSEMBLING OF UNITS—DEPARTURE FROM NEW ZEALAND

THE trip from Simon's Town to Melbourne was disappointing on account of the absence of fair winds. We had a few gales, but finer weather than we expected, and took advantage of the ship's steadiness to work out the details for the sledge journeys and depot plans. The lists of those who were to form the two shore parties were published, together with a skeleton list for the ship. The seamen had still to be engaged in New Zealand to complete this party.

A programme was drawn up for work on arrival at winter quarters, a routine made out for McMurdo Sound or Cape Crozier, if it so happened that we could effect a landing there, weights were calculated for the four men sledging-units, sledge tables embellished with equipment weights, weekly allowances of food and fuel, with measures of quantities of each article in pannikins or spoonfuls, provisional dates were set down in the general plan, daily ration lists constructed, the first season's depot party chosen and, in short, a thoroughly comprehensive handbook was made out for our guidance which could be referred to by any member of the Expedition. Even an interior plan of the huts was made to scale for the carpenter's edification.

It was an enormous advantage for us to have our leader with us now, his master mind foresaw every situation so wonderfully as he unravelled plan after plan and organised our future procedure.

Meantime, the seamen were employed preparing the sledge gear, sewing up food bags, making canvas tanks and sledge harness, fitting out Alpine ropes, repair bags, thongs, lampwick bindings, and travelling equipment generally. Gran overlooked the ski and assigned them to their future owners, Petty Officer Evans prepared the sewing outfits for the two shore parties, the cooks assembled mess-traps and cooking utensils, and Levick and Atkinson, under Dr. Wilson's guidance, assembled the medical equipment and fixed up little surgical outfits for sledge parties. By the time we arrived at Melbourne, our next port of call, a great deal had been accomplished and people had a grasp of what was eventually expected of them.

Scott left us again at Melbourne and embarked on yet another begging campaign, whilst I took the ship on to Lyttelton, where the *Terra Nova* was dry-docked with a view to stopping the leak in her bows. The decks, which after her long voyage let water through sadly, were caulked, and barnacles six inches long were taken from her bottom and sides. Whilst in New Zealand all the stores were landed, sorted out and restowed. On a piece of waste ground close to the wharves at Lyttelton the huts were erected in skeleton in order to make certain that no hitch would occur when they were put up at our Antarctic base. Davis, the carpenter, with the seamen told off to assist him, marked each frame and joist, the tongued and grooved boards were roughly cut to measure and tied into bundles ready for sledge transport in case it happened that we could not put the ship close to the winter quarters. Instruments were adjusted, the ice-house re-insulated and prepared to receive the 150 frozen sheep and ten bullocks which were presented to us by New Zealand farmers. Stables were erected under the forecastle and on the upper deck of the *Terra Nova*, ready for the reception of our ponies, and a thousand and one alterations and improvements made. The ship was restowed, and all fancy gear, light sails and personal baggage put ashore., We took on board 464 tons of coal and embarked the three motor sledges, petrol, and paraffin.

We spent four weeks in Port Lyttelton, four weeks of hard work and perfect happiness. Our prospects looked very rosy in those days, and as each new member joined the Expedition here he was cordially welcomed into the *Terra Nova* family.

Mr. J. J. Kinsey acted as agent to the Expedition, as he had done for the National Antarctic Expedition of 1901-4, and, indeed, for every Polar enterprise that has used New Zealand for a base.

New Zealanders showed us unbounded hospitality ; many of us had visited their shores before and stronger ties than those of friendship bound us to this beautiful country.

When we came to Lyttelton, Meares and Bruce had already arrived with nineteen Siberian and Manchurian ponies and thirty-four sledge dogs, and these were now housed at Quail Island in the harbour. All the ponies were white, animals of this colour being accepted as harder than others for snow work, and the dogs were as fine a pack as one could select for hard sledging and rough times. Meares had had adventure in plenty when selecting the dogs and told us modestly enough of his journeys across Russia and Siberia in search of suitable animals. Scott was lucky to get hold of such an experienced traveller as Meares, and the *Terra Nova* gained by the inclusion of Lady Scott's brother, Wilfred Bruce, in the Expedition. Wilfred Bruce was christened " Mumbo," and, although a little older than the rest of the officers, he willingly took a subordinate place, and Pennell, writing of him after the Expedition was finished, said that he withheld his advice when it was not asked for and gave it soundly when it was.

Lieut. Bruce joined Meares at Vladivostock, and he must have thought he was joining a travelling circus when he ran into this outfit. Meares crossed by Trans-Siberian Railway to Vladivostock, thence made preparation to travel round the Sea of Okotsk to collect the necessary dogs. He started off by train to Kharbarovsk, where he got in touch with the Governor-General of Eastern Siberia, General Unterberger, who helped him immensely, got him a good travelling sledge for the trip down the Amur River to Nikolievsk, and wrote a letter which he gave Meares to show at the post-houses and whenever in difficulties. The Governor-General ordered frozen food to be got ready for Meares's journey. A thousand versts[1] had to be traversed, and this only took seven days ; the going was interesting at times, and Meares had good weather on the sledge journey to Nikolievsk, although the cold was intense and sometimes the road was very bad. The sledges were horse-drawn between the post-houses.

Mr. Rogers, the English manager of the Russo-

[1] Roughly 660 miles.

Chinese Bank of Nikolievsk, helped Meares considerably in securing the dogs. Most of them were
picked up in the neighbourhood of that place, but
were not chosen before they had been given some
hard driving tests. In one of the trial journeys the
dogs pulled down a horse and nearly killed it before
they could be beaten off. Some of them have a good
deal of the wolf in their blood.

A settlement of " fish-skin " Indians was visited
in the dog search, and Meares told us of natives who
dressed in cured skins of salmon. These people
were expert hunters who trekked weeks on end with
just a pack of food on their backs, their travelling
being done on snowshoes.

After taking great pains, thirty-four fine dogs
were collected, all used to hard sledge travelling,
and these Meares shipped on board steamer which
took him and his menagerie by river to Kharbarovsk. The journey to Vladivostock was by
train. The Russian officials allowed him to hitch
on a couple of cattle trucks containing the dogs
to the mail train for that part of the journey.

Russian soldiers and Chinamen were detailed by
the Governor-General to assist the procession
through the streets of Vladivostock to their kennels
here. A slight upset was caused by a mad dog
rushing in amongst them, but fortunately it was
killed before any of our dogs were bitten. Some
of them were flecked by the foam from the mad
dog's jaws, but none were any the worse after
a good carbolic bath. After the dogs were settled
and in good shape the ponies were collected and
brought from up-country in batches. On arrival
at the Siberian capital they were examined by the
Government vet., after which Meares and an

Australian trainer picked the best, until a score were purchased. Horse boxes were obtained now and feed tins made for the voyage and, after minor troubles with shipping firms, Meares, Bruce, and three Russians sailed from Vladivostock in a Japanese steamer which conveyed them to Kobe. Here they transhipped into a German vessel that took then via Hong-kong, Manila, New Guinea, Rockhampton, and Brisbane, to Sydney. There the animals were inoculated for the N'th time and a good deal of palaver indulged in before they were again shifted to the Lyttelton steamer. The poor beasts suffered from the heat, particularly the dogs, although they had been close-clipped for the long and trying voyage.

At Wellington, New Zealand, Meares was compelled to tranship the animals to yet another steamer. When the travelling circus was safely installed in Quail Island our dogs and ponies had undergone shipments, transhipments, inoculations and disinfectings sufficient to make them glad to leave civilisation, and we had to thank Meares for his patience in getting them down without any losses.

We sailed from Lyttelton on November 25 for Port Chalmers, had a tremendous send-off and a great deal of cheering as the ship moved slowly away from the piers. Bands played us out of harbour and most of the ships flew farewell messages, which we did our best to answer.

Some members went down by train to Dunedin and joined us at Port Chalmers. We filled up here with what coal we could squeeze into our already overloaded ship and left finally for the Great Unknown on November 29, 1910.

Lady Scott, Mrs. Wilson, and my own wife came out with us to the Heads and then went on board the *Plucky* tug after saying good-bye. We were given a rousing send-off by the small craft that accompanied us a few miles on our way, but they turned homeward at last and at 3.30 p.m. we were clear with all good-byes said—personally I had a heart like lead, but, with every one else on board, bent on doing my duty and following Captain Scott to the end. There was work to be done, however, and the crew were glad of the orders that sent them from one rope to another and gave them the chance to hide their feelings, for there is an awful feeling of loneliness at this point in the lives of those who sign on the ships of the "South Pole trade"—how glad we were to hide those feelings and make sail—there were some dreadfully flat jokes made with the best of good intentions when we watched dear New Zealand fading away as the spring night gently obscured her from our view.

CHAPTER IV

THROUGH STORMY SEAS

AFTER all it was a relief to get going at last and to have the Expedition on board in its entirety, but what a funny little colony of souls. A floating farm-yard best describes the appearance of the upper deck, with the white pony heads peeping out of their stables, dogs chained to stanchions, rails, and ring-bolts, pet rabbits lolloping around the ready supply of compressed hay, and forage here, there, and everywhere. If the *Terra Nova* was deeply laden from Cardiff, imagine what she looked like leaving New Zealand. We had piled coal in sacks wherever it could be wedged in between the deck cargo of petrol. Paraffin and oil drums filled up most of the hatch spaces, for the poop had been rendered uninhabitable by the great wooden cases containing two of our motor sledges.

The seamen were excellent, and Captain Scott seemed delighted with the crowd. He and Wilson were very loyal to the old *Discovery* men we had with us and Scott was impressed with my man, Cheetham, the Merchant Service boatswain, and could not quite make out how " Alf," as the sailors called him, got so much out of the hands—this little squeaky-voiced man—I think we hit on Utopian conditions for working the ship. There were no wasters, and our seamen were the pick of the British Navy and Mercantile Marine. Most of the Naval men were intelligent petty officers and were as fully alive as the merchantmen to "Alf's" windjammer[1] knowledge. Cheetham was quite a character, and besides being immensely popular and loyal he was a tough, humorous little soul who had made more Antarctic voyages than any man on board.

The seamen and stokers willingly gave up the best part of the crew space in order to allow sheltered pony stables to be built in the forecastle ; it would have fared badly with the poor creatures had we kept them out on deck on the southward voyage.

A visit to the Campbell Islands was projected, but abandoned on account of the ship being unable to lay her course due to strong head winds on December 1. We therefore shaped to cross the Antarctic Circle in 178° W. and got a good run of nearly 200 miles in, but the wind rose that afternoon and a gale commenced at a time when we least could afford to face bad weather in our deeply-laden conditions. By 6 p.m. I had to heave the ship to under lower topsails and fore topmast staysail. Engines were kept going at slow speed to keep the ship under control, but when night fell the prospect was gloomy enough. Captain Scott had consented to my taking far more on board than the ship was ever meant to carry, and we could not expect to accomplish our end without running certain risks. To sacrifice coal meant curtailing the Antarctic cruising programme, but as the weather grew worse we had to consider throwing coal overboard to lighten the vessel. Quite apart from this, the huge waves which washed over the

[1]Sea phrase for sailing ships.

ship swamped everything and increased the deck weights considerably. Ten tons of coal were thrown over to prevent them from taking charge and breaking petrol cases adrift. In spite of a liberal use of oil to keep heavy water from breaking over, the decks were continually swept by the seas and the rolling was so terrific that the poor dogs were almost hanging by their chains. Meares and Dimitri, helped by the watch, tended them unceasingly, but in spite of their combined efforts one dog was washed overboard after being literally drowned on the upper deck. One pony died that night, Oates and Atkinson standing by it and trying their utmost to keep the wretched beast on its feet. A second animal succumbed later, and poor Oates had a most trying time in caring for his charges and rendering what help he could to ameliorate their condition. Those of his shipmates who saw him in this gale will never forget his strong, brown face illuminated by a hanging lamp as he stood amongst those suffering little beasts. He was a fine, powerful man, and on occasions he seemed to be actually lifting the poor little ponies to their feet as the ship lurched heavily to leeward and a great sea would wash the legs of his charges from under them. One felt somehow, glancing into the ponies' stalls, which Captain Scott and I frequently visited together, that Oates's very strength itself inspired his animals with confidence. He himself appeared quite unconscious of any personal suffering, although his hands and feet must have been absolutely numbed by the cold and wet.

In the middle watch Williams, the Chief Engineer, reported that his pumps were choked and that as fast as he cleared them they choked again, the water coming into the ship so fast that the stoke-hold plates were submerged and water gaining fast. I ordered the watch to man the hand-pump, but that was soon choked too. Things now looked really serious, since it was impossible to get to the pump-well while terrific seas were washing over the ship and the afterhatch could not be opened. Consequently we started to bail the water out with buckets and also rigged the small fire-engine and pumped with this as well.

The water in the engine room gradually gained until it entered the ashpit of the centre furnace and commenced to put the fires out. Both Williams and Lashly were up to their necks in water, clearing and re-clearing the engine room pump suctions, but eventually the water beat them and I allowed Williams to let fires out in the boiler. It could not be otherwise. We stopped engines, and with our cases of petrol being lifted out of their lashings by the huge waves, with the ponies falling about and the dogs choking and wallowing in the water and mess, their chains entangling them and tripping up those who tried to clear them, the situation looked as black and disheartening as it well could be.

When dawn broke the greater part of the lee bulwarks had been torn away and our decks laid open to the sea, which washed in and out as it would have over a rock. The poor ship laboured dreadfully, and after consultation with Captain Scott we commenced to cut a hole in the engine room bulkhead to get at the hand pump-well.

Meanwhile I told the afterguard off into watches, and, relieving every two hours, they set to work, formed a chain at the engine room ladder way and bailed the ship out with buckets. In this way they must have discharged between 2000 and 3000 gallons of water. The watch manned the hand pump, which, although choked, discharged a small stream, and for twenty-four hours this game was kept up, Scott himself working with the best of them and staying with the toughest.

It was a sight that one could never forget: everybody saturated, some waist-deep on the floor of the engine room, oil and coal dust mixing with the water and making every one filthy, some men clinging to the iron ladder way and passing full buckets up long after their muscles had ceased to work naturally, their grit and spirit keeping them going. I did admire the weaker people, especially those who were unhardened by the months of physical training of the voyage out from England.

When each two-hour shift was relieved, the party, coughing and spluttering, would make their way into the ward-room where Hooper and Neale, the stewards, mere boys, supplied them with steaming cocoa. How on earth the cooks kept the galley fires going I could never understand: they not only did this, but fed us all at frequent intervals.

By 10 p.m. on the 2nd December the hole in the engine room bulkhead was cut completely. I climbed through it, followed by Bowers, the carpenter, and Teddy Nelson, and when we got into the hold there was just enough room to wriggle along to the pump-well over the coal. We tore down a couple of planks to get access to the shaft and then I went down to the bottom to find out how matters stood. Bowers came next with an electric torch, which he shone downwards whilst I got into the water, hanging on to the bottom rungs of the ladder leading to the bilge. Sitting on the keel the water came up to my neck and, except for my head, I was under water till after midnight passing up coal balls, the cause of all the trouble. Though, of course, we had washed out the bilges in New Zealand, the constant stream of water which leaked in from the topsides had carried much coal-dust into them. This, mixed with the lubricating oil washed down from the engines, had cemented into buns and balls which found their way down and choked both hand and engine pump suctions. I sent up twenty bucketfuls of this filthy stuff, which meant frequently going head under the unspeakably dirty water, but having cleared the lower ends of the suction pipe the watch manning the hand pump got the water down six inches, and it was obvious by 4 o'clock in the morning that the pump was gaining. We therefore knocked the afterguard off bailing, and the seamen worked steadily at the pump until 9 a.m. and got the water right down to nine inches, so we were able to light fires again and once more raise steam. We made a serviceable wire grating to put round the hand pump suction to keep the bigger stuff from choking the pipes in future. It was days before some of us could get our hair clean from that filthy coal-oil mixture.

One more pony died during the gale, but when the weather moderated early on the 3rd, the remaining seventeen animals bucked up and, when not eating their food, nonchalantly gnawed great gaps in the stout planks forming the head parts of their stalls. At last the sun came out and helped to dry the dogs. Campbell and his seamen cleared up the decks and re-secured the top hamper in the forenoon, we reset sail, and after tea Scott,

Oates, Atkinson, and a few more of us hoisted the two dead ponies out of the forecastle, through the skylight, and over the side. It was a dirty job, because the square of the hatch was so small that a powerful purchase had to be used which stretched out the ponies like dead rabbits.

We only made good twenty-three miles that day and, although the gale had abated, it left us a legacy in the shape of a heavy uncomfortable swell. Most of the bunks were in a sad state, the ship having worked so badly that the upper deck seams opened everywhere and water had literally poured into them.

Looking at the fellows' faces in the ward-room at dinner that night there was no trace of anxiety, worry, or fatigue to be seen. We drank to sweethearts and wives, it being Saturday evening, and those who had no watch were glad to turn in early.

More fresh wind next day but finer weather to follow. Gran declared he saw an iceberg on the 5th December, but it turned out to be a whale spouting. Our runs were nothing to boast of, 150 miles being well above the average, but the lengthening days told us that we were rapidly changing our latitude and approaching the ice.

CHAPTER V

ANTARCTICA—THROUGH THE PACK ICE TO LAND

WE sighted our first iceberg in latitude 62° on the evening of Wednesday, December 7. Cheetham's squeaky hail came down from aloft and I went up to the crow's-nest to look at it, and from this time on we passed all kinds of icebergs, from the huge tabular variety to the little weathered water-worn bergs. Some we steamed quite close to and they seemed for all the world like great masses of sugar floating in the sea.

From latitudes 60° to 63° we saw a fair number of birds : southern fulmars, whale birds, molly-mawks, sooty albatrosses, and occasionally Cape-pigeons still. Then the brown-backed petrels began to appear, sure precursors of the pack ice—it was in sight right enough the day after the brown-backs were seen. By breakfast time on December 9, when nearly in latitude 65°, we were steaming through thin streams of broken pack with floes from six to twelve feet across. A few penguins and seals were seen, and by 10 a.m. no less than twenty-seven icebergs in sight. The newcomers to these regions were clustered in little groups on the forecastle and poop sketching and painting, hanging over the bows and gleefully watching this lighter stuff being brushed aside by our strong stem.

We were passing through pack all day, but the ice hereabouts was not close enough nor heavy enough to stop us appreciably. The ship was usually conned by Pennell and myself from the crow's-nest, and I took the ship very near one berg for Ponting to cinematograph it. We now began to see snow petrels with black beaks and pure white bodies, rather resembling doves. Also we saw great numbers of brown-backed petrels the first day in the pack, whole flights of them resting on the icebergs. The sun was just below the horizon at midnight and we had a most glorious sunset, which was first a blazing copper changing to salmon pink and then purple. The pools of water between the floes caught the reflection, the sea was perfectly still and every berg and ice-floe caught something of the delicate colour. Wilson, of course, was up and about till long after midnight sketching and painting. The Antarctic pack ice lends itself to water-colour work far better than to oils.

When conning the ship from up in the crow's-nest one has a glorious view of this great changing ice-field. Moving through lanes of clear blue water, cannoning into this floe and splitting it with iron-bound stem, overriding that and gnawing off a twenty ton lump, gliding south, east, west, through leads of open water, then charging an innocent-looking piece which brings the ship up all-standing, astern and ahead again, screwing and working the wonderful wooden ship steadily southward until perhaps two huge floes gradually narrow the lane and hold the little lady fast in their frozen grip.

This is the time to wait and have a look round : on one side floes the size of a football field, all

jammed together, with their torn up edges showing
their limits and where the pressure is taken. Then
three or four bergs, carved from the distant Barrier,
imprisoned a mile or so away, with the evening
sun's soft rays casting beautiful shadows about
them and kissing their glistening cliff faces.

Glancing down from the crow's nest the ship
throws deep shadows over the ice and, while the
sun is just below the southern horizon, the still
pools of water show delicate blues and greens that
no artist can ever do justice to. It is a scene from
fairyland.

I loved this part of the voyage, for I was in my
element. At odd times during the night, if one can
call it night, the crow's-nest would have visitors,
and hot cocoa would be sent up in covered pots by
means of signal halyards. The pack ice was new
to all the ship's officers except myself, but they soon
got into the way of conning and working through
open water leads and, as time went on, distinguished
the thinner ice from the harder and more dangerous
stuff.

On December 10 we stopped the ship and secured
her to a heavy floe from which we took in sufficient
ice to make eight tons of fresh water, and whilst
doing this Rennick sounded and obtained bottom
in 1964 fathoms, fora-minifera and decomposed
skeleton unicellular organs, also two pieces of black
basic lava. Lillie and Nelson took plankton and
water bottle samples to about 280 fathoms. A few
penguins came round and a good many crab-eater
seals were seen. In the afternoon we got under way
again and worked for about eight miles through the
pack, which was gradually becoming denser. About
2.30 p.m. I saw from the crow's-nest four seals on

a floe. I slid down a backstay, and whilst the officer on watch worked the ship close to them, I got two or three others with all our firearms and shot the lot from the forecastle head. We had seal liver for dinner that night ; one or two rather turned up their noses at it, but, as Scott pointed out, the time would come when seal liver would be a delicacy to dream about.

Campbell did not do much conning except in the early morning, as his executive duties kept him well occupied. The Polar sledge journey had its attractions, but Campbell's party were to have interesting work and were envied by many on board. For reasons which need not here be entered into Campbell had to abandon the King Edward VII. Land programme, but in these days his mob were known as the Eastern Party, to consist of the Wicked Mate, Levick, and Priestley, with three seamen, Abbott, Browning, and Dickason. Campbell had the face of an angel and the heart of a hornet. With the most refined and innocent smile he would come up to me and ask whether the Eastern Party could have a small amount of this or that luxury. Of course I would agree, and sure enough Bowers would tell me that Campbell had already appropriated a far greater share than he was ever entitled to of the commodity in question. This happened again and again, but the refined smile was irresistible and I am bound to say the Wicked Mate generally got away with it, for even Bowers, the incomparable, was bowled over by that smile.

We crossed the Antarctic Circle on the morning of the 10th, little dreaming in those happy days that the finest amongst us would never recross it again.

We took a number of deep-sea soundings, several of over 2000 fathoms, on this first southward voyage. Rennick showed himself very expert with the deep-sea gear and got his soundings far more easily than we had done in the *Discovery* and *Morning* days.

We were rather unfortunate as regards the pack ice met with, and must have passed through 400 miles of it from north to south. On my two previous voyages we had had easier conditions altogether, and then it had not mattered, but all with these dogs and ponies cooped up and losing condition, with the *Terra Nova* eating coal and sixty hungry men scoffing enormous meals, we did not seem to be doing much or getting on with the show. It was, of course, nobody's fault, but our patience was sorely tried.

We made frequent stops in the pack ice, even letting fires out and furling sail, and sometimes the ice would be all jammed up so that not a water hole was visible—this condition would continue for days. Then, for no apparent reason, leads would appear and black water-skies would tempt us to raise steam again. Scott himself showed an admirable patience, for the rest of us had something to occupy our time with. Pennell and I, for instance, were constantly taking sights and working them out to find our position and also to get the set and drift of the current. Then there were magnetic observations to be taken on board and out on the ice away from the magnetic influence of the ship, such as it was. Simpson had heaps to busy himself with, and Ponting was here, there, and everywhere with his camera and cinematograph machine. Had it not been for our anxiety to make southward progress,

the time would have passed pleasantly enough,
especially in fine weather. Days came when we
could get out on the floe and exercise on ski, and
Gran zealously looked to all our requirements in
this direction.

December 11 witnessed the extraordinary sight
of our company standing bareheaded on deck whilst
Captain Scott performed Divine Service. Two
hymns were sung, which broke strangely the great
white silence. The weather was against us this day
in that we had snow, thaw, and actually rain, but
we could not complain on the score of weather
conditions generally. Practically all the ship's
company exercised on the floes while we remained
fast frozen. Next day there was some slight
loosening of the pack and we tried sailing through
it and managed half a degree southward in the
forty-eight hours. We got along a few miles here
and there, but when ice conditions continued
favourable for making any serious advance it
was better to light up and push our way onward
with all the power we could command. We got
some heavy bumps on the 13th December and
as this hammering was not doing the ship much
good, since I was unable to make southing then at
a greater rate than one mile an hour, we let fires
right out and prepared, as Captain Scott said,
" To wait till the clouds roll by." For the next
few days there was not much doing nor did we
experience such pleasant weather.

Constant visits were made to the crow's-nest in
search of a way through. December 16 and 17 were
two very gray days with fresh wind, snow, and some
sleet. Affectionate memories of Captain Colbeck
and the little relief ship, *Morning*, came back when

the wind soughed and whistled through the rigging.
This sound is most uncanny and the ice always
seemed to exaggerate any noise.

I hated the overcast days in the pack. It was
bitterly cold in the crow's-nest however much one
put on then, and water skies often turned out to be
nimbus clouds after we had laboured and cannoned
towards them. The light, too, tired and strained
one's eyes far more than on clear days.

When two hundred miles into the pack the ice
varied surprisingly. We would be passing through
ice a few inches thick and then suddenly great floes
four feet above the water and twelve to fifteen feet
deep would be encountered. December 18 saw us
steaming through tremendous leads of open water.
A very funny occurrence was witnessed in the evening when the wash of the ship turned a floe over
under water and on its floating back a fish was left
stranded. It was a funny little creature, nine
inches in length, a species of notathenia. Several
snow petrels and a skua-gull made attempts to
secure the fish, but the afterguard kept up such a
chorus of cheers, hoots and howls that the birds
were scared away till one of us secured the fish
from the floe.

Early on the 19th we passed close to a large
iceberg which had a shelving beach like an island.
We began to make better progress to the south-
westward and worked into a series of open leads.
We came across our first emperor penguin, a young
one, and two sea-leopards, besides crab-eater seals,
many penguins, some giant petrels, and a Wilson
petrel. That afternoon tremendous pieces of ice
were passed ; they were absolutely solid and
regular floes, being ten to twelve feet above water

and, as far as one could judge, about 50 feet below. The water here was beautifully clear.

We had now reached latitude 68° and, as penguins were plentiful, Archer and Clissold, the cooks, made us penguin stews and " hooshes " to eke out our fresh provisions. Concerning the penguins, they frequently came and inspected the ship. One day Wilson and I chased some, but they continually kept just out of our reach ; then Uncle Bill lay down on the snow, and when one, out of curiosity, came up to him he grabbed it by the leg and brought it to the ship, protesting violently, for all the world like a little old man in a dinner jacket. Atkinson and Wilson found a new kind of tapeworm in this penguin, with a head like a propeller. This worm has since been named after one of us !

We were now down to under 300 tons of coal, some of which had perforce to be landed, in addition to the 30 tons of patent fuel which were under the forward stores. I had no idea that Captain Scott could be so patient. He put the best face on everything, although he certainly was disappointed in the *Terra Nova* and her steaming capacity. He could not well have been otherwise when comparing her with his beloved *Discovery*. Whilst in the pack our leader spent his time in getting hold of the more detailed part of our scientific programme and mildly tying the scientists in knots.

We had some good views of whales in the pack. Whenever a whale was sighted Wilson was called to identify it unless it proved to belong to one of the more common species. We saw Sibbald's whale, Rorquals, and many killer whales, but no Right whales were properly identified this trip.

I very much wanted to show Scott the island we

had discovered in the first Antarctic Relief Expedition and named after him, but when in its vicinity snow squalls and low visibility prevented this.

On the 22nd Bowers, Wright, Griffith Taylor and myself chased a lot of young penguins on the ice and secured nine for our Christmas dinner. We spent a very pleasant Christmas this year, devoting great attention to food. We commenced the day with kidneys from our frozen meat store. Captain Scott conducted the Christmas church service and all hands attended since we had no steam up and were fast held in the pack. The ward-room was decorated with our sledge flags and a new blue tablecloth generally brightened up our Mess. We had fresh mutton for lunch and the seamen had their Christmas dinner at this time. The afterguard dined at 6.30 on fresh penguin, roast beef, plum pudding, mince pies, and asparagus, while we had champagne, port, and liqueurs to drink and an enormous box of Fry's fancy chocolates for dessert. This " mortal gorge " was followed by a sing-song lasting until midnight, nearly every one, even the most modest, contributing. Around the Christmas days we made but insignificant headway, only achieving thirty-one miles in the best part of the week, but on the 29th the floes became thin and the ice showed signs of recent formation, though intermingled with heavier floes of old and rotten ice. There was much diatomacea in the rotten floes. About 2.40 a.m. the ship broke through into a lead of open water six miles in length.

I spent the middle watch in the crow's-nest, Bowers being up there with me talking over the

Expedition, his future and mine. He was a wonderful watch companion, especially when he got on to his favourite subject, India. He had some good tales to tell of the Persian Gulf, of days and weeks spent boat-cruising, of attacks made on gun-running dhows and kindred adventure. He told me that one dhow was boarded while he was up the Gulf, when the Arabs, waiting until most of the boat's crew of bluejackets were on board, suddenly let go the halyards of their great sail and let it down crash over the lot, the boom breaking many heads and the sail burying our seamen, while the Arabs got to work and practically scuppered the crowd.

Soon after 4 a.m. I went below and turned in, confident that we were nearing the southern extreme of the pack. Captain Scott awoke when I went into the cabin, pleased at the prospect, but after so many adverse ice conditions he shook his head, unwilling to believe that we should get clear yet awhile. I bet him ten sardine sandwiches that we should be out of the pack by noon on the 30th, and when I turned out at 8 o'clock I was delighted to find the ship steaming through thin floes and passing into a series of great open water leads. By 6 p.m. on the 29th a strong breeze was blowing, snow was falling, and we were punching along under steam and sail. Sure enough we got out of the pack early on the 30th and, cracking on all our canvas, were soon doing eight knots with a following wind.

Later in the day the wind headed us with driving snow, fine rain, and, unfortunately, a considerable head swell. This caused the ship to pitch so badly that the ponies began to give trouble again. Oates asked for the speed to be reduced, but we got over this by setting fore and aft sail and keeping the ship's head three or four points off the wind. New Year's Eve gave us another anxious time, for we encountered a hard blow from the S.S.E. It was necessary to heave the ship to most of the day under bare poles with the engines just jogging to keep the swell on her bow. A thin line of pack ice was sighted in the morning and this turned out to be quite a blessing in disguise, for I took the ship close to the edge of it and skirted along to leeward. The ice formed a natural breakwater and damped the swell most effectually. The swell and sea in the open would have been too much for the ponies as it must be remembered that they had been in their stalls on board for five weeks.

We had now reached the Continental Shelf, the depth of water had changed from 1111 fathoms on the 30th to 180 fathoms this day. The biologists took advantage of our jogging along in the open water to trawl, but very few specimens were obtained. At midnight the "youth of the town" made the devil of a din by striking sixteen bells, blowing whistles on the siren, hooting with the foghorn, cheering and singing. What children we were, but what matter !

1911 came like the opening of a new volume of an exciting book. This was the year in which Scott hoped to reach the Pole, the ideal date he had given being December 21. This was the year that Campbell and his party were looking forward to so eagerly—if only they could be successful in landing their gear and equipment in King Edward VII. Land—and, for the less showy but more scientific sledgers, 1911 held a wealth of excitement in store.

Griffith Taylor and Debenham knew pretty well
that next New Year's Day would see them in the
midst of their Western journey with the secrets
of those rugged mountains revealed perhaps. I
do not know what my own feelings were, it would
be impossible to describe them. I read up part of
Shackleton's diary and something of what his
companion Wilde had written. Just this :

12 miles, 200 yards.—1/1/08.

" Started usual time. Quan (pony) got through
the forenoon fairly well with assistance, but after
lunch the poor chap broke down and we had to take
him out of harness. Shackleton, Adams, and Marshall dragged his sledge, and I brought the ponies
along with the other load. As soon as we camped
I gave Quan the bullet, and Marshall and I cut him
up. He was a tough one. I am cook this week with
Marshall as my tent mate."

The more one read into Shackleton's story the more
wonderful it all seemed, and with our resources
failure appeared impossible—yet that telegram
which Captain Scott had received at Melbourne :

" Beg leave to inform you proceeding Antarctic.
                                —AMUNDSEN."

We all knew that Amundsen had no previous
Antarctic sledging experience, but no one could
deny that to Norwegians ice-work, and particularly
ski-ing, was second nature, and here lay some good
food for thought and discussion. Where would the
Fram enter the pack ? Where would Amundsen

make his base ? The answers never once suggested anything like the truth.

Actually on New Year's Day Amundsen was between 500 and 600 miles north of us, but of Roald Amundsen more anon.

How strange to be once more in open water, able to steer whatever course we chose, with broad daylight all night, and at noon only a couple of days' run from Cape Crozier. Practically no ice in sight, but a sunlit summer sea in place of the pack, with blue sky and cumulo stratus clouds, so different from the gray, hard skies that hung so much over the great ice field we had just forced. The wind came fair as the day wore on and by 10 p.m. we were under plain sail, doing a good six knots. High mountains were visible to the westward, part of the Admiralty Range, two splendid peaks to be seen towering above the remainder, which appeared to be Mounts Sabine and Herschell. Coulman Island was seen in the distance during the day.

What odd thrills the sight of the Antarctic Continent sent through most of us. Land was first sighted late on New Year's Eve and I think everybody had come on deck at the cry " Land oh ! " To me those peaks always did and always will represent silent defiance ; there were times when they made me shudder, but it is good to have looked upon them and to remember them in those post-War days of general discontent, for they remind me of the four Antarctic voyages which I have made and of the unanimous goodwill that obtained in each of the little wooden ships which were our homes for so long. How infinitely distant those towering mountains seemed and how eternal their loneliness.

As we neared Cape Crozier Wilson became more and more interested. He was dreadfully keen on the beach there being selected as a base, and his enthusiasm was infectious. Certainly Scott was willing enough to try to effect a landing even apart from the advantage of having a new base. The Cape Crozier beach would probably mean a shorter journey to the Pole, for we should be spared the crevasses which radiated from White Island and necessitated a big detour being made to avoid them.

As we proceeded the distant land appeared more plainly and we were able to admire and identify the various peaks of the snow-clad mountain range. The year could not have opened more pleasantly. We had church in a warm sun, with a temperature several degrees above freezing point, and most of us spent our off-time basking in the sunshine, yarning, skylarking, and being happy in general.

We tried to get a white-bellied whale on the 2nd January, but our whale-gun did not seem to have any buck in it and the harpoon dribbled out a fraction of the distance it was expected to travel.

The same glorious weather continued on January 2, and Oates took five of the ponies on to the upper deck and got their stables cleared out. The poor animals had had no chance of being taken from their stalls for thirty-eight days, and their boxes were between two and three feet deep with manure. The four ponies stabled on the upper deck looked fairly well but were all stiff in their legs.

Rennick took soundings every forty or fifty miles in the Ross Sea, the depth varying from 357 fathoms comparatively close up to Cape Crozier to 180 fathoms in latitude 73°.

Cape Crozier itself was sighted after breakfast on the 3rd, and the Great Ice Barrier appeared like a thin line on the southern horizon at 11.30 that morning. We were close to the Cape by lunch time, and by 1.30 we had furled sail in order to manœuvre more freely. The *Terra Nova* steamed close up to the face of the Barrier, then along to the westward until we arrived in a little bay where the Barrier joins Cape Crozier. Quite a tide was washing past the cliff faces of the ice ; it all looked very white, like chalk, while the sun was near the northern horizon, but later in the afternoon blue and green shadows were cast over the ice, giving it a softer and much more beautiful appearance. Ponting was given a chance to get some cinema films of the Barrier while we were cruising around, and then we stopped in the little bay where the Ice Barrier joins Cape Crozier, lowered a boat, and Captain Scott, Wilson, myself, and several others went inshore in a whaler. We were, however, unable to land as the swell was rather too heavy for boat work. We saw an Emperor penguin chick and a couple of adult Emperors, besides many Adèlie penguins and skua-gulls. We pulled along close under the great cliffs which frown over the end of the Great Ice Barrier. They contrasted strangely in their blackness with the low crystal ice cliffs of the Barrier itself. In one place we were splashed by the spray from quite a large waterfall, and one realised that the summer sun, beating down on those black foothills, must be melting enormous quantities of ice and snow. A curious ozone smell, which must have been the stench of the guano from the penguin rookeries, was noticed, but land smells of any sort were pleasant enough now for it brought home to us the fact that we should shortly embark on yet another stage of the Expedition.

Pennell conned the ship close under the cliffs and followed the boat along the coast. The *Terra Nova* was quite dwarfed by the great rocky bluffs and we realised the height of the cliffs for the first time.

Whilst we were prospecting Nelson obtained water-bottle samples and temperatures at 10, 50, 100, and 200 fathoms. The deep water apparently continued to the foot of the cliff in most places but there were two or three tiny steep beaches close to the junction of the Barrier and Ross Island.

Captain Scott being satisfied that no landing was possible, we in the boat returned to the ship and proceeded in her to the penguin rookery, a mile or so farther west. When half a mile from the shore, we found the bottom rapidly shoaling, the least depth being $9\frac{1}{2}$ fathoms. Several small bergs were ashore hereabouts, but the swell breaking on the beach plainly told us that a landing was out of the question. After carefully searching the shore with glasses while the ship steamed slowly along it, all ideas of a landing were abandoned and we set course for McMurdo Sound. As soon as the ship was headed for her new destination we commenced to make a running survey of the coast to Cape Bird. This took until ten o'clock at night, and we found a great bight existed in Ross Island which quite changed its shape on the map. After 10 p.m. we ran into some fairly heavy pack ice, gave up surveying, and had a meal.

I went up to the crow's-nest in order to work the ship to the best advantage, and spent eleven hours on end there, but the excitement of getting the *Terra Nova* round Cape Bird and into McMurdo Sound made the time fly. Occasionally the ship crashed heavily as she charged her way through the ice masses which skirted the shore. Whilst I conned the ship leadsmen sounded carefully, and I was able to work her close in to the coast near Cape Bird and avoid some heavy ice which we could never have forced. At 4.30 a.m. I broke through the Cape Bird ice-field and worked the ship on as far as Cape Royds, which was passed about 6.30 a.m. Looking through our binoculars we noticed Shackleton's winter hut looking quite new and fresh.

Leaving Cape Royds we made our way up McMurdo's Sound as far as Inaccessible Island, where we found the Strait frozen over from east to west. Skirting along the edge of the sea ice I found there was no way in, although I endeavoured to break into it at several points to reach what looked like open water spaces a mile or two from the ice edge. Accordingly, we stopped and I came down to report on the outlook. Captain Scott, Wilson, and I eventually went aloft to the cross-trees and had a good look round ; we finally decided to land and look at a place where there appeared to be a very good beach. In *Discovery* days this spot was known as the skuary, being a favourite nesting place for skua-gulls, a sort of little cape. I piloted the ship as close I could to this position, which is situate midway between Cape Bird and Cape Armitage on Ross Island. An ice anchor was laid out and then Scott, Wilson, and

I landed on the sea ice and walked a mile or so over it to the little cape in question.

It appeared to be an ideal winter quarters, and was then and there selected as our base. Captain Scott named it Cape Evans, after me, for which I was very grateful. Wilson already had a Cape named after him on the Victoria Land coast in latitude 82°.

We now returned on board and immediately commenced landing motor sledges, ponies, etc. For better working, once the various parties were landed, we adopted the standard time of meridian 180°, in other words, twelve hours fast on Greenwich Mean Time.

We now organised ourselves into three parties and I gave up the command of the *Terra Nova* to Pennell till the ship returned from New Zealand next year. The charge of the transport over the one and a half miles of sea ice which lay between the ship and shore was given to Campbell, whilst I took charge of the Base Station, erection of huts, and so forth, Captain Scott himself supervising, planning and improving.

We continued getting stuff out on the ice until late at night, and by dinner time, 7 p.m., we had put two motor sledges, all the dogs and ponies ashore, besides most of the ordinary sledges and tents.

Next day we turned out all hands at 4.30, breakfasted at 5, started work at 6, and landed all the petrol, kerosene, and hut timber. Most of the haulage was done by motors and men, but a few runs were made with ponies. We erected a big tent on the beach at Cape Evans and in this the hut-building party and those who were stowing

stores and unloading sledges on the beach got
their meals and sleep. We worked continuously
until 10 p.m. with only the shortest of meal intervals, and then, tired but contented, we " flattened
out " in our sleeping bags, bunks, or hammocks.

The following day the same routine was continued
and nearly the whole of the provision cases came
ashore and were stacked in neat little piles under
Bowers's direction. This indefatigable little worker
now devoted himself entirely to the western party
stores. He knew every case and all about it. Each
one weighed approximately 60 lb. We had purposely arranged that this should be so when ordering
stores in London to save weight and space. The
cases were made of Venesta 3-ply wood. Of course,
the instruments and heavier scientific gear could
not stow in these handy packages, but the sixty-
pound-Venesta was adhered to whenever possible.
The ponies were not worked till the afternoon of
the 6th, and then only the best of them with light
loads.

Davis, the carpenter, had with him seaman Ford,
Keohane, and Abbot. Their routine was a little
different from ours : they worked at hut building
from 7 a.m. till midnight usually, and their results
were little short of marvellous. Odd people helped
them when they could, and of these Ponting showed
himself to be *facile princeps* as carpenter. I never
saw anything like the speed in which he set up
tongued and grooved match boarding.

Day, Nelson, and Lashly worked with the motor
sledges ; the newest motor frequently towed loads
of 2500 lb. over the ice at a six mile an hour speed.
The oldest hauled a ton and managed six double
trips a day. Day, the motor engineer, had been

down here before—both he and Priestley came from the Shackleton Expedition. The former had a decidedly comic vein which made him popular all round. From start to finish Day showed himself to be the most undefeated sportsman, and it was not his fault that the motor sledges did badly in the end.

Perhaps my diary from January 7, 1911, to the 8th gives a good idea of the progress we were making with the base station and of the general working day here. It reads as follows:

" *Saturday, January 7, 1911.*

" All hands hard at work landing stores. Meares and Dimitri running dog teams to and fro for light gear.

" Captain Scott, Dr. Wilson, Griffith Taylor, Debenham, Cherry-Garrard, and Browning leading ponies. Campbell, Levick, and Priestley hauling sledges with colossal energy and enormous loads, the majority of the ship's party unloading stores, Bowers, two seamen, Atkinson, and I unloading sledges on the beach and carrying their contents up to their assigned positions, Simpson and Wright laying the foundations for a magnetic hut, and so on. Every one happy and keen, working as incessantly as ants. I took on the job of ice inspector, and three or four times a day I go out and inspect the ice, building snow bridges over the tide cracks and thin places. The ice, excepting the floe to which the ship is fast, is several feet thick. The floe by the *Terra Nova* is very thin and rather doubtful. We, ashore, had dinner at 10 p.m. and turned in about 11."

But the following day, although included here, was by no means typical.

"*Sunday, January* 8.

" This morning a regrettable accident took place. The third and newest motor sledge was hoisted out and, while being hauled clear on to the firm ice, it broke through and sank in deep water. Campbell and Day came in with the news, which Captain Scott took awfully well.

" It was nobody's fault, as Simpson and Campbell both tested the floe first and found it quite thick and apparently good. However, there it is, in about 100 fathoms of water.

" We stopped sledging for the day and those on board shifted the ship by warping, but could not get her into a satisfactory billet, so raised steam.

" We spent the day working on the hut and putting chairs and benches together. Captain Scott put the sledge meters together and I helped him. These are similar to the distance meters on motor-cars. They register in nautical miles (6084 feet) and yards, to 25 yards or less by interpolation.

" Took a True Bearing and found the approximate variation for Simpson (149° E.)."

On the following day those on board the ship shifted her to a new position alongside the fast ice, just under a mile from our beach. The transportation of stores continued and we got ashore a great number of bales of compressed fodder, also some Crown Preserve Patent Fuel. As there was nothing much to do on the beach my party lent a hand with the landing of fodder, and I led the ponies Miki, Jehu, and Blossom ; the latter, having suffered greatly on the outward voyage, was in poor condition. Still, most of the ponies were doing well, and at night were picketed on a snowdrift behind the hut. They occasionally got adrift, but I usually heard them and got up to make them fast, my small sleeping-tent being right alongside their tethering space.

Nelson continued working with me unless the requirements of his biological work called him away. In less than a week we had the whole of our stores and equipment landed, and from the beginning many of us took up our quarters at Cape Evans itself. We pitched several small tents on the beach, and it was an agreeable change to roll up and sleep in a fur bag after the damp, cold berths we had occupied in the ship. Teddy Nelson became my particular friend in the shore party and shared a sledging tent with me. The rest of the shore staff paired off and slept in the small tents, while Captain Scott had one to himself. We called it the " Holy of Holies," and from the privacy of this tiny dwelling Scott issued his directions, supervised, planned, and improved whenever improvement could be made in anything. He had a marvellous brain and a marvellous way of getting the best possible work out of his subordinates, still he never spared himself. One did with extraordinary little sleep, and in the sunny days it became necessary to leave tent doors wide open, otherwise the close-woven wind-proof tent cloth kept all the fresh air out and one woke with a terrific head.

To rightly get hold of our wintering place one must imagine a low spit of land jutting out into a fiord running, roughly north and south and bounded on both sides by a steep-to coast line indented with glaciers of vast size. Here and there gigantic snow-slopes were to be seen which more gradually lowered into the sea, and all around ice-covered mountains with black and brown foothills. A few islands rose to heights of 300 or 400 feet in McMurdo Sound, and these had no snow on them worth speaking of even in the winter. The visible land was of black or chocolate-brown, being composed of volcanic tuff, basalts, and granite. There were occasional patches of ruddy brown and yellow which relieved the general black and white appearance of this uninhabitable land, and close to the shore on the north side of Cape Evans were small patches of even gritty sand. In the neighbourhood of our Cape hard, brittle rocks cropped up everywhere, rocks that played havoc with one's boots. Sloping up fairly steeply from Cape Evans itself we had more and more rock masses until a kind of rampart was reached, on which one could see a number of extraordinary conical piles of rock, which looked much as if they had been constructed by human hands for landmarks or surveying beacons—these were called debris cones. This part above and behind Cape Evans was christened The Ramp, and from it one merely had to step from boulders and stones on to the smooth blue ice-slope that extended almost without interruption to the summit of Erebus itself. From The Ramp one could gaze in wonder at that magnificent volcano, White Lady of the Antarctic, beautiful in her glistening gown of sparkling crystal with a stole of filmy smoke-cloud wrapped about her wonderful shoulders.

We used to gaze and gaze at that constantly changing smoke or steam which the White Lady breathes out at all seasons, and has done for thousands of years.

Those were such happy days during the first Cape Evans summer. For the most part we had hot weather and could wash in the thaw pools which formed from the melting snow, and even draw our drinking water from the cascades which bubbled over the sun-baked rock, much as they do in summer-time in Norway.

The progress made by Davis and his crew of voluntary carpenters was amazing. One week after our arrival at the Cape, Nelson, Meares, and I commenced to cut a cave out of the ice cap above our camp for stowing our fresh mutton in. When knock-off work-time came Bowers, Nelson, and I made our way over to the ship with a hundred gallons of ice from this cave to be used for drinking water, it all helped to save coal and nobody made a journey to or fro empty handed if it could be helped. Once on board we took the opportunity to bath and shave. In this country it is certainly a case of " Where I dines I sleeps," so after supper on board we coiled down in somebody's beds and slept till 5.30 next morning when we returned to camp and carried on all day, making great progress with the grotto, which was eventually lit by electric light. We had plenty of variety in the matter of work ; one part of the grotto was intended for Simpson's magnetic work, and this was the illuminated section. Whenever people visited the ice caves we got them to do a bit of picking and hewing, even roping in Captain Scott, who did a healthy half-hour's work when he came along our way.

Scott and Wilson got their hands in at dog-driving

now, as I did occasionally myself. Nobody could touch Meares or Dimitri at dog-team work, although later on Cherry-Garrard and Atkinson became the experts.

The hut was finished externally on January 12 and fine stables built up on its northern side. This complete, Bowers arranged an annexe on the south side from which to do the rationing and provision issues. How we blessed all this fine weather; it was hardly necessary to wear snow glasses, in spite of so much sunshine, for the glare was relieved by the dark rock and sand around us. When all the stores had been discharged from the ship she lightened up considerably, and Campbell then set to work to ballast her for Pennell. Meares amused the naval members of our party by asking, with a childlike innocence, " Had they got all the cargo out of the steamer ? " There was nothing wrong in what he said, but the *Terra Nova*, Royal Yacht Squadron—and " cargo " and " steamer " —how our naval pride was hurt !

Incidentally we called the sandy strand (before the winter snow came, and covered it, and blotted it all out) Hurrah Beach; the bay to the north- ward of the winter quarters we christened Happy Bay. Although our work physically was of the hardest we lived in luxury for a while. Nelson provided cocoa for Captain Scott and myself at midnight just before we slept. He used to make it after supper and keep it for us in a great thermos flask. We only washed once a week and we were soon black with sun and dirt but in splendid training. In the first three weeks my shore gang, which included the lusty Canadian physicist, Wright, carried many hundreds of cases, walked

miles daily, dug ice, picked, shovelled, handed
ponies, cooked and danced. Outwardly we were
not all prototypes of " the Sentimental Bloke,"
but occasionally in the stillness of the summer
nights, we some of us unbent a bit, when the
sun stood low in the south and all was quiet and
still, and we did occasionally build castles in the air
and draw home-pictures to one another, pictures of
English summers, of river picnics and country life
that framed those distant homes in gold and made
them look to us like little bits of heaven—however,
what was more important, the stores were all out
of the *Terra Nova*, even to stationery, instruments,
and chronometers, and we could have removed
into the hut at a pinch a week before we did, or
gone sledging, for that matter, had we not purposely
delayed to give the ponies a chance to regain condition. It was certainly better to let the carpenter
and his company straighten up first, and in our slack
hours we, who were to live in the palatial hut, got
the house in order, put up knick-knacks, and settled
into our appointed corners with our personal gear
and professional impedimenta only at the last
moment, a day or two before the big depot-laying
sledge journey was appointed to start. Simpson
and Ponting had the best allotments in the hut,
because the former had to accommodate anemo-
meters, barometers, thermometers, motors, bells,
and a diversity of scientific instruments, but yet
leave room to sleep amongst them without being
electrocuted, while the latter had to arrange a
small-sized dark room, 8 ft. by 6 ft. floor dimension,
for all his developing of films and plates, for
stowing photographic gear and cinematograph,
and for everything in connection with his

important and beautiful work as camera artist to the Expedition. Ponting likewise slept where he worked, so a bed was also included in the dark room.

Before moving the chronometers ashore Pennell, Rennick, and I myself took astronomical observations to determine independently the position of the observation spot on the beach at Cape Evans. The preliminary position gave us latitude 77° 38′ 23″ S. longitude 166° 33′ 24″ E., a more accurate determination was arrived at by running meridian distances from New Zealand and taking occultations during the ensuing winter, for longitude: latitudes were obtained by the mean results of stars north and south and meridian altitudes of the sun above and below pole.

Before getting busy with the preliminaries for the big depot journey, I took stock of the fresh meat in the grotto. The list of frozen flesh which I handed over to Clissold, the cook, looked luxurious enough, for it included nothing less than 700 lb. of beef, 100 sheep carcasses, 2 pheasants, 3 ox-tails, and 3 tongues, 10 lb. of sweetbread, 1 box of kidneys, 10 lb. of suet, 82 penguins, and 11 skua-gulls ! The cooks' corner in the hut was very roomy, and, if my memory serves me aright, our cooking range was of similar pattern to one supplied to the Royal yacht, *Alexandra.*

On January 19 a snow road was made over to the ice foot on the south side of Cape Evans in order to save the ponies' legs and hoofs. The Siberian ponies were not shod, and this rough, volcanic rock would have shaken them considerably.

A great deal of the bay ice had broken away and drifted out of the Sound, so that by the 20th the

ship was only a few hundred yards from Hurrah
Beach. This day Rennick, smiling from ear to ear,
came across the ice with the pianola in bits conveyed on a couple of sledges. He fixed it up with
great cleverness at one end of the hut and it was
quite wonderful to see how he stripped it on board,
brought it through all sorts of spaces, transported
it undamaged over ice and rocky beach, re-erected
it, tuned it, and then played " Home, Sweet Home."
What with the pianola going all out, the gramophone giving us Melba records, and the ship's
company's gramophone squawking out Harry
Lauder's opposition numbers, Ponting cinemato-
graphing everything of interest and worthy of
pictorial record, little Anton rushing round with
nosebags for the ponies, Meares and Dimitri
careering with the dog teams over ice, beach,
packing cases, and what not, sailors with coloured
tam-o'-shanters bobbing around in piratical style,
the hot sun beating down and brightening up
everything, one might easily have imagined this
to be the circus scene in the great Antarctic joy-
ride film. Everything ran on wheels in these days,
and it was difficult to imagine that in three months
there would be no sun, that this sweltering beach
would be encrusted with ice, and that the cold,
dark winter would be upon us.

The 21st was quite an exciting day. Captain
Scott woke me at 4 a.m. to tell me that the ship was
in difficulties. I got up at once, called the four
seamen, and with Uncle Bill we all went out on to
the floe. The ice to which the ship was fast had
broken away, and so we helped her re-moor with her
ice-anchors. Petty Officer Evans went adrift on the
floe, but we got him back in the pram. We turned

in again at 5.15 and set a watch, but at 6.30 the
Terra Nova hoisted an ensign at the main, a prearranged signal, and so all hands again went out and
got her ice anchors; she slipped the ends of the
wire hawsers holding them and stood out into the
Sound. The ice was breaking up fast, a swell rolling
in causing the big floes to grind and crunch in rather
alarming fashion. Fortunately, Pennell had raised
steam, which was just as well for before he got clear
the ship was only half a cable from Cape Evans,
which lay dead to leeward—she was well out of it.
We took the wire hawsers, pram and ice anchors to
our winter quarters and kept them in readiness for
the ship's return, then had a delightful breakfast,
with appetites sharpened from the early morning
exercise and chill wind. Afterwards we continued
the preparations for the depot trip and got eight out
of eleven sledges fitted up with the bulk of their gear
and a portion of stores.

At about 3 p.m. the *Terra Nova* came in, and just
as she was turning to come alongside the fast ice she
struck a rock with only twelve feet of water on it.
This pinnacle, as it proved to be, lay within twenty
feet of a sounding of eleven fathoms. Pennell
immediately sounded all round, shifted several tons
weight aft, and with the engines going full speed
astern, he made his crew run from side to side and
roll ship. Scott sent me out in the whaler with a
party to assist the ship; we sounded all round and
quickly made a plan of the relative disposition of
the soundings round the *Terra Nova*. However, as
we finished, the ship moved astern and successfully
floated, the crew gave three cheers, and we cheered
lustily from the whaler. Pennell, as usual, was quite
equal to the occasion when the ship struck; he was

absolutely master of the situation, cool, decided, and successful. I was thankful to see the ship floating again, for, unlike the *Discovery* expedition, we had no plans for a relief ship.

When I told Captain Scott that the *Terra Nova* had run ashore he took it splendidly. We ran down to the beach, and when we beheld the ship on a lee shore heeling over to the wind, a certain amount of sea and swell coming in from the northward, and with the ultimate fate of the Expedition looking black and doubtful, Scott was quite cheerful, and he immediately set about to cope with the situation as coolly as though he were talking out his plans for a sledge journey.

After the *Terra Nova* got off this intruding rock she was steamed round to the edge of the fast ice, near the glacier tongue which juts out between Cape Evans and Cape Barne. We placed her ice-anchors, and after that Wilson and I went on board and had a yarn with Pennell, whom we brought back to tea. Scott was awfully nice to him about the grounding and told him of his own experience in 1904, when the *Discovery* was bumping heavily in a gale just after freeing herself from the ice at Hut Point.

Nelson, Griffith Taylor, Meares, and Day helped me with the sledge packing until 11.30 p.m. when we rolled into our bunks tired out and immediately fell asleep.

The next day, a Sunday, was entirely devoted to preparing personal gear for the depot journey : this means fitting lamp wick straps to our fur boots or finnesko, picking from our kits a proportion of puttees and socks, sewing more lamp wick on to our fur gloves so that these could hang from our shoulders when it was necessary to uncover our hands. We also had to fit draw-strings to our wind-proof blouses and adjust our headgear according to our individual fancy, and finally, tobacco and smokers' requisites would be added to the little bundle, which all packed up neatly in a pillow-slip. This personal bag served also as a pillow.

CHAPTER VI

SETTLING DOWN TO THE POLAR LIFE

THE following members were selected for the depot journey which Captain Scott elected to lead in person : Wilson, Bowers, Atkinson, Oates, Cherry-Garrard, Gran, Meares, Ford, Crean, Keohane, and myself. It was decided to take eight pony-sledges and two dog-sledges, together with about a ton of pony food, sledging rations, dog biscuit, and paraffin to a position on the Great Ice Barrier as far south as we could get before the first winter set in. This decision was arrived at by Scott after consultation with Oates and others, and, as will be seen by reference to the list of those chosen for the journey, none of the scientific staff were included except Wilson himself.

The ponies selected were either those in the best condition or the weaker beasts which from Oates's viewpoint would hardly survive the rigours of the winter. Apart from the animals picked for this journey, we had nine beasts left to be taken care of by the little Russian, Anton, and the trusty Lashly, whose mechanical knowledge and practical ability were needed to help get the Base Station going.

On January 3 I was sent on board with all the sledges, including two for a western geological reconnaissance and a small spare sledge for use in case of breakdown or accident to the depot-laying people. By this time no ice remained in the bay north of Cape Evans and the transport out to the *Terra Nova* had perforce to be done by boat.

I was glad to have this chance of working out the errors and rates of our chronometer watches, and, although I was up at 5 a.m., I could not resist having a long yarn, which continued far into the night, with those never-to-be-forgotten friends of mine, Campbell, Pennell, Rennick, and Bruce, the worthy and delightful lieutenants of the Expedition. Like little Bowers, Pennell and Rennick have made the supreme sacrifice, and only Campbell, Bruce and myself remain alive to-day.

January 24 was a busy day. Captain Scott was fetched from the shore directly after breakfast, and at 10 a.m. the ship left for Glacier Tongue to shadow as it were, the string of white Siberian ponies which were being led round over the fast ice in the bay to the southward of Cape Evans.

On arriving at the Tongue, Pennell selected a nice, natural wharf to put his ship alongside, and, this done, I got a picketing line out on the ice for the horses and then got the sledges on to the glacier. It is as well here to describe Glacier Tongue briefly, since frequent reference will be made to that icy promontory in this narrative.

Glacier Tongue lies roughly six miles to the S.S.E. of Cape Evans and is a remarkable spit of ice jutting out, when last surveyed, for four miles into McMurdo Sound. Soundings showed that it was afloat for a considerable part of its length, and as Scott found subsequently, a great portion of it broke adrift in the autumn or winter of 1911 and was carried by the winds and currents of the Sound to a position forty miles W.N.W. of Cape

Evans, where it grounded, a huge flat iceberg two miles in length. Glacier Tongue was an old friend of mine, for it was here in the 1902-4 Relief Expedition that the crew of the little *Morning* dumped twenty tons of coal for the *Discovery* to pick up on her way northward, when the time for her to free herself from the besetting ice which held her prisoner off Hut Point.

The ponies were marched to their tethering place without further accident than one falling through into the sea, but he was rescued none the worse. Oates showed himself to advantage in managing the ponies : he was very fond of telling us that a horse and a man would go anywhere, and I believe if we sailor-men had had the bad taste to challenge him he would have hoisted one of those Chinese ma[1] up to the crow's-nest !

We all had tea on board and then, after checking the sledge loads and ascertaining that nothing had been forgotten, the depot party started out with full loads and marched away from Glacier Tongue for seven miles, when our first camp was made on the sea ice. To commence with I went with Meares and No. 1 dog-sledge ; the dogs were so eager and excited that they started by bolting at a breakneck speed and, in spite of all that we could do, took us over the glacier edge on to the sea ice. The sledge capsized and both Meares and I were thrown down somewhat forcibly. We caught the sledge, however, and got the dogs in hand after their initial energy had been expended. Scott and Wilson managed their dog sledge better as Meares gave them a quieter team.

It was about nine o'clock when we camped,

[1] Chinese for horse.

Meares, Wilson, Scott and I sharing a tent. Uncle Bill was cook, and I must say the first sledging supper was delightful.

We went back to Glacier Tongue the next day to relay the fodder and dog biscuit which was to be depoted. We had brought the provisions for depot along the eve before. I went in with Meares and Nelson, who had come out on ski to " speed the parting guest." We had a rare treat all riding in on the dog sledge at a great pace. Had lunch on board and then Captain Scott gave us an hour or two to ourselves, for it was the day of farewell letters, everybody sitting round the ward-room table sucking pens or pencils, looking very wooden-faced and nonchalant despite the fact that we were most certainly writing to our nearest and dearest, sending through our letters an unwritten prayer that we should be spared after steadfastly performing our alloted tasks with credit to our flag and with credit to those at whose feet we yearned to lay the laurels we hoped to win. Even as I wrote my farewell letters Captain Scott, Wilson, Bowers, and Nelson found time to write to my wife ; Scott's letter may well be included here for it shows his thoughtfulness and consideration :

> " *January*, 25, 1911,
>> Glacier Tongue,
>>> " McMurdo Sound.

" DEAR MRS. EVANS,—I thought you might be glad to have a note to tell you how fit and well your good man is looking, his cheery optimism has already helped me in many difficulties and at the present moment he is bubbling over with joy at the ' delights ' of his first sledge trip.

" He will have told you all the news and the ups and downs of our history to date, and you will have guessed that he has always met the misfortunes with a smile and the successes with a cheer, so that very little remains for me to say—except that I daily grow more grateful to you for sparing him for this venture. I feel that he is going to be a great help in every way and that it will go hard if, with so many good fellows, we should fail in our objects.

" Before concluding I should really like to impress on you how little cause you have for anxiety. We have had the greatest luck in finding and establishing our winter quarters, and if I could go shopping to-morrow I should not know what to buy to add to our comfort. We are reaping a full reward for all those months of labour in London, in which your husband took so large a share—if you picture us after communication is cut off it must be a very bright picture, almost a scene of constant revelry, with your husband in the foreground amongst those who are merry and content—I am sure we are going to be a very happy family and most certainly we shall be healthy and well cared for.

" With all kind regards and hopes that you will not allow yourself to be worried till your good man comes safely home again.

" Yours sincerely,
" R. Scott."

I said my good-byes after an early tea to the fellows of the *Terra Nova* and also to the Eastern party, the lieutenants saw me over the side, and I went away with a big lump in my throat, then Nelson and I took out a 10-ft. sledge with 530 lb. of fodder on it—rather too heavy a load, but it all helped, and the sea ice surface was none too bad. We did not get to camp till 10.35 p.m. : Meares, with his usual good-heartedness, came out from the tent and helped us in for the last miles or so. He had driven the dogs out with another load after tea time. Uncle Bill had a fine pemmican supper awaiting us. My job kept me in camp next day to adjust theodolites, but the rest of the party went out to bring the final relay of depot stores from the *Terra Nova*. During the following days we relayed the depot stuff along to a position near the edge of the Barrier, and whilst so engaged most of us found time to visit Hut Point. While Captain Scott was selecting the position for dumping a quantity of compressed fodder bales the remainder of the party dug the snow out of the old hut left by the *Discovery* in 1904. It looked a very deserted place, and the difference between the two winter quarters, Hut Point and Cape Evans, was amazing. One could quite understand the first expedition here selecting Hut Point for its natural harbour, but for comfort and freedom from unwelcome squalls and unpleasant gusts of wind commend me to Cape Evans. Never in my life had I seen anything quite so dreary and desolate as this locality. Practically surrounded by high hills, little sunshine could get to the hut, which was built in a hollow. Of course, we saw the place at its worst, for the best summer months had passed. The hut itself had been erected as a magnetic observatory and it contrasted shabbily with our 50-ft by 25-ft. palace. We did not finish clearing the snow away, although with so many willing workers we made considerable progress. In parts the midsummer sun had melted the snow, which in turn had re-frozen into blue ice, and this we found troublesome because the slender woodwork of the hut would not stand any heavy pick work.

We christened the place on the Barrier edge Fodder Camp, and it was the general opinion that we could risk leaving the bales of hay here until the depot stuff had been taken south. Accordingly, all the more important stores were relayed on January 29 to a position two miles in from the Barrier edge. Whilst doing this relay work I went in with Meares to Hut Point to bring out some 250 lb. of dog biscuit, and our dogs, being very fresh, scented a seal, took charge of the light sledge, and, in spite of all the brakeing and obstructing Meares and I put up, the dogs went wildly forward until they reached the seal. The second they came to it Meares and I found ourselves in the midst of a snapping, snarling, and biting mixture, with the poor seal floundering underneath. While we were beating the dogs off the seal it bit Meares in the leg ; he looked awfully surprised and showed great forbearance in not giving the seal one for himself with the iron-shod brake stick. I never saw anybody less vicious in nature than " Mother " Meares : he never knocked the dogs about unless it was absolutely necessary. Even Osman, the wild wolf-like king-dog, showed affection for him.

Whilst moving the sledging stores to Safety Camp, as we called the depot, two miles in, we came across two tents left by Shackleton two or three years before. They contained a few stores and a Primus stove, which proved to be most useful later on. On January 30 and 31 we completed the depot at Safety Camp and then reorganised the depot party, owing to Atkinson's developing a very sore heel, which made it impossible for him to accompany us. It did not matter very much, because we had heaps of people to work the depot-laying journey, only it meant a disappointment for Atkinson, which he took to heart very much. The question of sledging experience made us wish to have Atkinson on this trip, but he gained it a few weeks later. Accordingly, I took over Crean's pony, Blossom, whilst he took charge of our sick man and returned with him to Hut Point. Scott himself took Atkinson's pony, and on the 2nd February the caravan proceeded in an E.S.E. direction to make for a point in approximately 78° S. 169° E. Most of the ponies had 600 lb. loads on their sledges, Meares's dog team 750, and Wilson's 600. We found the surface very bad, most of the ponies sinking deep in the snow. After doing roughly five miles we halted and had a meal. Oates was called into our tent and consulted with a view to bettering the conditions for the ponies. As a result it was decided to march by night and rest during the day when the sun would be higher and the air warmer. There was quite a drop in the temperature between noon and midnight, and it was natural to suppose that we should get better and harder surfaces with the sun at its lower altitude. We still, of course, had the sun above the horizon for the full twenty-four hours, and should have for three weeks yet ; the choice was altogether a wise one and we therefore turned in during the afternoon and remained in our sleeping bags until 10 p.m. when we arose and cooked our breakfast.

Camp was broken at midnight and the march resumed. For three hours we plodded along, a little

SOUTH WITH SCOTT   91

leg weary perhaps, on account of the unusual time
for marching and working physically. We had
lunch about 3 a.m. and rested the ponies for a couple
of hours. The surface was still very bad, the ponies
labouring heavily, and my own animal, Blossom,
suffered through his hoofs being very small, so that
he sank into the snow far more than did the other
horses. It was on his account that we only covered
nine miles. I did some surveying work after our
7.30 a.m. supper and turned in at 10 o'clock until
7 p.m. Captain Scott took over cook in our tent
and made the breakfast.

For the next few days we continued marching
over the Great Ice Barrier, the distances covered
depending on the condition of Blossom and another
pony, Blücher. Both of these animals caused
anxiety from the start, and, owing to their weakness
the depot-laying distances scarcely exceeded ten
miles daily. There is nothing to be gained from a
long description of this autumn journey, it was
merely a record of patiently trudging and of carefully watching over the ponies. Generally speaking,
the weather was not in our favour, the sky being
frequently overcast, and we experienced an unpleasant amount of low drift.

February 5 and 6 were blizzard days during which
no move could be made, and it was not until nearly
11 p.m. on the 7th that the hard wind took off and
the snow ceased to drift about us. The blizzards
were not serious but were quite sufficient to try the
ponies severely—Blossom, Blücher, and a third
animal, James Pigg, could in no way keep up with
the van, although their loads were lightened considerably. The bluejackets, Forde and Keohane,
showed extraordinary aptitude in handling the

ponies, but in spite of their efforts their animals were quite done up by February 12, as also was poor old Blossom. It would have been cruel to continue with them, they were so wasted, and even their eyes were dull and lustreless. Accordingly, Scott decided to send Blücher, James Pigg, and Blossom back with Forde, Keohane, and myself. A reorganisation was made near the 79th parallel, and whilst the main party proceeded southward, Forde, Keohane, and I took our feeble ponies northward with the intention of getting them home to Hut Point before the temperature fell, until the cold would be too great for them to stand. It was annoying for me to be sent back, still there was plenty of survey work to be done between the turning-point and Safety Camp. Blücher failed from the start and lay down in the snow directly the depot party left us. Forde lifted him up, but his legs were limp and would not support him. We rubbed the poor pony's legs and did what we could for him, poor old Forde being practically in tears over the little beast. To give one an idea of this wretched animal's condition, when it was decided to kill him for humanity's sake and his throat was cut by Keohane with a sailor's knife, there was hardly any blood to let out. It was a rotten day for all three of us, blowing too hard to travel until very late, and a second pony, Blossom, was doing his best to die. We made some little way homeward, Keohane, James Pigg and myself pulling the sledge with our gear on it, and Forde lifting, carrying, and pushing Blossom along. I felt I ought to kill this animal but I knew how angry and disappointed Scott would be at the loss, so kept him going although he showed so much distress. It was surprising what spirit the little brute had : if we started to march away Blossom staggered along after us, looking like a spectre against the white background of snow. We kept on giving him up and making to kill him, but he actually struggled on for over thirty miles before falling down and dying in his tracks. We built a snow-cairn over him and planted what pony food we had no further use for on the top of the cairn.

The third pony, James Pigg, was kept fit and snug under a big snow-wall whenever we were not marching, and he won home to Safety Camp with very little trouble, frequently covering distances equal to our own marching capability. Once Safety Camp had been regained we got good weather again and James Pigg became quite frisky, ate all that we could give him, and, to our delight, his eyes regained their brightness and he began to put on flesh.

We spent a couple of days at Safety Camp before Captain Scott returned with the dog teams. In order to cut off corners he shaved things rather fine, and getting rather too close to White Island, the dog teams ran along the snow-bridge of a crevasse, the bridge subsided, and all the dogs of Scott's and Meares's sledge, with the exception of Osman, the leader, and the two rear animals, disappeared into a yawning chasm. Scott and Meares secured their sledge clear of the snow bridge and with the assistance of their companions, Wilson and Cherry-Garrard, who had the other team, they were lowered by means of an Alpine rope into the crevasse until they could get at the dogs. They found the poor animals swinging round, snapping at one another and howling dismally, but in an awful tangle. The dogs were rescued a pair at a time and, fortunately for all concerned, they lay down and rested when hauled up to the surface by Uncle Bill and "Cherry." When all the animals were up and Scott and Meares themselves had regained safety, a dog fight took place between the two teams. Apart from this excitement things had gone very well. Scott was most enthusiastic about the capabilities of Meares's dogs, and he then expressed an opinion that he would probably run the dogs light on the Polar journey and do the final plateau march to the Pole itself with them. What a pity he didn't ! Had he done so he might have been alive to-day.

We learnt from the dog-drivers that the depot had been established in 79° 30" S. 169° E., practically one hundred and fifty miles distant from the base, and here a ton or so of sledging stores awaited us preparatory for the great sledge journey to the Pole.

Bowers, Oates, and Gran had been left to build up the depot and lead back the other five ponies with their empty sledges. We waited for them at Safety Camp before transporting some of the stuff we had left here out to Corner Camp, the position thirty-five miles E.S.E. of Safety Camp, where the crevasses ended. Some of us went into Hut Point to see if the ship had been there with any message. Little did we dream whilst we sauntered in over the ice of the news that awaited us. We found that the *Terra Nova* had been there the day before Atkinson and Crean had got there ; she had also made a second visit on the 9th or 10th February, bringing the unwelcome news that Amundsen's expedition had been met with in the Bay of Whales. The *Terra*

Nova had entered the bay and found the *Fram* there
with the Norwegians working like ants unloading
their stores and hut-building in rather a dangerous
position quite close to the Barrier edge. Amundsen's
people had about 120 dogs and a hard lot of men,
mostly expert ski-runners. They were contem-
plating an early summer journey to the Pole and
not proposing to attempt serious scientific work
of any sort. Further, to our chagrin, the
eastern party had not effected a landing, for
Campbell realised that it would be profitless to set up his base alongside that of the
Norwegians.

The ice conditions about King Edward VII. Land
had been found insuperable, great masses of land
ice barring the way to their objective, and so poor
Campbell and his mates left news that they were
reluctantly seeking a landing elsewhere. We spent
a very unhappy night, in spite of all attempts to
be cheerful. Clearly, there was nothing for us but to
abandon science and go for the Pole directly the
season for sledging was advanced enough to make
travelling possible after the winter. It now became
a question of dogs versus ponies, for the main bulk
of our stuff must of necessity be pony-drawn unless
we could rely on the motor sledges—nobody believed
we could. However, all the arguing in the world
wouldn't push Amundsen and his dogs off the
Antarctic continent and we had to put the best face
on our disappointment. Captain Scott took it very
bravely, better than any of us, I think, for he had
done already such wonderful work down here. It
was he who initiated and founded Antarctic sledge
travelling, it was he who had blazed the trail, as it
were, and we were very very sorry for him, for such

news, such a menace, could hardly be expected to give him a happy winter.

Scott did the best thing under the circumstances : he set us all to work on the 23rd February to get out three weeks' men provisions for eight men from the stores at Safety Camp, and these collected and packed, he, Cherry-Garrard, and Crean took a 10-ft. sledge, and Forde, Atkinson, and myself a 12-ft. one, while Keohane and James Pigg pulled another big sledge containing oats and paraffin, and we all set out in a bunch for Corner Camp, thirty odd miles away. All this depot work meant an easy start next season, since the transport of great loads over sea ice and the deep, soft snow, which is usually encountered when first getting on to the Barrier hereabouts, would strain the ponies' legs and break the hearts of the dogs. Scott thought all this out and certainly overcame preliminary difficulties by getting so much pony food, provision, and paraffin out to One Ton Camp and Corner Camp. He felt the benefit next springtime. This second little run out is not worth describing ; we sighted Bowers's party coming back with the five ponies whilst we were camped one night, and we noted that they were travelling very quickly, which proved all was well with these animals.

On arrival at Corner Camp Scott left us in order to get back and see the five ponies safely conducted to Hut Point. He instructed me to make easy marches with our friend James Pigg as there was no further work for him this season. Cherry-Garrard and Crean accompanied Scott, and the three pushed on at their utmost for blizzard weather had come again and the snow fall was considerable.

We must now follow Captain Scott's and Bowers's party, who, in conjunction, engaged on the problem of getting five ponies and two dog teams to Hut Point. There did not seem to be anything in doing this, but if ever a man's footsteps were dogged by misfortune, they surely were our leader's.

Scott sent Cherry-Garrard and Crean with Bowers and four ponies across the sea ice from the Barrier edge to reach Hut Point on March 1. He himself had remained with Oates and Gran to tend the pony Weary Willie, a gutless creature compared to the others, which was showing signs of failing. Weary Willie died for no apparent reason, unless his loss of condition was due to the blizzards we encountered on the depot journey.

Bowers and Co. made a good start, but the ponies they had were undoubtedly tired and listless after their hard journey, they were also in bad condition and frequently had to be rested. When they had advanced some way towards Hut Point over good strong sea ice, cracks became apparent and a slight swell showed Bowers that the sea ice was actually on the move. Directly this was appreciated his party turned and hastened back, but the ice was drifting out to sea. The ponies behaved splendidly, jumping the ever widening cracks with extraordinary sagacity, whilst Bowers and his two companions launched the sledges over the water spaces in order not to risk the ponies' legs. Eventually they reached what looked like a safe place and, since men and ponies were thoroughly exhausted, camp was pitched and the weary party soon fell asleep, but at 4.30 the next morning Bowers awoke hearing a strange noise. He opened the tent and found the party in a dreadful plight—the ice had again

D

commenced to break up and they were surrounded
by water. One of the ponies had disappeared into
the sea. Camp was again struck and for five hours
this plucky little party fought their way over three-
quarters of a mile of drifting ice. They never for an
instant thought of abandoning their charge,
realising that Scott's Polar plans would in all probability be ruined if four more ponies were lost
with their sledges and equipment. Crean, with great
gallantry, went for support, clambering with difficulty over the ice. He jumped from floe to floe
and at last climbed up the face of the Barrier
from a piece of ice which swung round in the
tideway and just touched the ice cliff at the right
moment. Cherry-Garrard stayed with Bowers at
his request, for this undaunted little seaman would
never give up his charge while a gleam of hope
remained.

For a whole day these two were afloat on a floe
about 150 ft. square, all the ice around was broken
up into similar floes, which were rising and falling
at least a foot to the heavy swell. A moderate breeze
was blowing from the eastward, and nothing was
visible above the haze and frost smoke except the
tops of two islands named White and Black Islands,
and the hills around Hut Point. Whilst Crean was
clambering over bits of ice and jumping by means
of connecting pieces from one big floe to another, his
progress was watched by Bowers through the
telescope of a theodolite. One can gather how
delighted Bowers must have been to see Crean
eventually high up on the Barrier in the distance,
for it meant that he would communicate with
Captain Scott, whose intelligent, quick grasp in
emergency would surely result in Gran being

despatched on ski over to Cape Evans, for he alone could do this. Once there, a boat could have been launched and the floe party rescued. Bowers's satisfaction was short-lived, however, since Killer whales were noticed cruising amongst the loose ice, and these soon became numerous, some of them actually inspecting the floe by poking their noses up and taking an almost perpendicular position in the water, when their heads would be raised right above the floe edge. The situation looked dangerous, for the whales were evidently after the ponies. The wind fell light as the day progressed and the swell decreased and vanished altogether. This fortunately resulted in the floes closing near to the Barrier, and the open water spaces decreased then to such a degree that the party were able to bridge the cracks by using their sledges until they worked the whole of their equipment up to the Barrier face, where Bowers and Cherry-Garrard were rescued by Scott, Oates, Gran, and Crean. After a further piece of manœuvring a pony and all the sledges were recovered, the three other ponies were drowned. Only those who have served in the Antarctic can realise fully what Bowers's party and also Scott's own rescue party went through.

The incident which terminated in the loss of three more of our ponies cast a temporary gloom over the depot party when we reassembled in the safety of the old ramshackle magnetic lean-to at Hut Point. I use the word lean-to because one could hardly describe it as a hut, for the building was without insulation, snow filled the space between ceiling and roof, and whenever a fire was kindled or heat generated, water dripped down in steady pit-a-pat until there was no dry floor space worth the name.

It might be interesting to touch on the experiences of our friend James Pigg, for this pony can only be described as a quaint but friendly little rogue. He and Keohane seemed to have their own jokes apart from us. We were left to ourselves on the 27th February, while Scott, as stated, pushed forward to Safety Camp, " we," meaning Atkinson, Forde, Keohane, and myself. We were kept in camp on the 27th by a strong blizzard, and the next day when the weather abated, during our forenoon march James Pigg fell into a crevasse, quite a small one, and his girth, through so much high feeding, jammed him by his stomach and prevented him falling far down. The whole situation was ridiculous. We parbuckled him out by means of the Alpine rope, which was quickly detached from the sledge, James Pigg taking a lively interest in the proceedings, and finally rolling over on his back and kicking himself to his feet as we four dragged him up to the surface. This done, Keohane looking very Irish and smiling, bent over and peered down into the bluey depths of the crevasse and, to our intense amusement, James Pigg strolled over alongside of him and hung his head down too. He then turned to Keohane, who patted his nose and said, " That was a near shave for you, James Pigg ! "

We got to Safety Camp on the evening of March 1 and found two notes from Captain Scott directing us to make for Hut Point via Castle Rock, and notifying us that the sea ice was all on the move. We had an interesting climb next day, but a very difficult one, for we were on the go from 9 a.m.

until after 11 that night. First we found our way over the Barrier Ice to the foot of the slope leading up to the ice ridge northward of Castle Rock. Here we tethered James Pigg and spent some hours getting our gear and sledges up the slope. We had no crampons for this work as they were all on Scott's own sledge, so that it was necessary at times to pull up the slopes on hands and knees, assisted by our ski sticks, an unusual procedure but the only one possible to employ on the steeper blue ice. We took the sledges up one by one and then went down with an Alpine rope to help James Pigg. We found the pony very bored at our long absence; he neighed and whinnied when we came down to him, and, to our great surprise, went up the long, steep slope with far greater ease than we did ourselves.

It was out of the question for us to proceed the four and a half miles along the ridges which led down to Hut Point, for darkness had set in and we had no wish to repeat the performance of an earlier expedition when a man lost his life hereabouts through slipping right over one of these steep slopes into the sea on the western side of the promontory ridge which terminates at Hut Point.

It was snowing when we turned in and still snowing on March 3 when we turned out of our sleeping-bags. James Pigg, quite snug, clothed in his own, Blossom's, and Blücher's rugs, had a little horseshoe shelter built up round him. We did not know at this time of the pony disaster, but, thinking Captain Scott might be anxious if he got no word as to our whereabouts or movements, Atkinson and I started to march along the ice ridges of Castle Rock and make our way to Hut Point. It

was blowing hard and very cold, but the joy of
walking on firm ice without a sledge to drag was
great. When finally we came to the old *Discovery*
hut at lunch time, we found Wilson, Meares, and
Gran in very low spirits. They told us that Bowers
and Cherry-Garrard were adrift on an ice floe and
the remainder of the party had gone to the rescue
along the Barrier edge. We were much downcast
by this news, and after a meal of biscuit and tea,
started back for our camp. The weather was now
clearer, and we could see some way out over the
Barrier ; we could also see the sea looking very
blue against the white expanse of ice.

On the way back we discussed a plan and arranged that we should leave Keohane with the pony,
take a sledge, and make our way along the ice edge
of the Barrier searching for Scott and joining up
with him, but just before descending to the hollow
where our tent was we spied a sledge party on the
Barrier and, on reaching our camp, were delighted
to see through my telescope six men. Thank God !
This meant that all were safe. We went out to
meet the party, reaching them about 8 p.m. where
they had camped, a couple of miles from Cape
Armitage, between two pressure ridges that formed
great frozen waves. Bowers told me that when
Scott's party attempted to save the horses at the
Barrier edge, rotten ice and open water leads were
the cause of their downfall, and when the horses
slipped into the sea, that he had been compelled
to kill his own pony with a pickaxe to save him
being taken alive by one of the Orcas or Killer
whales. The only horse saved was Captain Scott's,
one of the best we had in that Expedition.

I think the Irish sailors must have spoilt James

Pigg, for, when eventually we got Scott's sledge loads up to the hill-crest where our camp was, James Pigg, instead of welcoming the other pony, broke adrift, and jumping into the new-comer's shelter, leapt on him, kicked him and bit him in the back. On March 5 we all started for Hut Point, having previously sent in Atkinson with the good news that no men's lives were lost. Wilson and party met us near Castle Rock and led the ponies in while we dropped the laden sledges, full of pony harness, tents, and sledging gear, with a sufficiency of pony fodder for a fortnight, down the ski-slope to Hut Point. It was a fine bit of tobogganing and Captain Scott showed himself to be far more expert than any of us in controlling a sledge on a slippery slope.

We soon got into the way of climbing around on seemingly impossible slopes and could negotiate the steepest of hills and the slipperiest of steep inclines. It was largely a question of good crampons, which we fortunately possessed.

The month of March and the first half of April, 1911, proved to be the most profitless and unsatisfactory part of the Expedition. This was due to a long compulsory wait at Hut Point, for we could not cross the fifteen miles that lay between our position there and the Cape Evans Station until sea ice had formed, which could be counted on not to break away and take us into the Ross Sea in its northward drift. Time after time the sea froze over to a depth of a foot or even more and time and again we made ready to start for Cape Evans to find that on the day of departure the ice had all broken and drifted out of sight. As it was, we were safely, if not comfortably, housed at Hut Point, with the two dog teams and the two remaining ponies, existing in rather primitive fashion with seal meat for our principal diet. By the end of the first week in March we had converted the veranda, which ran round three sides of the old magnetic hut, into dog and pony shelters, two inner compartments were screened off by bulkheads made of biscuit cases, a cook's table was somehow fashioned and a reliable stove erected out of petrol tins and scrap-iron. Our engineers in this work of art were Oates and Meares. For a short while we burnt wood in the stove, but the day soon came when seal blubber was substituted, and the heat from the burning grease was sufficient to cook any kind of dish likely to be available, and also to heat the hut after a fashion.

Round the stove we built up benches to sit on for meals, and two sleeping spaces were chosen and made snug by using felt, of which a quantity had been left by Scott's or Shackleton's people. The " Soldier " and Meares unearthed some fire bricks and a stove pipe from the debris heap outside the hut and then we were spared the great discomfort of being smoked out whenever a fire was lit. An awning left by the *Discovery* was fixed up by several of us around the sleeping and cooking space, and although rather short of luxuries such as sugar and flour, we were never in any great want of good plain food.

On March 14 the depot party was joined by Griffith Taylor, Debenham, Wright, and Petty Officer Evans.

Taylor's team had been landed by the *Terra Nova* on January 27, after the start of the depot party, to make a geological reconnaissance. In the course of their journeying they had traversed the Ferrar Glacier and then come down a new glacier, which Scott named after Taylor, and descended into Dry Valley, so called because it was entirely free from snow. Taylor's way had led him and his party over a deep fresh-water lake, four miles long, which was only surface frozen—this lake was full of algæ. The gravels below a promising region of limestones rich in garnets were washed for gold, but only magnetite was found. When Taylor had thoroughly explored and examined the region of the glaciers to the westward of Cape Evans, his party retraced their footsteps and proceeded southward to examine the Koettlitz Glacier. Scott had purposely sent Seaman Evans with this party of geologists, reasoning with his usual thoughtfulness that Evans's sledging experience would be invaluable to Taylor and his companions.

Taylor and his party made wonderful maps and had a wonderful store of names, which they bestowed upon peak, pinnacle, and pool to fix in their memories the relative positions of the things they saw. Griffith Taylor had a remarkable gift of description, and his Antarctic book, *The Silver Lining*, contains some fine anecdotes and narrative.

According to Taylor's chart the Koettlitz Glacier at its outflow on to the Great Ice Barrier is at least ten miles wide. The party proceeded along the north of the glacier for a considerable distance, sketching, surveying, photographing, and making copious notes of the geological and physiographical conditions in the neighbourhood, and one may say fearlessly that no Antarctic expedition ever sailed yet with geologists and physicists who made better use of the time at their disposal, especially whilst doing field work.

This party hung on with their exploration work until prudence told them that they must return from the Koettlitz Glacier before the season closed in. Their return trip led them along the edge of the almost impenetrable pinnacle of ice which is one of the wonders of the Antarctic. Their journey led them also through extraordinary and difficult ice-fields that even surprised the veteran sledger Evans. Their final march took them along the edge of the Great Ice Barrier and brought them to Hut Point on March 14.

We now numbered sixteen at this congested station; the sun was very little above the horizon and gales were so bad that spray dashed over the small hut occasionally, whilst all round the low-lying parts of the coast wonderful spray ridges of ice were formed. We had our proportion of blizzard days and suffered somewhat from the cold, for it was rarely calm. Some of us began to long for the greater comforts of the Cape Evans Hut; there was no day, no hour in fact, when some one did not climb up the hillock which was surmounted by the little wooden cross put up in memory of Seaman Vince of the *Discovery* expedition, to see and note the ice conditions.

Winter was coming fast and night shadows of cruel dark purple added to the natural gloom of Hut Point and its environments. Wilson was the one man amongst us who profited most from our sojourn here. In spite of bad light and almost frozen fingers he managed to make an astonishing collection of sketches, portraying the autumn scenes near this corner of Ross Isle. How sinister and relentless the western mountains looked, how cold and unforgiving the foothills, and how ashy gray the sullen icefoots that girt this sad, frozen land.

There was, of course, no privacy in the crowded hut-space, and when evening came it was sometimes rather a relief to get away to some sheltered corner and look out over the Sound. The twilight shades and colours were beautiful in a sad sort of way, but the stillness was awful. Whenever the wind fell light new ice would form which seemed to crack and be churned up with every cat's-paw of wind. The currents and tidal streams would slowly carry these pancakes of ice up and down the Strait until the weather was calm enough and cold enough to cement them together till they formed floes, which in their turn froze fast into great white icefields strong enough to bear us and any weights we liked to take along. One often turned in, confident that a passage could be made over the frozen sea to Glacier Tongue at least, but in the morning everything would be changed and absolutely no ice would be visible floating in the sea. When Taylor's party had rested a little at Hut Point they threw in their lot with the rest of us and made occasional trips out on the silent Barrier as far as Corner Camp, to add sledge loads of provisions now and again to the stores already depoted there in readiness for the southern sledge journey, on which we built our hopes for ultimate triumph.

Eight of us went out for a week's sledging on March 16, but the temperatures were now becoming too low to be pleasant and touching 40° or so below zero. What tried us more than anything else was

thick weather and the fearfully bad light on days
when no landmarks were visible to guide us to the
depot. Our sleeping-bags also were frozen and
uncomfortable, thick rime collecting on the insides
of our tents which every puff of wind would shake
down in a shower of ice. When sitting round on our
rolled-up sleeping-bags at meal times we could not
help our heads and shoulders brushing off patches
of this frost rime, which soon accumulated in the fur
of the sleeping-bags and made life at night a clammy
misery. The surfaces were very heavy, and dragging
even light sledges when returning from the depot
proved a laborious business.

This autumn time gave a series of gales and
strong winds with scarcely ever more than a few
hours of calm or gentle breeze, sandwiched in
between. Sometimes we used ski, but there are
occasions when ski are quite useless, owing to snow
binding in great clogs underneath them. The
Norwegians use different kinds of paraffin wax
and compositions of tar and other ingredients for
overcoming this difficulty. Gran had brought from
Christiania the best of these compositions, nevertheless there were days when whatever we put on
we had difficulty with ski and had to cast them
aside. There were people who preferred foot-
slogging to ski at any time, and there were certainly
days when teams on foot would literally dance
round men pulling on ski. In the light of experience,
however, the expert ski-runner has enormous
advantage over the " foot-slogger," however good
an athelete.

What strikes me here is the dreadful similarity in
weather condition, wind, temperature, etc., surface
and visibility to that which culminated in the great

disaster of our expedition and resulted in poor
Scott's death exactly a year later. Here is a day
taken haphazard from my diary :

" From Corner Camp to Hut Point :

" March 18, 1911.—Called the hands at 6.15 and
after a fine warming breakfast started off on ski.
The light was simply awful and the surface very
bad, but we did six miles, then lunched. After
lunch carried on with a strong wind blowing, but
after very heavy dragging we were forced to camp
when only nine and a half miles had been laid
between us—we really couldn't see ten yards. Just
after we camped the wind increased to about
force 6, alternately freshening up and dying away,
and a good deal of snow fell. Temperature 32·5
below zero."

One year later Scott was facing weather conditions and surfaces almost identical, but the difference lay in that he had marched more than sixteen
hundred miles, was short of food, and his party
were suffering from the tragic loss of two of their
companions and the intense disappointment of
having made this great sledge journey for their
country's honour to find that all their efforts had
been in vain, and that they had been anticipated
by men who had borne thither the flag of another
nation.

When Scott found that we sledgers were getting
temperatures as low as minus forty he decided to
discontinue sledging rather than risk anything in
the nature of severe frostbite assailing the party
and rendering them unfit for further work, for it

must be remembered that we had already been away from our base ten weeks, that many of us had never sledged before, and that the depot journey was partly undertaken to give us sledging experience and to point out what improvements could be made in our clothing and equipment.

The first and second weeks in April brought the ice changes that we had so long awaited, and after one or two false starts two teams set out from Hut Point on April 11 to make their way across the fifteen miles of sea ice to Cape Evans.

This turned out to be a somewhat hazardous journey, since it had to be made in the half light with overcast weather and hard wind. Scott took charge of one tent and had with him Bowers, Griffith Taylor, and Petty Officer Evans, while I had in my party Wright, Debenham, Gran, and Crean. The seven who remained at Hut Point in charge of dogs and ponies helped us out a league or so for the first part of our journey.

The route led first up the steep ice slope overhanging Hut Point, and then to the summit of the ridge, which is best described as the Castle Rock promontory. Our sojourn at Hut Point had given us plenty of chance to learn the easier snow roads and the least dangerous, and Scott chose the way close eastward of Castle Rock to a position four miles beyond it, which his first expedition had named Hutton Cliffs. From Castle Rock onward the way took us to the westward of two conical hills which were well-known landmarks—a hitherto untrodden route—but the going was by no means bad. Bitingly cold for faces and finger-tips, still, no weights to impede us. We camped for lunch after covering seven miles, for the light was bad, but it improved surprisingly whilst we were eating our meal. Accordingly, we put on our crampons about 3 p.m. and struck camp, securely packing the two green tents on the sledges, and casting a careful eye round the loads, tightened a strap here, hitched there, and then led by Scott we made a careful descent to the precipitous edge of the ice cap which overlays the promontory. We got well down to a part that seemed to overhang the sea and, to our delight, found a good solid-looking ice-sheet below us which certainly extended as far as Glacier Tongue. The drop here was twenty-five feet or so and Taylor and I were lowered over the cornice in an Alpine rope, then Wright and then the sledges, after that the remainder of the party. An ash-pole was driven into the snow and the last few members sent down in a bowline at one end of the rope whilst we below eased them down with the other part. The two parts of the Alpine rope working round the pole cut deeply into the overhanging snow and brought a shower of ice crystals pouring over the heads and shoulders of whoever was sitting in the bowline. It was a good piece of work getting everything down safely, and I admired Scott's decision to go over ; a more nervous man would have fought shy because, once down on the sea ice there was little chance of our getting back and we had got to fight our way forward to Cape Evans somehow.

When Taylor and I got first down we were greeted with a weird and wonderful sight : constant drifts of snow had formed a great overhang and the ice cliff was wreathed in a mass of snowy curtains and folds which took all manner of fantastic turns and shapes. A fresh wind was blowing continuously that made it most unpleasant for those above, and it was a relief to us all when the last man was passed down in safety, it was Scott himself.

We quickly harnessed up again and swung out over the sea ice towards Glacier Tongue, the cliffs of which stood out in a hard, white line to the northward, a couple of miles away. Arrived at the Tongue, Bowers and I clambered up a ten-foot cliff face by standing on Wright's and Crean's shoulders. We then reached down and hauled up the sledges and the others, harnessed up again, and proceeded to cross the Glacier, which was full of small crevasses. We reached the northern side of it and went down an easy snow slope to the sea ice beyond. As far as one could see this ice continued right up to and around Cape Evans, seven miles away to the N.W. It was now 6.30 p.m.; Scott halted us and discussed our readiness to make a night march into the winter quarters. There was not one dissentient voice, and we gladly started off at 8 o'clock for a night march to our snug and comfortable hut, picturing to ourselves a supper of all things luxurious. Our feet seemed suddenly to have taken wings, but, alas, the supper was not to be, for thick weather set in, and when, by 10 o'clock the wind was blowing hard and it was pitch dark, Scott suddenly decided to camp under the shelter of Little Razorback Island, where by that time we had arrived. We passed a filthy night here, for the snow on the sea ice was saturated with brine and, in no time, our sleeping-bags became wet and sticky.

Next day we were called at six to find a blizzard with a high drift making it impossible to move, so we remained in our bags until 4 p.m., when we shifted on to the narrow platform of rock situated on the south side of Little Razorback. We had one small meal here, but our condition was not a pleasant one, since little food remained and fuel was short. There was undoubtedly a chance that the sea ice would break up and drift away in this high wind. Had that happened we should have been left to starve on the tiny island. The position was not an enviable one. We got back into our bags, which were, as stated, wet and beastly, after a scanty supper and tried to sleep, but our feet were wet too, and cold, so that few of us could do more than close our eyes. The night passed slowly enough, and we turned out at 7 a.m. to cook what remained of our food before attempting to make Cape Evans. We were glad that it had stopped snowing and, although the light was bad enough, we could just make out the ice foot showing up bold and white on the south side of the Cape. After the meal we struck camp, formed marching order, and started half running for winter quarters. Covering a couple of miles we found, to our great relief, that the fast ice not only extended up to the Cape but right round into North Bay. We soon sighted the hut, and shortly after saw some people working outside. Directly they saw us in they ran to bring the others out at full speed, and coming to meet us they cheered and greeted us, then hauled our sledges in. It appeared they were unable to recognise any of us owing to our dirty and dishevelled state. This was not to be wondered at, for we had not washed nor had we shaved for eighty days. We all talked hard and exchanged news. Ponting lined us up to be photographed—the first nine Bolshevists—we looked such awful black-guards.

Now, April 13, 1911, as communication had been established between Hut Point and Cape Evans, we settled down for the winter. I shall never forget the breakfast that Clissold prepared for us at 10.30 that morning. It was delicious—hot rolls, heaps of butter, milk, sugar, jam, a fine plate of tomato soup, and fried seal cooked superbly. The meal over, we shaved, bathed, and put on clean clothes, smoked cigarettes, and took a day's holiday. At 10 o'clock that evening, by prearrangement, Very's lights were fired to let them know at Hut Point of our safe arrival. Our own signal was answered by a flare. Gramophone records were dug out and we lazily listened to Melba singing and to musical comedy tunes, those who had energy and sufficient inclination got the pianola going, and finally each man unfolded his little story to another member of the Expedition who had taken no part in the sledging.

Captain Scott was delighted at the progress made by those left in our hut under Dr. Simpson, everything was in order, the scientific programme in full swing, and nothing in the shape of bad news beyond the loss of an ill-tempered pony called Hackenschmidt, and one more dog that appeared to have died from a peculiar disease—a minute thread-worm getting to his brain, this according to Nelson who had conducted the post-mortem.

CHAPTER VII

ARRANGEMENTS FOR THE WINTER

LESS than a fortnight from the day of our return to Cape Evans, on April 23 to be exact, the sun left us to remain below the horizon for four long weary months. Of course, there was a considerable amount of twilight, and even on midwinter's day at noon there was some gray light in the north. Different people took the winter in different fashion, according to their temperaments. There were some who never could have faced a second winter with any degree of cheerfulness, but taking it all round, we did well enough, and when summer came again our concrete keenness and zeal had not one whit abated. That is especially true in the case of those who were chosen to make the great journey southward, even though it was obvious that certain members could only accompany their leader for a mere fraction of the great white way.

During the four months' winter darkness each one occupied himself with his special subject, and Dr. Wilson not only proved himself to be an efficient chief of our scientific staff, but a sound friend and companion to the executive members, Bowers, Oates, Meares, and myself. Uncle Bill was our Solomon and it was to him that we all went for sympathy and practical advice. It was to him the staff went, that is to say, the officers and scientists, for the smoothing over of those little difficulties, roughnesses, and unevennesses that were bound to arrive from time to time during the course of winter. The sailors came more to Bowers, Oates, and myself, for, in their conservative naval way, they could never quite get over the fact that the hut was not a ship and that there were other members who, although they had never come under any sort of naval or military discipline, were men of greater age and experience in fending for themselves than youngsters like Bowers and myself. Still, things went beautifully, and so they should have, when one considers the great care our leader had exercised in the selection of his personnel.

If Scott had had his choice again and if he had been allowed to select from the whole world, one can say without hesitation he would have chosen Wilson to captain our splendid scientific team and to be his human book of reference. Wilson was more nearly Scott's own age than the other important members of this enterprise, and Wilson, it must be remembered, had pulled shoulder to shoulder with Scott on his southern sledge journey in 1902-3.

Before taking a peep at the individuals forming the rest of our party and at their delicate scientific work at the base station, I must not forget to mention that Scott, with his indomitable energy, was away again four days after his return to Cape Evans with Bowers, Crean, and five fresh men to Hut Point for the dual purpose of replenishing that station with fuel, lighting material, etc., and getting those who should be at Cape Evans for certain work and duty back there. Scott returned by the way we had come, *i.e.* the Glacier Tongue-Castle

Rock route, and then left the dog-boy with Meares to take charge of these animals, Lashly and Keohane to nurse and exercise the two ponies, and Nelson and Forde to get into the way of winter roughing it, besides which he left Day over at Hut Point, where his clever fingers found plenty to do to ameliorate the condition of those living there. Day had learnt much under Shackleton in these parts, and by some of us he was nicknamed " Handy Andy." Meares was now appointed " Governor of Hut Point." As a matter of fact he and his dogs were better off here than at Cape Evans, because the dogs could use the big sheltered verandas already mentioned, whereas they had no such shelter at Cape Evans.

Scott was back in the hut by April 21, having left Meares definite orders that James Pigg and Punch the ponies were not to leave Hut Point for Cape Evans until the entire journey could be made over the sea ice under conditions of absolute safety. This meant a wait of three weeks to a month before everything suited, and the " Governor of Hut Point " did not come in until the 13th May, when he arrived in pomp and splendour with all the dogs and the two ponies fit and well—his party, black with soot and blubber, their windproof clothing smelly and greasy, a dirty but robust and cheerful gang.

The next few paragraphs give an idea of the arrangement of the hut. Starting at the left hand top corner we find Simpson's laboratory, and we usually found Simpson in it at work, always at work, except when he was engaged in scientific argument or when, just after lunch, he stretched himself out on his bunk at the end of a large cigar ! Simpson was no novice to work in the frigid zones, for he had already wintered within the Arctic circle in northern Norway. Weather did not worry him much nor apparently did temperatures, for since his investigations midst the snows of the Vikings' land, Simpson had worked extensively in India. His enduring good humour and his smiling manner earned for him the sobriquet of Sunny Jim.

In the first year the self-registering instruments that found themselves in Simpson's corner, or in the small hut which contained his magnetic observatory, gave us an admirable record of temperatures, barometric pressures, wind force and direction, atmospheric electricity, sunshine when the sun did shine, and the elements of terrestrial magnetism. Thanks to Simpson, we also had investigations of the upper air currents, aurora observations, atmospheric optics, gravity determination and what is more, some fine practical teaching that enabled the various sledging units properly to observe and collect data of meteorological importance. Simpson's place was essentially at the base station ; and his consequent work as physicist and meteorologist prevented him from taking an active part in our sledge journeys. When he was recalled to Simla in 1912 his work was ably continued by Wright, our Canadian chemist, who, as I have said elsewhere, accompanied us south to make a special study of ice structure and glaciation.

Wright lived in the bunk above Simpson's, and when not devoting his energy and magnificent physique to sledging and field work, he gave himself up to the study of ice physics, a somewhat new scientific line of research. Wright was originally

introduced to the Expedition by Griffith Taylor,
and Scott, advised by Wilson, was so keen on the
inclusion of this young Canadian chemist in our
scientific staff that really the study of ice structure
and glaciation was made for Wright and his science
coined for him. He photographed ice flowers
formed in the sea, he found out how long ice took to
freeze down our way, cast aspersions on the bearing
capabilities of our beloved sea ice and, generally,
brought his intelligence to bear in a way that commanded the approbation of Wilson and our chief.
Wright was one of the strongest members of our
Expedition, and he had the most powerful flow
of language. He made some beautiful photographs
of ice crystals and surprised the simple sailor like
myself with his ability as a navigator and
astronomer.

Moving along from Wright and Simpson we
come to Nelson and Day. Teddy Nelson, our marine
biologist, did both winters at Cape Evans, and he
not only carried out biological work but studied the
tides. His corner was pleasant to look upon, with
its orderly row of enamelled and china trays and
dishes. During the winter months holes were made
in the sea ice through which were lowered tow-nets,
for collecting drifting organisms and so on. Special
thermometers of German make were lowered by
Nelson through the ice holes to get sea temperatures, and likewise reversing water bottles were
employed to obtain samples of sea-water daily.

Day, the motor engineer, was responsible for the
lighting by acetylene. He was wonderfully clever
as a mechanic and also a good carpenter. He took
charge of our petrol, paraffin, and spirit store, and
was never idle for a minute.

Moving along to the right we come to the last cubicle, where the " Rubbleyubdugs " lived. These were Tryggve Gran, Griffith Taylor, and Frank Debenham. (All libel actions in connection with the Ubdugs I am prepared to settle out of port in the long bar at Shanghai.) Quoting from the *South Polar Times* : " ' The Ubdug Burrow ' is festooned with kodaks, candles and curtains ; they (the Ubdugs) are united by an intense love of the science of autobiography, their somewhat ambiguous motto is ' the pen is mightier than the sword, but the tongue licks them both ! ' " Griffith Taylor and Debenham were both Australians : the former was probably the wittiest man in the Expedition, and, in my opinion, the cleverest contributor to the *South Polar Times*, excepting of course the artistic side. The *South Polar Times* was our winter magazine, beautifully illustrated by Wilson's water colours and Ponting's photographs. Taylor's motto was " Advance, Australia ! "—most certainly he helped it to. People were always welcome in the Ubduggery, where they seemed to have an un-limited supply of cigarettes and good novels.

Debenham was certainly nurse to the Ubdugs, that is to say he was the least untidy, but then of course he was the smallest. In this cubicle the most voluminous of diaries were kept, and at least two books have been published therefrom. Gran kept his diary mostly in Norwegian, but there were many words coined in our Expedition which had no Scandinavian equivalent, and Gran failed to translate them, in spite of his having more im-agination than any one amongst us.

Crossing over the hut to the cubicle opposite one arrives at the somewhat congested space in which

Cherry-Garrard was housed, with Bowers above him. In their corner were store lists, books, and mystery bags which contained material for the *South Polar Times*, toys and frivolous presents to liven us up at the midwinter and other festivities. Bowers and Cherry-Garrard were, in a way, worse off than the others, for they had the darkest part of the hut, yet in this gloomy tenement all kinds of calculations were made and much other good work done.

Oates came next, with his bunk more free of debris than anybody else's, for he was the horse man, pure and simple, and his duties freed him from that superabundance of books, instruments, stationery, specimens, charts, and what-not with which we others had surrounded ourselves. Any spare gear he kept in the saddle room, a specially cleared space in the stables, where he was assisted by the little Russian groom, Anton, who soon became devoted to his hard-working and capable master. The two men, so unlike in appearance and character, etc., and such miles apart in social standing and nationality, worked shoulder to shoulder in the stables throughout the long winter night. By the dim candle-light which illuminated our pony-shelter, one could see Oates grooming his charges, clearing up their stall, refitting their harness, and fixing up the little improvements that his quick, watchful eye continually suggested. At the far end of his stables he had a blubber stove, where he used to melt ice for the ponies' drinking water and cook bran mashes for his animals. Here he would often sit and help Meares make dog pemmican out of seal meat—they made about 8 cwt. of this sustaining preparation.

Moving along from the Château, Oates, Meares's and Atkinson's two bunks came next, Meares above and Atkinson below. These two sleeping berths likewise were not conspicuous by any superfluity of scientific oddments, for Meares's work took him outside of the hut as a rule, unless he was engaged in making dog harness. Meares and Oates were the greatest friends, and these two, Atkinson, Cherry-Garrard and Bowers, were, if I remember rightly, known collectively as the Bunderlohg. Although numerically superior to their *vis-à-vis*, the Ubdugs, and always ready to revile them, the Ubdugs kept their end up and usually came out victorious in discussions or in badinage.

Finally, the Holy of Holies, where Captain Scott and the library occupied one end and Uncle Bill and myself the far corner, with the ceaselessly ticking chronometers and many sledging watches. There was an air of sanctity about this part : all the plotting was done here, charts made and astronomical observations worked out. Wilson worked up his sketches at the " plotting table," interviewed the staff here, and above his bunk kept a third of the shore party's library. We had two comfortable trestle beds up our end and our leader also had a bed in preference to the built-up bunk adopted by most of the afterguard. Ours was the Mayfair district : Wilson and I lived in Park Lane in those days, whilst Captain Scott occupied Grosvenor Street ! He had his own little table covered with " toney " green linoleum, and also had a multiplicity of little shelves on which to keep his pipes, tobacco, cigars, and other household gods. It was well illuminated in this part, and, although hung around with fur mitts, fur boots, socks, hats and woollen clothing, there was something very chaste about this very respectable corner. For the rest of it we had our Arctic library, and the spare spaces on the matchboard bulkhead, which fenced it on three sides, were decorated with photographs. In place of eiderdown Scott's old uniform overcoat usually covered his bed, while peeping out from under his sleeping place one could espy an emblem of civilisation and prosperity in the shape of a very good suit-case.

The foregoing pages illustrate sufficiently the grouping of the afterguard, and if one adds an anthracite stove, a 12 ft. by 4 ft. table, a pianola, gramophone, and a score of chairs, with a small shelf-like table squeezed in between the dark-room and Simpson's corner, one completes the picture of the officers' quarters in the Cape Evans Hut.

A bulkhead of biscuit cases and so on divided us from the men's accommodation. They were very well off, each seaman having a trestle bed similar to Captain Scott's, unless he preferred to build a bunk for himself, as one or two did. They had a table 6 ft. by 4 ft., and the cook had a kitchen table 4 ft. square, and certainly no crew space was ever provided on a Polar Expedition that gave such comfortable and cosy housing room.

CHAPTER VIII

THE WINTER CLOSES IN

THE closing down of the Polar night was very swift now and the few hours of gray daylight were employed collecting what data was required by certain members for working on during the forthcoming days of darkness. Young Gran was handed over to me to help with the survey work and astronomical observations which had to be taken from time to time. He was a most entertaining assistant. Without complaint, he stood patiently shivering in that cutting winter wind whilst I swung around the theodolite telescope and took angles for him to write down in my notebook. I don't think anybody has made a triangulated survey under conditions worse than we endured that epoch : the weather was beastly and we spent much time dancing when nearly sick with cold, our fingers tucked under our arms to recover their feelings. When one's extremities did get frost-bitten it was no joke—frost-bitten finger tips gave us little peace at night with their sharp burning pain.

The most interesting part of the survey work was what is known to the surveyor as coast-lining. This meant walking along the edge of the sea ice, fixing one's position by sextant angle every five hundred yards or so, and sketching in a notebook the character and features of the ever changing coast between the various " fixes." One could keep warm doing this and one saw more of the land and ice formation than the others, for it meant following carefully round-cape and glacier edge, penetrating inlets and delineating every islet, promontory, cliff, and talus.

In spite of the cold, the gloom, and the sad whistling wind that heralded the now fast approaching darkness, I felt glad to work with my sextant and sketch-book under the shadow of those fantastic ice-foots hung round with fringes of icicle. I loved to go with Gran into the deep bays and walk for miles under the overhanging of the vast ice cliffs all purple in the reflection of the early winter noon, and to come out sometimes as we did on to the sea ice clear of a jutting glacier, to face suddenly northward over the frozen sea where nothing but a great waste of ice stretched away to meet the horizon and the rosy, copper glow of the departed sun's rays. Some of the cloud effects at the end of April were too wonderful for mere pen or brush to describe. To appreciate them one must go there and see them, those wonderful half-light tints.

Then there were the ice caves and grottos which were formed in the grounded icebergs that had overturned before we came, and the still more wonderful caves in the ice-sheet where it over-rode Ross Island and formed a cliff-face between Cape Evans and Glacier Tongue, extraordinarily like the white chalk cliffs of Studland Bay I found them, with here and there outstanding pinnacles which a little imagination would liken to Old Harry Rocks when the gray light was on them.

At the most we could only take sextant and theodolite angles for two hours on either side of noon, so Gran and I went without our lunch, taking a few biscuits and some chocolate out with us on our survey days, and as we worked farther and farther from our base we found it necessary to start out in the darkness in order to take full advantage of what light was vouchsafed us. It was good healthy work and we developed glorious appetites, so that our mouths ran with water when perhaps we met a couple of fellows leading the little white ponies on the sea ice for exercise, and they told us what they had had for lunch and what was being kept for us. We found it all most interesting and, although I detested that sunless winter, I loved the changing scenery, which never seemed monotonous when there was any daylight or moonlight. To mark our "stations" we used red and black bunting flags, and they showed up very well. We gave them all sorts of weird names, such as Sardine, Shark, and so forth, and we knew almost to a yard their distances from one another, as also their bearings, which helped us when we were overtaken by bad weather. Eventually it became too dark for any survey work, but there was always plenty to do indoors for the majority of us. Apart from our specialist duties some one was always to be found who could give employment to the willing— there were no idlers or unwilling folk amongst us. Simpson, for example, would employ as many volunteers as he could get to follow the balloons which he frequently sent up to record temperature and pressure. To each of these balloons a fine silk thread was attached, or rather the thread was attached to the little instrument it carried. When any strain was put on the thread it broke the thread connecting the small temperature and pressure instrument to the balloon, the former dropped on to the ice and was recovered by one of the volunteers, who followed the silk thread up until he came to the instrument where it had fallen. One required good eyesight for this work as for everything else down here, and I have never ceased to marvel at the way Cherry-Garrard got about and worked so well when one considers that he was very shortsighted indeed.

Everybody exercised generously, whether by himself on ski, leading a pony, digging ice for the cook or ice to melt for the ponies' drinking water, or even with a whole crowd playing rather dangerous football on the sea ice north of Cape Evans.

When the real winter came I used to walk, after winding the chronometers, until breakfast time to begin with. This gave me half an hour, then again before lunch I would put on ski and go for a run with anybody who had not a pony to exercise. The visibility was frequently limited, particularly on overcast days ; one would glide along over the sea ice, which was in places wind-swept and in others covered with snow. Nothing in sight but the gray-white shadow underfoot and the blue-black sky above, a streak or band just a mere smudge of daylight in the north, but this would be sufficient to give one direction to go out on. Then slowly, dim, spectre-like shapes would appear which would gradually sort themselves out into two lots, black and white—these were Titus's ponies—the white shapes, the black were the men leading them. On they came, seemingly at a great pace, and one heard a crunching noise as the hoofs of the ponies trod down the snow crust, but one could not hear the footfalls of the men. One exchanged a " Hallo " with the leading man and passed on until a much bigger white shape loomed up in the obscurity of the noon-twilight, the going underfoot changed and skis fetched up against a great lump of ice which was scarcely discernible in the confusing darkness, and one realised that what little light there was to the northward had been blotted out by one of the big grounded icebergs. Directly one realised which berg it was a new course would be shaped, say to the end of the Barne Glacier ; the cliffs of this reached, one proceeded homeward a league to the hut. This could not be missed on the darkest day if the coast-line was followed, and, at last, when stomach cried out like a striking clock, one realised that it was 2 p.m. or so, and a little glow indicated the where-abouts of the hut. Approaching it, one saw the tall chimney silhouetted against the sky, then the black shapes which oddly proclaimed themselves to be motor-sledges, store heaps or fodder dumps, and finally the hut itself. One stumbled over the tide-crack and up on to the much trodden snow which covered the Cape Evans's beach. Six or seven pairs of skis stuck in the snow near the hut door indicated that most people had come in to lunch, so there was need to haste. Off came one's own skis, and with a lusty stab in they went heel downwards into the snow alongside the other ones, so that when a new fall came they would stand up vertically and be easily found again.

The sticks one took into the hut, because even in our well-appointed family there were pirates who borrowed them and forgot to replace them. Entering the hut after kicking much snow from boots one passed first through the acetylene smelling porch—Handy Andy's pride—as we called Day's gas plant, then in to the seamen's quarters, where the smell of cooking delighted and the sight of those great, hefty sailors scoffing the midday meal hustled one still more.

In the officers' half of the hut most people were already busy with their knives and forks, two or three perhaps just sitting down, the night watchman probably sitting up on the edge of his bunk putting on his slippers, and cheerfully accepting the friendly insults from his pals at table who told him the date and year—down went ski-sticks on the bed, room would be made at the table, and half a dozen dishes pushed your way, and although the mess-traps were enamelled, the food you shuffled down from the tin plate and the cocoa you lapped from the blue and white mug had not its equal at the Carlton, the Ritz, or the Berkeley.

Concerning the night watchman and his duties, although we had so many self-recording instruments, there were certain things which called for attention during the silent hours. Aurora observations had to be made which no instrument would record, movement of clouds had to be noted in the meteorological log, the snow cleared from the anemometer and so forth, then of course rounds had to be made in case of fire, ponies and dogs visited, the galley fire lit or kept going according to requirements, and so on. Night watch-keeping duty was only undertaken by certain members chosen from the afterguard. Scott himself always took a share in this, as he did in everything else that mattered. One came to welcome the night on, for the attendant work was not very strenuous

E

and the eight hours' quietude gave the watchman a chance to write up a neglected diary, to wash clothes, work out observations, and perhaps make contributions to the *South Polar Times* undisturbed by casual well-wishers who were not meant to see the article in question until the day of publication. We were allowed to choose from the stores more or less what we liked for consumption in the stillness of the night watch. I always contributed special China or Ceylon tea for the benefit of the lonely watchman—I had two big canisters of the beverage, a present from one of our New Zealand well-wishers, Mrs. Arthur Rhodes of Christchurch, and these lasted the afterguard watch-keepers through the Expedition.

The auroras were a little disappointing this first winter as seen from Cape Evans, they were certainly better seen from the Barrier. We only got golden bands and curtains splaying in the heavens, except for one or two rare occasions when there were distinct green rays low down amongst the shafts of weird light farthest from the zenith.

In view of the possibility of a second winter one kept a few letters going which contained a little narrative of our work to date. We had most imposing note-paper which was used for these occasions : the crest consisted of a penguin standing on the South Pole with the southern hemisphere underfoot, a garter surrounding this little picture inscribed with " British Antarctic Expedition— *Terra Nova* R.Y.S." Alas, some of the letters were never delivered, for death not only laid his hand upon certain members of the Expedition, but also upon some of our older friends, supporters, and subscribers.

One passed out of the hut hourly at least and, on moonlight nights especially, one found something beautiful in the scenery about Cape Evans. At full moon time everything turned silver, from towering Erebus with gleaming sides to the smooth ice slopes of Ross Island in the north-east, while away to the southward the high black Dellbridge Islands thrust up from a sea of flat silver ice. Even the conical hills and the majestic Castle Rock, fifteen miles away, stood out quite clearly on occasions. The weirdest thing of all was to hear the dogs howling in the middle of the night, they made one think of wolves and of Siberia.

All things considered, the winter passed quickly enough : we had three lectures a week, and our professional occupations, our recreations and different interests soon sped away the four months' winter darkness. The lectures embraced the technical and the practical side of the Expedition ; thus, besides each of the scientific staff lecturing on his individual subject, Oates gave us two lectures on the care and management of horses ; Scott outlined his plans for the great southern journey, giving probable dates and explaining the system of supporting parties which he proposed to employ ; Ponting told us about Japan, and illustrated his subject with beautiful slides made from photographs that he himself had taken ; Bowers lectured on Burma, until we longed to be there ; and Meares gave us a light but intensely interesting lecture on his adventures in the Lolo country, a practically unknown land in Central Asia.

In connection with the work of Simpson at the base station, I must not forget the telephones.

Certain telephones and equipment sufficient for our needs were presented to us in 1910 by the staff of the National Telephone Co., and they were very largely used in scientific work at the base station as well as for connecting Cape Evans to Hut Point, fifteen miles away. Simpson made the Cape Evans-Hut Point connection in September, 1911, by laying the bare aluminium wire along the surface of the snow-covered sea ice, and for a long time there was no difficulty in ringing up by means of magnetos. However, when the sun came back and its rays became reasonably powerful, difficulty in ringing and speaking was experienced.

We used the telephones almost daily for taking time, and Simpson used to stand inside the hut at the sidereal clock whilst I took astronomical observations outside in the cold. We also telephoned time to the ice cave in which the pendulums were being swung when determining the force of gravity. Telephones were quite efficient in temperatures of 40° and more below zero.

Midwinter Day arrived on June 22, and here one must pay an affectionate and grateful tribute to Bowers, Wilson, Cherry-Garrard, and Clissold the cook.

To start with, we had to discuss whether we would hold the midwinter festival on the 22nd or 23rd of June, because in reality the sun reached its farthest northern Declination at 2.30 a.m. on the 23rd by the standard time which we were keeping. We decided to hold it on the evening of the 22nd, this being the dinner time nearest the actual culmination. A Buszard's cake extravagantly iced was placed on the tea-table by Cherry-Garrard, his gift to us, and this was the first of the dainties with which we proceeded to stuff ourselves on this memorable day. Although in England it was midsummer we could not help thinking of those at home in Christmas vein. The day here was to all intents and purposes Christmas Day ; but it meant a great deal more than that, it meant that the sun was to come speeding back slowly to begin with, and then faster and faster until in another four months or so we should find ourselves setting out to achieve our various purposes. It meant that before another year had passed some of us, perhaps all of us, would be back in civilisation taking up again the reins of our ordinary careers which, of necessity, would lead us to different corners of the earth. The probability was that we should never all sit down together in a peopled land, for Simpson was bound to be racing back to India with Bowers and probably Oates, whose regiment was at Mhow ; Gran would away to Norway, and the other Ubdugs to Australia. One or two of us had been tempted to settle in New Zealand, and the old Antarctics amongst us knew how useless it had been to arrange those Antarctic dinners which never came off as intended.

But to return to the menu for Midwinter Day. When we sat down in the evening we were confronted with a beautiful water-colour drawing of our winter quarters, with Erebus's gray shadow looming large in the background, from the summit of which a rose-tinted smoke-cloud delicately trended northward, and, standing out from the whole picture a neatly printed tablet which proclaimed the nature of this much-looked-forward-to meal :

Consomme Seal.

Roast Beef and Yorkshire Pudding.

Horseradish Sauce.

Potatoes à la mode and Brussels Sprouts.

Plum Pudding.   Mince Pies.

Caviare Antarctic.

Crystallised fruits.   Chocolate Bonbons.

Butter Bonbons.   Walnut Toffee.

Almonds and Raisins.

Wines.

Sherry, Champagne, Brandy Punch, Liqueur.

Cigars, Cigarettes, and Tobacco.

Snapdragon.

Pineapple Custard.   Raspberry Jellies.

and what was left of the Buszard's cake !

The menu was, needless to say, Wilson's work, the exquisite dishes Clissold produced, the maître d'hotel was Birdie, and Cherry-Garrard the producer of surprises in the shape of toys which adorned the Christmas Tree that followed on the dinner. Everybody got something from the tree, which was in reality no tree at all, for it was a cleverly constructed dummy, with sticks for branches and coloured paper leaves. Still, it carried little fairy candles and served its purpose well.

Then I must not forget the greatest treat of all : an exhibition of slides showing the life about our winter quarters and the general work of the Expedition from the starting away in New Zealand to this actual day almost in the hut. The slides were wonderful and they showed every stage of the ice through which we had come and in which we lived. There were penguin pictures, whales and seals, bird life in the pack, flash light photographs of people and ponies, pictures of Erebus and other splendid and familiar landmarks, and, in short, a magnificent pictorial record of events, for Ponting had been everywhere with his camera, and it is only to be regretted that the Expedition did not take him to the Pole. This was, of course, impossible, when everything had to give way to food. Following the photographic display and the Christmas Tree came the only Antarctic dance we enjoyed. Few of us remember much about it for we were very merry, thanks to the wine, and there was considerable horseplay. I remember dancing with the cook whilst Oates danced with Anton. Everybody took a turn, and associated with this dance I might mention that Clissold so far forgot himself as to call Scott "Good old Truegg." Truegg was the composition used by us for cooking in various ways omelets, buttered eggs, puddings, and cakes of all kinds, and, although it was a great boon to the Expedition, we had by this time tired of it. Still, we used it as a term of endearment, but nobody in his sober senses would have dreamt of calling our much respected Commander "Good old Truegg"; the brandy punch must have been responsible for Clissold's mixing up of names ! We had now arrived at the stage when it was time to shut up, the officers became interested in an aurora display and gradually rolled off to bed. It was left to me to see the seamen turned in; they were good-humoured but obstreperous, and not until 2 a.m. did silence and order once more reign in the hut.

Very wisely our leader decided on June 23 being kept as a day of rest ; our digestions were upset and we took this time off to make and mend clothes, and returned to our winter routine, a little subdued perhaps, on June 24.

CHAPTER IX

PRELIMINARY EXPLORATIONS

So much for the winter life up to date ; no great excitements, nothing untoward, but a remarkable *bonhomie* obtaining in our little company despite the tedium of so many days of winter gloom. On June 27 Dr. Wilson with Bowers and Cherry-Garrard started on a remarkable journey to Cape Crozier, nearly seventy miles distant from Cape Evans, via Hut Point and the Barrier. The object of these intrepid souls was to observe the incubation of the Emperor Penguins at their rookery, which was known to exist near the junction point of the Barrier Edge with the rocky cliff south of Cape Crozier. It must be borne in mind that this was the first Antarctic midwinter journey, and that the three men must of necessity face abnormally low temperatures and unheard of hardships whilst making the sledge journey over the icy Barrier. We had gathered enough knowledge on the autumn sledge journeys and in the days of the *Discovery* expedition to tell us this, so that it was not without considerable misgivings that Captain Scott permitted Wilson to carry the winter expedition to Cape Crozier into being. The scope of my little volume only permits me to tell this story in brief. No very detailed account has yet been published, although Cherry-Garrard, the only survivor of the three,

137

wrote the far too modest memoir of the journey which has been published in Volume II of *Scott's Last Expedition.*

Apart from the zoological knowledge Wilson hoped to gain from the Cape Crozier visit in midwinter, there was a wealth of other information to be collected concerning the Barrier conditions, particularly the meteorological conditions, but above all we knew that with such quick and reliable observers as Wilson and his companions we must derive additional experience in the matter of sledging rations, for the party had agreed to make experiments in order to arrive at the standard ration to be adopted for the colder weather we must face during the second half of the forthcoming Polar journey.

Wilson took two small 9 ft. sledges, and after being photographed was helped out to Glacier Tongue by a small hurrah party. In the bad light he was handicapped from the very first, and it took the party two days to get on to the Ice Barrier. Their progress was dreadfully slow, which was not to be wondered at, for they were pulling loads of 250 lb. per man, the surfaces were beyond anything they had faced hitherto, and the temperatures seldom above 60°. Relay work had to be resorted to, and in consequence the party took eighteen days to reach Cape Crozier. They met with good weather, that is, calm weather, to begin with, but the bad surfaces handicapped them severely. After rounding Cape Mackay they reached a windswept area and met with a series of blizzards. Their best light was moonlight, and they were denied this practically by overcast skies. Picture their hardships : frozen bags to sleep in, frozen finnesko to put their feet in every time they struck camp, finger-tips always getting frost-bitten and sometimes toes and heels; no comfort was to be derived within camp, for, at the best, they could only sit and shiver when preparing the food, and once the bags were unrolled to sleep in more trouble came. It is on record that Cherry-Garrard took as long as three-quarters of an hour to break his way into his sleeping-bag, and once inside it he merely shook and froze. The party used a double tent for this journey, that is to say, a light lining was fitted on the inner side of the five bamboo tent poles, so that when the ordinary wind-proof tent cloth was spread over the poles an air space was provided. There was, I may say, a sharp difference of opinion as to the value of the tent; Wilson's party swore by it and Scott was always loud in its praise. The sailors hated it and despised it; they always argued, when consulted on the subject of the double tent, that it collected snow and rime and added much to the weights we had to drag along. Perhaps they were right, and I remember one occasion when two members of the Expedition dumped the inner lining after carrying it many hundred miles with the remark, " Good-bye, you blighter, you've had a damn good ride ! "

The scene inside the little green tent baffles description : the three men's breath and the steam from the cooker settles in no time on the sides of the tent in a thick, white rime ; the least movement shakes this down in a shower which brings clammy discomfort to all ; the dimmest of light is given by the sledging lantern with its edible candle (for Messrs. Price and Co. had made our candles eatable and not poisonous), everything is frozen stiff, fur boots, bags and fur mitts break if roughly handled, for they are as hard as boards. The cold has carved deep ruts in the faces of the little company who, despite their sufferings and discomforts, smile and keep cheerful without apparent effort. This cheerfulness and the fragrant smell of the cooking pemmican are the two redeeming features of a dreadful existence, but the discomforts are only a foretaste of what is to come—one night the temperature fell to 77° below zero, that is 109° of frost. There is practically no record of such low temperature, although Captain Scott found that Roald Amundsen in one of his northern journeys encountered something nearly as bad. One cannot wonder that Wilson's party scarcely slept at all, but their outward experiences were nothing to what they put up with at Cape Crozier, which was reached on July 15. To get on to the slopes of Mount Terror near Crozier the party climbed over great pressure ridges and up a steep slope to a position between the end of a moraine terrace and the conspicuous hillock known as The Knoll. In the gap here the last camp was made in a windswept snow hollow, a stone hut was constructed behind a land ridge above this hollow, the party using a quantity of loose rocks and hard snow to build with. Cherry-Garrard did most of the building, while the others provided the material, for, in his methodical way, Cherry had built a model hut before leaving Cape Evans. The hut was 800 ft. above sea-level, roofed with canvas, with one of the sledges as a rafter to support the canvas roof.

On the 19th July the party descended by the snow slopes to the Emperor penguin rookery. They had great trouble in making this descent, on account of crevasses in the ice slopes which overhung the level way under the rock cliffs. As a matter of fact, the attempt on the 19th proved abortive, although the little band got close to the rookery. They reached it successfully on the 20th when the light was almost failing, and were mortified to find only about one hundred Emperor penguins in place of the two or three thousand birds which the rookery had been found to contain in the *Discovery* days. Possibly the early date accounted for the absence of Emperors; however, half a dozen eggs were collected, and three of these found their way home to England. Wilson picked up rounded pieces of ice at the rookery which the stupid Emperors had been cherishing, fondly imagining they were eggs; evidently the maternal instinct of the Emperor penguin is very strong.

The party killed and skinned three birds and then returned to the shelter of the stone hut, not without difficulty, it is true. It is worthy of note that the three birds killed by the party were very thickly blubbered, and the oil obtained from them burned well.

The Ross Sea was found to be frozen over as far as the horizon. When the party got back to their shelter two eggs had burst and saturated Cherry-Garrard's mitts. This optimistic young man found good even in this, for he said that on the way home to Cape Evans his mitts thawed out far more easily than Bowers's did, and attributed the little triumph to the grease in the broken egg! That night they slept for the first time in the stone hut; perhaps it was fortunate that they did so for it was blowing hard and the wind developed into a terrific storm.

One of the hurricane gusts of wind swept the roof of the hut away, and for two days the unfortunate party lay in their bags half smothered by fine drifting snow. The second day was Dr. Wilson's birthday; he told me afterwards that had the gale not abated when it did all three men must have perished. They had not dared to stir out of the meagre shelter afforded by their sleeping-bags. Wilson prayed hard that they might be spared. His prayer was answered, it is true, but before another year had passed two of this courageous little band lost their lives in their eager thirst for scientific knowledge.

When the three men crept out of their bags into the dull winter gloom they groped about and searched for their tent, which had blown away from its pitch near the stone hut. By an extraordinary piece of good fortune it was recovered, scarcely damaged, a quarter of a mile away. Cherry-Garrard describes the roar of the wind as it whistled in their shelter to have been just like the rush of an express train through a tunnel.

Wilson, Bowers, and Cherry-Garrard started home after this, but were caught by another blizzard, which imprisoned them in their tent for another forty-eight hours. They were now running short of oil for warming and cooking purposes, but the little party won through after a very rough march full of horrible hardships and discomforts, and reached Cape Evans on the 1st August, when they had faced the dreadful winter weather conditions on the cruel Ice Barrier for five weeks. What forlorn objects they did look : it was pathetic to see them as they staggered into the hut. Wilson, when he could give a collected account of what he and his party had faced, was loud in the praise of Birdy and Cherry.

The party were examined by Atkinson, who gave some direction and advice concerning their immediate diet—they seemed to want bread, butter, and jam most, and the little loaves provided by Clissold disappeared with extraordinary speed. They were suffering from want of sleep, but were all right in a few days. One of the remarkable features of this journey was the increase of weights due to ice collecting in their sleeping-bags, gear and equipment. Their three bags, which weighed forty-seven pounds on leaving Cape Evans, had increased their weight to one hundred and eighteen at the conclusion of the trip. Other weights increased in the same proportion, and the sledge had dragged very heavily in consequence.

The three men when they arrived were almost encased with ice, and I well remember undressing poor Wilson in the cubicle which he and I shared. His clothes had almost to be cut off him.

From this journey, as stated, we evolved the final sledging ration for the Summit, it was to consist of:

16	ozs.	biscuit.
12	,,	pemmican.
3	,,	sugar.
2	,,	butter.
0.7	,,	tea.
0.6	,,	cocoa.

daily   34.3 ozs.

It may seem little enough for a hungry sledger, but no one could possibly eat that amount in a temperate climate ; it was a fine filling ration even for the

Antarctic. The pemmican consisted of the finest beef extract, with 60 per cent. pure fat, and it cooked up into a thick tasty soup. It was specially made for us by Messrs. Beauvais of Copenhagen.

No casualties occurred during the winter, but Dr. Atkinson sustained a severely frost-bitten hand on July 4 when we had one of our winter blizzards. Certain thermometers had been placed in positions on the sea ice and up on the Ramp by Simpson, and these we were in the habit of visiting during the course of our exercise ; the thermometer reading was done by volunteers who signified their intention to Simpson in order to avoid duplication of observation. On blizzard days we left them alone, but Atkinson, seeing that the wind had modified in the afternoon, zealously started out over the ice and was absent from dinner. Search parties were sent in various directions, each taking a sledge with sleeping-bags, brandy flask, thermos full of cocoa, and first-aid equipment. Flares were lit and kept going on Wind Vale Hill, Simpson's meteorological station overlooking the hut. Search was made in all directions by us, and difficulty was experienced due to light snowfall. Atkinson fetched up at Tent Island, apparently, which he walked round for hours, and, in trying to make the Cape again, became hopelessly lost, and, losing one of his mitts for a time, fell into a tide crack and did not get home till close upon midnight. Search parties came in one by one and were glad to hear the good news of Atkinson's return. My own party, working to the south of Cape Evans, did not notice how time was passing, and we—Nelson, Forde, Hooper, and myself—fetched up at 2 a.m. to be met by Captain Scott and comforted with cocoa.

Atkinson's hand was dreadful to behold; he had blisters like great puffed-out slugs on the last three fingers of his right hand, while on the forefinger were three more bulbous-looking blisters, one of them an inch in diameter. For days and days the hand had constantly to be bandaged, P. O. Evans doing nurse and doing it exceedingly well. Considering all things, we were fairly free of frostbite in the Scott expedition, and there is no doubt that Atkinson's accident served as an example to all of us to " ca' canny."

Although we had our proportion of blizzard days I do not think our meteorological record showed any undue frequency of high wind and blizzards ; but, as Simpson in his meteorological discussion points out, we suffered far more in this respect than Amundsen, who camped on the Ice Barrier far from the land. It is a bitter pill to swallow, but in the light of after events one is compelled to state that had we stuck to our original plan and made our landing four hundred miles or so to the eastward of Ross Island, we should have escaped, in all probability, the greater part of the bad weather experienced by us. Comparison with Framheim, Amundsen's observation station, shows that we at Cape Evans had ten times as much high wind as the Norwegians experienced. Our wind velocities reached greater speeds than 60 miles an hour, whereas there does not appear to be any record of wind higher than 45 miles an hour at Amundsen's base at the Bay of Whales. Some of our anemometer records were very interesting. In the month of July, when Wilson's party was absent, we recorded 258 hours of blizzards, that is, of southerly winds of more than 25 miles an hour speed. This was the record for the winter months, but while we were depot-laying and waiting for the sea to freeze over at Hut Point, no less than 404 hours of blizzard were recorded in one month—March. Think of it, well over half the month was blizzard, with its consequent discomfort and danger. The blizzard which nearly caused the loss of the Cape Crozier party measured a wind force up to 84 miles an hour ; no wonder the canvas roof of the stone hut there was swept away !

Our minimum temperature at the hut meteorological station was 50° below zero in July, 1911, and the maximum temperature during the winter occurred in June when the thermometer stood as high as +19°.

Our ten ponies stood the winter very well, all things being considered. One nearly died with cramp, but he pulled round in extraordinary fashion after keeping Oates and myself up all night nursing him. In spite of the names we assigned to the animals, largely on account of their being presented to us by certain schools, institutions, and individuals, the ponies were called by names conferred on them by the sailors and those who led them out for exercise. The ten animals that now survived were James Pigg, Christopher, Victor, Nobby, Jehu, Michael, Snatcher, Bones, Snippets, and a Manchurian animal called Chinaman, who behaved very badly in that he was always squealing, biting, and kicking the other ponies. A visitor to the stables, if he lent a hand to stir up the blubber which was usually cooking there, found himself generally welcome and certain to be entertained. Oates, and Meares, his constant companion, had both served through the South African War, and had many delightful stories to tell of their experiences in this campaign ; their anecdotes are not all printable, but no matter. Of Oates it is correct to say that he was more popular with the seamen than any other officer. He understood these men perfectly and could get any amount of work out of them, this was a great advantage, because he only had his Russian groom permanently to assist him, and he generally used volunteer labour after working hours to carry out his operations. In the two lectures he gave us on " The Care and Management of Horses," to which reference has been made, Oates showed how much time and thought he had devoted to his charges, and to the forthcoming pony-sledge work over the Great Ice Barrier.

During the latter half of the winter Oates and I saw a good deal of one another, as we daily exercised our ponies on the sea ice when Wilson's party was away and afterwards also till the weather was light enough for me to continue surveying. Oates led two ponies out generally—Christopher, the troublesome, and Jehu, the indolent, while the care of the rogue pony, Chinaman, devolved on myself. When the ponies went well, which was usually the case, when they did not suffer from the weather, we used to have long yarns about our respective services and mutual friends. Oates would often discuss the forthcoming southern journey, and his ambition was to reach the top of the Beardmore Glacier ; he did not expect to be selected for the southern party, which was planned to contain four men only—two of these must have special knowledge of navigation, to check one another's observations—the third would be a doctor, and it was expected that a seaman would be chosen for the fourth. So Oates was convinced that he had no chance, never for a moment appreciating his own sterling qualities.

By the spring the ponies were all ready to start their serious training for the southern journey, and the proper leaders now took charge to daily exercise their animals in harness. The older sledges were used with dummy loads, varying in weight according to the condition and strength of the pony. So well in fact and so carefully did Oates tend his charges, that by the time they were required for the southern journey only Jehu caused him any anxiety, even so this beast managed to haul a reasonable load for a distance of nearly 280 miles.

As to the dogs, the list was as follows :

Poodle—killed during gale outward in ship.

Mannike Rabchick (Little Grouse)—died from fall into crevasse.

Vashka—died suddenly, cause unknown.

Sera Uki (Gray Ears)—died after cramp and paralysis of hind legs.

Seri   do.   do.

Deek   do.   do.

Stareek (Old Man)—sent back with first supporting party.

Deek the Wild One.

Brodiaga (Robber).

Biele Glas (White Eye).

Wolk (Wolf).

Mannike Noogis (Little Leader).

Kesoi (One Eye).

Julik (Scamp).

Tresor (Treasure).

Vida.

Kumugai.

Biela Noogis (White Leader).

Hohol (Little Russian).

Krisraviza (Beauty).

Lappe Uki (Lap Ears).

Petichka (Little Bird).

Cigane (Gipsy).

Giliak (Indian).

Osman.

Seri (Gray).

Sukoi (Lean).

Borup.

Rabchick (Grouse).

Ostre Nos (Long Nose).

Makaka (Monkey).

Chorne Stareek (Black Old Man).

Peary.

Note.—Borup and Peary were from the American North Polar Expedition puppies. Borup was used in Dimitri's dog team which got right on to the Beardmore Glacier, but Peary was never any use except for the other dogs to sharpen their teeth on. He was a regular pariah.

Apart from the sledge dogs, we had a bitch called Lassie for breeding purposes, but she was a rotten dog and killed her puppies, so we might as well have left her in New Zealand, where we got her.

The dogs came through the winter very well, and during blizzards they merely coiled themselves up into round balls of fur and let the snow drift over them. Meares and Dimitri kept a very watchful eye over the dog teams, and protected them against the prevailing winds with substantial snow-shelters, always taking the weaker or sick animals into the

annexe where Birdie kept his stores, or else into the
small dog hospital, which was made by Dimitri and
perfected by Meares.

The sun returned to us on the 22nd August. We
were denied a sight of it owing to bad weather, for
on the 22nd and 23rd August we had a blizzard
with very heavy snowfall, and the drift was so
great that, when it became necessary to leave the
hut for any purpose, the densely packed flakes
almost stifled us. We hoped to see the sun at noon
on the 23rd when it was denied us on the previous
day, but no such luck, the sun's return was heralded
by one of our worst blizzards, which continued with
very occasional lulls until August 26, when we
actually saw the sun, just a bit of it. I saw the upper
limb from out on the sea ice, and Sunny Jim at the
same time got a sight of it from his observatory hill.
How glad we were. We drank champagne to honour
the sun, people made poetry concerning it, some of
which—Birdie Bowers s lines—found their way
eventually into the *South Polar Times*. The animals
went half dotty over it, frisking, kicking, and
breaking away even from their leaders; they
seemed to understand so well, these little ponies,
that the worst part of the winter was gone—poor
ponies! Long before the sun again disappeared
below the northern horizon the ponies were no more.

There is not so very much in the statement that
the sun had now returned, but the fact, of little
enough significance to those without the Antarctic
Circle, left something in our minds, an impression
never to be effaced—the snowed-up hut surrounded
by a great expanse of white, the rather surprised
look on the dogs' faces, the sniffing at one's knees

and the wagging of tails as one approached to pat their heads, the twitching of the ponies' ears and nostrils, and the rather impish attitude the fitter animals adopted, the occasional kick out, probably meant quite playfully, and above all the grins on the faces of the Russian grooms. Yes, we were all smiling when the sun came back, even the horizon smiled kindly at us from the north. The Barne Glacier's snout lost its inexorable hard gray look and took on softer hues, and Erebus's slopes were now bathed in every shade of orange, pink, and purple. To begin with, we had very little of this lovely colouring, but soon the gladdening tints stretched out over morning and afternoon. We were never idle in the hut, but the sun's return seemed to make fingers lighter as well as hearts.

CHAPTER X

SPRING DEPOT JOURNEY

HOWEVER well equipped an expedition may be, there are always special arrangements and adaptions necessary to further the labour-saving contrivances and extend the radius of action.

For this reason the short autumn journeys had been undertaken to test the equipment as well as to give us sledging experience and carry weights of stores out on to the Barrier. And now that Wilson had added yet more knowledge to what we were up against, we set Evans and his seamen companions on to the most strenuous preparations for going South with sledges. Thus, while one lot of men were skilfully fitting sledges with convenient straps to secure the loads against the inevitable bumping, jolting, and capsizing, and lashing tank-like contrivances of waterproof canvas on, to contain the component units of food, another set of people would be fastening light wicker or venesta boxes athwart the sledge ends for carrying instruments and such perishable things as the primus stoves and methylated spirit bottles. These sledges were under the particular charge of Petty Officer Evans, and he took delightful pride in his office. What little gray dawn there was enabled him gleefully to inspect the completed sledges as they stood ready in their special groups outside our hut.

The more general type would be the 12 ft. sledge, constructed of light elm with hickory runners. On it were secured venesta wood trays for the tins of paraffin, usually in front, the aforesaid capacious canvas tank, and behind everything the oblong instrument box surmounted by light wooden chocks for holding the aluminium cooker.

All sledges had small manilla rope spans, secured in most seamanlike fashion, to take the towing strain and throw it fairly through the structure of these light but wonderfully strong sledges.

While the sledging equipment advanced, Bowers, aided by Cherry-Garrard, sorted out the rations, which he weighed and packed in the most business-like manner. Bowers was always well served, for he had the happy knack of enlisting volunteers for whatever his particular purpose called.

By September 1 Scott must have felt that no portion of his preparations was incomplete, for the travelling equipment had been taken in hand with a thoroughness that was the outcome of zeal and thoughtful attention to detail.

Previous to the departure of the large caravan for the Polar journey, a spring journey was proposed for the purpose of laying a small depot at Corner Camp and generally reconnoitring. On account of the low spring temperatures no animals were used for this trip, which was carried out by Gran, Forde, and myself.

We started on ski, pulling a heavy load of over six hundred pounds. We marched from eight o'clock in the morning until nine at night, with a short interval for lunch, and that first day out we covered twenty miles and arrived on the Great Ice Barrier at the close of our march. The Barrier in its bleak loneliness is probably the most desolate portion of the earth's surface, with the possible exception of the high plateau which forms the ice cap of the great Antarctic mountain ranges. Although only twenty miles from our winter quarters at Cape Evans, the temperature was 21° lower, as we afterwards found by comparison.

We were all three anxious to acquit ourselves well, and although the temperature on camping was 42° below zero we had not experienced any great discomfort until we encountered a sharp, cold breeze off Cape Armitage, which resulted in Forde having his nose badly frost-bitten. Directly this was noticed we quickly unpacked our sledge, erected our tent, and whilst Gran cooked the supper I applied what warmth I could to Forde's nose to bring the frozen part of it back to life.

Needless to say, the sharp air had keened our appetites, and we were all eager for the fragrant smelling pemmican. We sat round on our rolled-up fur sleeping-bags, warming our hands over the primus stove, and literally yearning for the moment to arrive when the pemmican would boil and we could absorb the delicious beverage and derive some badly needed warmth therefrom. Following the pemmican and biscuit came a fine brew of cocoa. This finished, the bags were unstrapped and laid out, when the three of us soon curled up and, huddling together for warmth, endeavoured to get to sleep. The thermometer, however, fell to 60° below zero, and the cold seemed to grip us particularly about the feet and loins. All night we shivered and fidgeted, feeling the want of extra heat in the small of our backs more than elsewhere.

We got little or no sleep that night, and my companions were as glad as I was myself when daylight came and we got busy with our breakfast.

We arrived at the old pony-food depot, Safety Camp, during the forenoon of September 9, and dug out the stores and bales of compressed hay, which we carefully tallied and marked by setting up a large black flag. Then we continued towards Corner Camp. We covered only eight or nine miles this second day on account of spending much time in digging out the depot at Safety Camp. The temperature seemed to fall as we advanced into the Barrier, and this night the thermometer fell to 62° below zero, which meant more shivering and even more discomfort, because now the moisture from our bodies and our breath formed ice in the fur of our sleeping-bags, especially at the head, hips, and feet. One can never forget the horrible ice-clammy feeling of one's face against the frozen fur. How I yearned for a whiff of mild New Zealand air and an hour of its glorious sunshine to thaw my frozen form.

In spite of the low temperature we did sleep this second night, for we were tired men, and Nature nursed us somehow into a sort of mild unconsciousness.

On the third day of our march a considerable effort was necessary to bring the sledge out of its settled position in the hard snow, but we soon got going, like willing horses swaying at our load. The day was very cold and our breath came out grayly steaming in the clear, crisp air.

At first our faces, feet, and fingers were quite painful from the cold, which bit right through, but as the march progressed the temperature rose kindly, until towards noon it was only about 30° below zero, warm enough after what we had experienced earlier.

As we trudged along we watched the mist which clothed the distant hills uncurl from their summits and roll back into rising sheets of vapour which finally dispersed and left a cloudless sky. The awful absence of life struck strong notes within us. Even our feet made no noise at all, clad in their soft fur boots, for we could no longer pull on ski owing to the increasing weight of ice collecting in our sleeping-bags and on the sledging equipment.

We were disappointed as the day progressed, for the sky became overcast and the wind blew stronger and stronger from the W.S.W. with low drifts, and at 8.30 p.m., it being too dark to see properly, we camped. By the time our tent was pitched a fair blizzard was upon us, and by 10 o'clock the camp was well snowed up. In spite of the howling wind we made all snug inside, and the temperature rose to such an extent that we got quite a good night's rest.

The blizzard continued throughout the night, but on the following day the wind took off somewhat, and by the afternoon it was fine enough for us to make a start again, which we did in a biting cold wind. We marched on until nightfall, covering about seven and a half miles.

On the 13th September, having shivered in my bag all night, at five o'clock I told my companions to get up, both of them being awake. The cold had been so dreadful that none of us had slept a wink, and we were not at all surprised on looking at the thermometer when we found the temperature was 73.3° below zero, Fahrenheit.

We cooked a meal and then prepared to scout for Corner Camp. I got a glimpse of Observation Hill, a well-known landmark, and took a bearing of that and another hill.

This gave me our whereabouts, and then we struck southward for a short distance until we saw just the top of the flagstaff of Corner Camp, which had been entirely buried up by the winter's snow-drifts. When we reached the Camp we pitched our tent and dug out all the forenoon, until eventually we had got all the stores repacked in an accessible fashion at the top of a great snow cairn constructed by the three of us. It was about the coldest day's work I ever remember doing.

The job finished, we made ourselves some tea and then started to march back to Hut Point, nearly thirty-five miles away. We proposed to do this distance without camping, except for a little food, for we had no wish to remain another minute at Corner Camp, where it was blowing a strong breeze with a temperature of 32° below zero all the time we were digging, in fact about as much as we could stick. When four miles on our homeward journey the wind dropped to a calm, and at 10.30 we had some pemmican and tea, having covered nine and a half miles according to our sledge meter. We started again at midnight, and, steering by stars, kept our course correct. The hot tea seemed to run through my veins; its effect was magical, and the ice-bitten feeling of tired men gave way once more to vigour and alertness.

As we started out again we witnessed a magnificent Auroral display, and as we dragged the now light sledge onward we watched the gold white streamers waving and playing in the heavens. The atmosphere was extraordinarily clear, and we seemed to be marching in fairyland, but for the cold which made our breath come in gasps. We were cased lightly in ice about the shoulders, loins, and feet, and we were also covered with the unpleasant rime which our backs had brushed off the tent walls when we had camped. On we went, however, confident but silent. No other sound now but the swish, swish of our ski as we sped through the soft new snow. In the light of the Aurora objects stood out with the razor-edge sharpness of an after-blizzard atmosphere, and the temperature seemed to fall even lower than at midnight. Our fingers seemed to be cut with the frost burn, and frost bites played all round our faces, making us wince with pain.

We were marching, as it were, under the shadow of Erebus, the great Antarctic volcano, and on this never-to-be-forgotten night the Southern Lights played for hours. If for nothing else, it was worth making such a sledge journey to witness the display. First, vertical shafts ascended in a fan of electric flame, and then the shafts all merged into a filmy, pale chrome sheet. This faded and intensified alternately, and then in an instant disappeared, but more flaming lights burst into view in other parts of the heavens, and a phantom curtain of glittering electric violet trembled between the lights and the stars.

No wonder Wilson and Bowers stated that the Aurora effects were much better and more variegated in colour this southern side of Mount Erebus. The awful splendour of this majestic vision gave us all a most eerie feeling, and we forgot our fatigue and the cold whilst we watched.

The Southern Lights continued for some hours, only vanishing with the faint appearance of dawn.

With daylight the well-known hills which surrounded our winter quarters thrust themselves into view, and gladdened by this sight we redoubled our efforts.

At 5 a.m. we had a light breakfast of tea and biscuits.

We were off again before six, and we continued marching until we came to the edge of the Great Ice Barrier shortly before 1 p.m. We did not stop for lunch, but marched straight to Hut Point, arriving at three o'clock at the Hut.

We cooked ourselves a tremendous meal, which we ate steadily from 4 to 5.30, and then we discussed marching on to our winter quarters at Cape Evans, fifteen miles farther.

Had we started we might have got in by 3 a.m., but not before. We had marched all through one night, and besides digging out Corner Camp, we had covered nearly thirty-five miles, which on top of a day's work we considered good enough. We therefore prepared the hut for the night ; two of us turned in about seven and soon fell asleep. Gran remained sitting at the stove, as his bag was in such a shockingly iced-up condition that he could not yet get into it. He awoke us about 10 p.m. with more food, cocoa and porridge, both of which were excellent. I full well remember that he put about four ounces of butter into each bowl of porridge, which we mightily enjoyed. We then slept again till morning a long, warm, dreamless sleep.

We had an easy march back to Cape Evans on the sea ice, and arrived in the evening at the Main Hut, which appeared to us like a palace after our cold spring journey.

CHAPTER XI

PREPARATIONS AND PLANS FOR THE SUMMER SEASON

WHILST the spring depot-laying party was absent, Scott, on September 15, took a small sledge party counting Bowers, Seaman Evans, and Simpson away westward. They covered over 150 geographical miles, and commenced by taking over to Butter Point a quantity of stores for Griffith Taylor's forthcoming western summer journey.

The provisions deposited, Scott marched up the Ferrar Glacier to Cathedral Rocks and did some scientific work and surveying. He found that the Ferrar Glacier moved 32 feet in seven months. He then came back down the Glacier and continued his march on sea ice, following the coast into the five mile deep bay known as New Harbour, thence outward and North Eastward to Cape Bernacchi and on past Marble Point, where the broken-off portion of Glacier Tongue was found aground as stated already.

After an examination of this ice mass the party pressed on past Spike Point to Dunlop Island, sledging coastwise parallel to the Piedmont Glacier, named by Griffith Taylor after Dr. Wilson. A thorough examination was made of Dunlop Island, revealing many facts of extraordinary scientific interest.

On 24th September the sledge team retraced their steps from Dunlop Island to a camp near Marble Point, and, after spending a night close to the remnant of Glacier Tongue, they shaped course direct for Cape Evans, which was reached about 1 a.m. on 29th September.

Travelling mostly on sea ice, and well away from the frigidity of the Ice Barrier, Scott was not troubled with any particularly low temperatures, but he experienced a nasty blizzard on the two days preceding his return to headquarters.

Apart from the value of this journey in observations of a technical nature, Scott gleaned much information, which he was able to impart to Griffith Taylor concerning the very important journey to be undertaken by the latter.

Once back in the Hut, Scott set to work to put the final touches to his elaborate plans, drew up instructions, got his correspondence in order lest he should miss the *Terra Nova* through a late return from the Pole, and even wrote a special letter urging that special promotion to Commander's rank should be given to Pennell and myself.

About this time he called on us severally to relieve him if we could of the responsibility of paying us for the second season. Most of us signed the document, but not all could afford to do so.

The general outline plan for the Polar journey was now understood by all concerned in it to be as follows:

The Motor Party.—Day, Lashly, Hooper, and myself to leave winter quarters about October 22, the two motors dragging fuel and forage.

The Pony Party, consisting of Scott, Wilson, Oates, Bowers, Cherry-Garrard, Atkinson, Wright,

F

Petty Officer Evans, Crean, and Keohane, to be independent of the success of the motors, to work light loads and easy distances out to Corner Camp, full loads and easy distances to One Ton Camp, and full distances beyond this point.

The Dog Teams, starting later, to rejoin Scott at One Ton Camp.

The first object was to get twelve men with 43 weekly food units provision (four men per weekly unit) to the foot of Beardmore Glacier. Thence, with 3 units of four men and 21 units of provision, it was hoped to extend the advance unit (Polar party of four men) the required distance. The route intended was the actual one taken as will be seen later.

All our instructions were clear, and we knew what was expected of us long before the start for the Southern journey was made.

The plans and instructions complete, we had a full month for our own individual work.

I had plenty to do in conjunction largely with Debenham, and accordingly he, I, and Gran set out on September 23 with sledge, tent, and a week's food supply to complete and extend our surveys, and in Debenham's case to " geologise."

We had an interesting but somewhat chilly time. Theodolite and plane table work are not suited to very cold climates. We all three worked long hours, usually turning out between 5 and 6 a.m. and not wasting time over meals.

Whilst away surveying we mostly worked on the sea ice, and pitched our tent there. On October 2 at midnight a terrific squall struck our tent. We knew what Wilson's experience had been and consequently we were out of our bags in a moment.

Being close to land we got Gran to collect rocks on the valance, while Debenham and I held on for our lives to it, otherwise the tent would have blown away via McMurdo Sound into the Ross Sea.

Eventually all was serene, the tent securely anchored by rocks piled close around, and we three were snoring in our bags.

We lay still until the following afternoon, by which time the blizzard had abated, and one could see a mile or two ; accordingly we were up and about, so that when the visibility suited, Debenham and I were once more at work and Gran was away to Cape Evans for the purpose of replenishing our food bag.

It is worthy of mention that Gran could easily carry sixty pounds weight in a " rygsaek,"[1] and hung about him whilst keeping up a speed on ski that made the best of us sweat.

Debenham whilst in the neighbourhood of the Turk's Head found much of interest to geologists, and was pleased at what we collected in the way of information. " Deb " was one of the best cooks in the expedition, so we fared well whilst he was with Gran and myself.

Gran kept us alive with his reminiscences, which were always amusing, and he certainly possessed the liveliest imagination in the Expedition. He ought to have been a brigand chief. Sometimes his imaginative foresight led him to commit slight breaches of discipline, as the following anecdote will show. On midwinter night when our table was gay and festive Gran noticed an unopened pint bottle of champagne towards the end of the feast, when

[1] Norwegian knapsack for ski running and towing.

" bubbley " was being superseded by port and liqueurs. Cleverly he coaxed the champagne bottle on to his lap, under his jersey, and finally into his bunk, where it remained hidden until such opportunity should arise for its consumption.

Gran was too generous to finish it himself, and too wise to divide it with many—a pint was for two and no more.

It so happened that whilst we two were working around Glacier Tongue this spring doing survey work we had to come in to Cape Evans for some purpose. We had a hard run out on ski to our camp, and my short legs found great effort necessary to keep pace with the swarthy ski-runner. Once arrived at the survey camp I puffed and blew and sank nearly exhausted on my sleeping-bag in the tent. I told Gran we must have some tea before re-commencing work, and reached out to get the cooker ready. Gran asked me what I fancied most in the world, and my reply was—a pint of champagne.

He laughed and asked me what I would give him for that same, to which I articulated, " FIVE POUNDS," and sank my tired head between my knees. Noiselessly the Norwegian glided from the tent to reappear with the stolen champagne bottle. I smiled delightedly, and soon we were hard at work cooking the champagne into its liquid state once more, for it was of course hard frozen in the low temperature.

When we got the stuff melted it had lost its " fizz," but it tasted nectar-like even from our aluminium sledge mugs, and such was the stimulus from it that we worked until darkness had set in. I have never paid the five pounds, for the reason that Gran chose a dinner party at the Grand Hotel, Christiania instead : from a financial point of view I should have gained by paying—but that is another story and has no connection with the Frozen South.

On October 13 we finished the coast survey in McMurdo Sound : generally the weather was wretched, but this notwithstanding we got along fairly well with our work. Once back in the Hut there was plenty to be done preparing for the Southern Journey.

My particular work consisted of rating chronometers, sewing, packing, stowing, making sundials, calibrating instruments, and preparing little charts which could be rolled up on a bamboo stick and carried in the instrument boxes of the sledges.

Poor Clissold, our cook, fell off an iceberg while posing for Ponting, and was on account of his severe shaking unable to accompany the Motor party for which Scott had detailed him.

After dinner on October 17 Day started his motors, and amidst a perfect furore of excitement he got one motor sledge down on to the sea ice. At the ice foot, alas, one of the rear axle cases fractured badly and the car was out of action 30 yards from the garage. The other car wouldn't start.

From the 18th until the 24th October, Day and Lashly were at work repairing the disabled car, and they made an excellent job of it, so that there was no delay in the starting date for the pioneer party with the motors.

We got all news by telephone from Hut Point with reference to the state of the surface on the Great Ice Barrier, as Meares and Dimitri returned on October 15 from a flying journey to Corner Camp and back with depot stores. Meares's dogs on this trip covered the seventy statute miles, out and home, in thirty-six hours, including their resting time.

Scott handed me my instructions on October 20, which read as follows:

Instructions for Motor Party.

Proceed at convenient speed to Corner Camp, thence to One Ton Camp, and thence due South to Latitude 80½° South. If motors successful (i) Carry forward from Corner Camp 9 bags forage, 1 bag of oilcake, *but* see that provision for ponies is intact, *viz.* : 3 sacks oats, 1 bag oilcake, 4 bags of forage. If motors pulling very well you can also take 9 cases emergency biscuit.

(ii) In addition carry forward from One Ton Camp all man food and fuel in depot, *viz.* : 7 units bagged provisions, 4 boxes biscuit, 8 gallons paraffin, but see that provision for ponies is intact, *viz.* : 5 sacks oats ; and deposit second bag of oilcake brought from Corner Camp. If motors pulling very well you can also take 2 or 3 bales of compressed fodder.

It being important that I should have latest news of your success I am arranging for dog teams to follow your tracks for some distance.

If motors break down temporarily you will have time for repairs.

If motors break down irretrievably, take 5 weeks' provision and 3 gallons extra summit oil on 10 foot sledge and continue South easy marches. Arrange as best you can for ponies to overtake you three or four marches due South One Ton Camp. Advance as much weight (man food) as you can conveniently carry from One Ton Camp, but I do not wish you to tire any of party. The object is to relieve the ponies as much as possible on leaving One Ton Camp, but you must not risk chance of your tracks being obliterated and pony party missing you.

(Signed)   R. F. SCOTT.

On October 23 I wrote my final letters to my wife and friends lest I should get back to Cape Evans after the departure of the *Terra Nova*: we had by now decided that another winter was imperious, and as far as possible those who were likely to remain a second winter wrote to this effect, and left their letters in Simpson's charge. Before my departure with the motors I also spent some time with my leader, and he gave me all his instructions to the various parties to read.

They are so explicit and comprehensive that I may well append certain of them here, for they clearly show how Scott's organisation covered the work of the ship, the base, the western party, the dog teams, and even the arrangements for Campbell's party.

I.—INSTRUCTIONS FOR COMMANDING OFFICER, *Terra Nova*.

October, 1911.

The expedition suffered a considerable loss of ponies in March, but enough remain to carry out the Southern Plan, under favourable circumstances.

This loss and experience with the remaining animals have decided me to start the Southern Journey at a later date than originally intended.

As at present arranged the Southern Party leaves at the end of this month (October), and it is estimated that if all goes well the earliest date at which the most advanced party can return to McMurdo Sound is March 15.

As it is probable the ship will be obliged to leave the Sound before this party has returned, arrangements have been made to pass a second winter at Cape Evans, and as is clearly desirable, the Scientific Staff will remain to continue their work.

If fresh transport is brought by the ship, other members of the Expedition will remain to work it, and it is probable that an attempt will be made to cross the Barrier in a S.S.E.ly direction in 1912-13.

The ship must be prepared to return to the Sound in 1912-13 to relieve those that remain for the second winter.

Details concerning past events can be learned from the bearers of these instructions.

In all that follows I want you to understand clearly that you should proceed in accordance with your judgment rather than the letter of these instructions, where the further information you possess may cause it to appear more expedient.

Subject to this condition I wish you to carry out the following programme :—

I assume that you arrive at the rendezvous, Granite Harbour, on or about January 15, and pick up the Western Geological Party as arranged.

The party will consist of Griffith-Taylor, Debenham, Gran, and Forde.

The first copy of this document may be found by you at the depot made by this party on the Bluff at the entrance of the Harbour, but I hope that Taylor himself will hand it to you.

In case the party should be absent it is well to quote Taylor's plan in brief :

To November 10—Exploring along coast North of Granite Harbour.

November 14 to 28—Exploring coast and inland South of Granite Harbour.

December 8 to January 8—Exploring inland of Granite Harbour region.

Taylor will make every effort to return to Granite Harbour in time to meet you, and should the party be absent you may assume that it has probably been delayed inland. On the chance that it may have been cut off you may proceed to search the coast in a Southerly direction if ice conditions permit.

The time occupied in the search must be left to your judgment, observing that the party will reach Granite Harbour with sufficient provision to last till April, 1912, and should be able to work its way back to this depot.

All things considered, I do not think you need be anxious about the party, even if you find a search impracticable, having regard to your future movements, and you will remember that the search will be more easily prosecuted as the season advances.

Should the party be recovered at once, as is most probable, I wish you to take it to Evans Coves, and land it without delay. The provisions carried by the party should be sufficient to support it for about two months, to provide for the possibility of the failure of the ship to return.

I imagine this landing will be effected about January 18 or 19, and the party should be instructed to be prepared to be re-embarked on February 15. It will, of course, be under your orders, and you should be careful that the place for relief is thoroughly understood by all concerned.

After landing this party you will proceed to Cape Evans, and should you reach it on or about January 23 you will have three weeks in McMurdo Sound before proceeding to finally relieve the Geological Party.

There will be a great deal of work to be done and very little assistance : the order in which it is performed must depend on the state of the ice, etc., but of course the practical work of relieving the station must take precedence in point of importance.

Simpson will remain in charge of the station, and is provided with complete lists of the stores remaining, together with the requirements for the future. Bowers will have left a letter for you concerning these matters. It is probable that a good many of the stores you bring will not be required on shore, and in any case you will easily determine what is wanted. If 10 tons of patent fuel remain, we shall not require more than 15 tons of additional fuel.

In addition to stores I hope you will be landing some fresh transport animals. Oates has drawn a plan for extending the stable accommodation, which will be left with Simpson. The carpenter should be landed for this work and for the few small alterations in the hut accommodation which may be necessary.

The Discovery Hut at Cape Armitage has now

been put into fairly good order, and anticipating that returning parties may have to remain there for some time, as we did last year, I am arranging to transport a quantity of stores to Hut Point. In case the ponies are unable to finish this work, I should like you to complete it at some convenient season. According to circumstances you will probably wait till the ice has broken well back.

Mails and letters for members of the Southern Party should be taken to Hut Point and left in clearly marked boxes.

Simpson will inform you of the plan on which the Southern Journey is being worked. The first returning parties from the South should reach Hut Point towards the end of January. At as early a date as convenient I should like you to proceed to the Western side of the Sound—

    (i) To find a snug berth in which the ship can take shelter during gales.

   (ii) To erect the meteorological hut if you have brought it with you.

From a recent sledge trip to the West I am inclined to think that excellent shelter could be found for the ship alongside the fast ice in the Ferrar Glacier Inlet or in New Harbour, and it might be well to make headquarters in such a place in time of disturbance. But it would be wise to keep an eye to the possibility of ice pressure across the Sound.

It might be possible to moor the ship under the shelter of Butter Point by a hawser secured to balks of timber buried deep in the snow ; she should lie easy at a long scope. In regards to the hut my idea is to place it in as sheltered a spot as possible, at or near a spot which commands a view of the Strait, the main object being to make it a station from which the phenomena of blizzards, etc., can be observed. Simpson, who was with me in the West, will give you some idea of our impressions.

You will understand that neither of the above objects are of vital importance.

On the proper date you will return to Evans Coves to pick up the Geological Party.

I must assume that Campbell has been landed in the region of Robertson Bay in a place that is fairly accessible at this season. If this is so I think it is desirable that you should visit his station after leaving Evans Coves to communicate fresh instructions to him.

Campbell was directed to be prepared to embark on February 25, and it is probable that he will have returned a few days before that date.

In view of the return of the ship in 1912-13 I propose to give Campbell's Party the choice of remaining another winter in their station under certain conditions or of returning to New Zealand. Should they decide to stay, the necessary stores for them can now be landed. Should they decide to return, inform Priestley that he is at liberty to remain at Cape Evans for a second winter if he wishes to do so.

Should the party be absent from the station you must leave the instructions and return to McMurdo Sound. I do not think you should delay beyond February 24 on this service.

You should be back in McMurdo Sound at the end of February or March, and after collecting fresh news, I hope you will be able to moor the ship and await developments for at least ten days.

The term of this stay must be left entirely to

your judgment, observing that whilst it is highly undesirable for you to miss the latest possible news, it would be more undesirable for you to be caught in the ice and forced to winter.

Concerning this matter I can only give you information as to what had happened in previous years—

Last year the Bays froze permanently on March 24.

Last year the Sound froze permanently on May 7 or 8.

By the Bays I mean the water south of Hut Point, inside Turtle Back Island, south of Glacier Tongue, inside the islands north of Glacier Tongue, and, I think, the western shores of the Sound.

The following gives the ice movements in the Sound in more detail:

March 24-25.		Ice forming and opening with leads.
„	26.	Sea clear.
„	27.	Strait apparently freezing.
„	28 (early).	Ice over whole Sound.
„	29.	All ice gone.
„	30.	Freezing over.
April	1.	Ice out, etc.

This sort of thing continued till May, with lengthening intervals, but never more than three days of frozen sea.

The dates of freezing over in 1902 were approximately the same, except that the Sound continued to open beyond the Glacier Tongue throughout the winter.

In 1903 the Bays did not break out, but the Sound was freezing and opening in March and April as in the other years. I think it is certain that the old ice lately broken as well as all the broken young ice drifts to the west, and that a ship on the western side of the Sound would be pretty certainly entangled at this season of the year.

I think it more than probable that you will find all the old ice broken out when you return from the north, and the Bay south of Cape Armitage completely open.

If so, this seems to me to be a good place for you to wait, moored to the edge of the Barrier, if possible. Young ice will constantly form about you, but I do not think you need fear its detaining you until after the third week in March. I am afraid it may be very cold and unpleasant waiting in such a situation, and possibly better and safer conditions for the ship can be found farther to the west and nearer to the decayed Glacier ice south of Black Island.

Moored here the ship would have a clear sea to leeward, whereas in the Bay beyond Cape Armitage she might have a lee shore. You will know best how to make a good permanent ice anchor.

There are shoals off Cape Armitage which may extend for one or even two miles, and careful navigation is needed in this immediate vicinity. The shoals off Hut Point and the west side of the Peninsula do not extend more than a ship's length from the shore. Otherwise, except inside the Islands, I believe the Sound to be free from such dangers.

In case you choose to wait in a spot somewhat remote from Hut Point I am arranging to attract your attention in the following manner :—Very's lights will be discharged and as large a flare as

possible will be burnt at Hut Point at midnight
or noon (you will remember we are keeping time
for 180th meridian).

As large a flag as possible will be displayed on
the skyline of the heights near by, and attempts
to heliograph with a looking-glass will be
made.

With a keen lookout for such signals you need
not frequently approach the Hut.

In the above I have referred to the young ice in
the Sound only ; there is no means of knowing
what is happening farther north, but I am of
opinion that as long as the *Terra Nova* is free to
move in the Southern Bays, she will have no great
difficulty in leaving the Ross Sea.

You will understand that the foregoing remarks
are intended as helpful suggestions and that I do
not wish them to interfere with your judgment of
the situation as it stands ; above all, I would not
have them to prompt you to take a risk in detaining
the ship beyond the time which you think proper
for her departure. I fully realise that at this critical
time, when gales are very frequent, your position
will be beset with difficulties, and I much regret
that it is necessary to ask you to undertake such an
uncomfortable service.

Apart from, but concurrently with, the services
which have been discussed, I know that you will be
anxious to help forward the scientific objects of the
Expedition. Having regard to your interests in
such matters, they also are left mainly to your judgment, and I wish only to specify some lines on
which any soundings taken would be especially
important.

These seem to be :

1. In the space occupied by the old Glacier Tongue (some two miles of the Tongue was broken off last summer).

2. Across the Sound in one or two places to give a section of the bottom elevations.

3. Across any fiords on the coast such as the Ferrar Glacier Inlet.

4. Off the end of ice tongues or the edge of ice walls.

5. Off the old pinnacled ice north of Black Island.

6. From a boat near the Barne Glacier.

7. From a boat around grounded bergs.

I have now to mention various matters of lesser importance to which I should like attention given if time and circumstances permit.

1. The Hut Galley is not in a very satisfactory condition. I should like Williams to overhaul it and try to make it more serviceable for a second season.

2. The coast of Victoria Land has been redrawn over the *Discovery* track. I should be glad to have definite evidence on this point. Any replotting of coast will of course be valuable.

3. Boot-leather, stout boot-nails, and useful paper are requirements which I hope you will be able to supply sufficiently for a second season.

4. The only want for the second season which I can foresee is reindeer pelts for repairing sleeping-bags. I very much fear you will not have brought any: anything you can provide to make good the want would be acceptable.

5. If convenient Williams might look at the blubber cooking stove in the Discovery Hut and

provide some sheet metal, etc., to keep it in good repair.

6. One of the old blubber stoves adapted as in stables and some chimney pipe should be placed in the Meteorological Hut if it is erected to the west.

7. To provide for possible difficulty in keeping up supply of blubber for Discovery Hut stove in March and April it might be useful to have a few bags of coal there, if you can spare them and land them conveniently. Last year we managed very well without coal.

8. If when erecting the stables, etc., the carpenter has not time to see to smaller matters, such as the repairing of the porch entrance, etc., will you please leave sufficient wood for the purpose. A drift screen would be an advantage outside door of porch.

9. If you erect the Meteorological Hut, and can conveniently do so, it would help for you to leave a few cases of provisions in it. Bowers leaves a note with Simpson on this point.

10. If at any time during the season it is convenient to you without undue expenditure of coal to land at Cape Crozier, I should like you to leave a small depot of provisions there. The object of this depot is to support a sledge party to visit the region early next season. Bowers leaves a note with Simpson concerning the stores required. They should be placed near the *Discovery* record post.

11. To assist the signalling to you from Hut Point you might land rockets or port-fires.

In regard to the constitution of the wintering party for the second winter, much must remain in doubt. The following members will return in any case :

1. Taylor, whose leave of absence transpires.
2. Ponting, who will have completed his work.
3. Anton, who has had enough of it.

Anton took the dark season very badly ; it preyed on his superstitions, but he has worked like a Trojan and is an excellent little man. Please recommend him highly if he wants to get work in New Zealand.

Meares may possibly return ; it depends on letters from home.

The following are certain to stay : Bowers, Simpson, Debenham, Wright, Nelson, Atkinson, Clissold, Hooper, Dimitri.

The movements of the following depend (i) on the date of the return from the South ; (ii) on the fresh transport which you have brought : Myself, Wilson, Evans, Oates, Cherry-Garrard, Gran, Day, and the seamen.

If you have brought fresh transport the probability is that all these will remain. If you have not brought fresh transport the majority, if not all, who are able to catch the ship will return. The decision is in every case voluntary and subject to alteration on receipt of home news or from other causes.

It is impossible for me to speak too highly of any member of the Expedition who has remained in this party, and you must do your best to see that the reasons of returning members are generally understood.

In regard to my agreement with the Central News

I am leaving with Simpson under separate cover a telegraphic despatch concerning the doings of this party, containing about 3000 words. I hope you will duly receive letters from me through returning sections of the Southern Party. I must leave it to you to complete the despatch with this material, with news from Campbell, and with an account of your own doings.

You will remember that the agreement is for a minimum of 6000 words, and we must not fail in the performance of our part, Drake must take special care to have the " Hereward " message correct.

As a matter of form, it will be well for you to remind every one returning in the ship of the terms of the ship's articles.

Ponting will be in charge of all the photographic material returning, and will see to the observance of the various agreements concerning it.

His own work is of the greatest importance, and it is probable that he will wish to be in the ship during your trip to recover the Geological Party and communicate with Campbell.

I should like you to give him every facility you can for his work, but of course you will remember that he is an enthusiast, and in certain circumstances might undervalue his own safety or that of the ship. I don't want you to run risks to get pictures.

I have hitherto made no mention of Amundsen, as we have no news of him beyond that which you brought. The circumstances do not appear to me to make it incumbent on you to attempt to visit his station. But should the *Fram* not have been heard of, or public opinion seem to point to the advisability, you are of course at liberty to go along the Barrier and to rearrange this programme as necessary for the purpose.

Finally, I wish you every sort of good fortune in the work that is to do, and better weather than you encountered last year. I am sure that you will do all that is possible under the circumstances.

(Signed) R. F. Scott.

II.—Instructions to Dr. G. C. Simpson.

My Dear Simpson,—In leaving you in charge of the Cape Evans Station I have little to do beyond expressing the hearty wish that all may be well with yourself and the other members of the Expedition remaining with you.

I leave in your charge a box containing instructions for the Commanding Officer of the *Terra Nova* and other documents which I wish you to deliver to the proper persons.

I think you are fully aware of my plans and wishes, beyond their expression in the various statements you have seen, and that it is needless to go further with written explanations.

As you know, it is arranged for Ponting, Hooper, and Anton to make a journey to the S.W. in December. Ponting will leave with you a written statement giving an outline of his intended movements. Later in the season he will probably visit Cape Royds and other interesting localities: please give him what assistance you can in his important work.

From time to time Meares may be visiting the station, and I hope that by this means, or through the telephone, you may receive information as to the progress of the Southern Party.

The thawing of the drifts in summer will have to be carefully watched and such measures as are necessary taken to avoid injury to the Hut and the stores. Cases should not be exposed to wet or tins to rust.

The breaking of the sea ice should be carefully watched, noted, and reported to Hut Point when possible.

Bowers will leave notes with you concerning store requirements and desirable expenditure. I anticipate the ship may have some difficulty in reprovisioning the station. You will of course render all the assistance you can.

Details as to the improvement of the Hut for a second winter will become more evident as the season advances. In addition to the probable renovation of the stables I can only suggest the following points at present :

1. An extension or rebuilding of the entrance porch so that the outer door faces north. Regard must be had to the possibility of bringing sledges into hut.

2. A shelter extension to latrine.

3. The construction of an air-tight embankment or other device at the base of the hut walls to keep the floor warmer

4. The betterment of insulation in your corner, and the provision of a definite air inlet there.

5. The caulking of small holes and slits in the inner roof.

6. The whale boat should be looked to and probably filled with water under advice from ship.

After departure of Southern Party all mattresses and bedding should be rolled up, and as opportunity occurs they should be thoroughly dried in the sun.

You will remember that as the summer advances certain places in the solid floe become dangerously weak. It should be well to keep watch on such places, especially should they occur on the road to Hut Point, over which parties may be travelling at any time. It is probable there will be a re-arrangement of the currents in the region of Tent Island since the breaking of the Glacier Tongue.

(Signed)   R. F. SCOTT.

III.—INSTRUCTIONS LEADER OF WESTERN PARTY.

1911.

The objects of your journey have been discussed, and need not here be particularised. In general they comprise the Geological exploration of the coast of Victoria Land.

Your party will consist of Debenham, Gran, and Forde, and you will cross the Sound to Butter Point on or about October.

You will depart from Butter Point with provision as under :

> 11 weeks' pemmican.
> 10 gallons oil.
> 18 weeks' remainder.
> 25 lb. cooking fat.

and make along the coast to Granite Harbour. You will leave at Butter Point two weeks' provision for your party, for use in case you are forced to retreat along the coast late in the season, and for the same eventuality you will depot a week's provision at Cape Bernacchi.

On arrival in Granite Harbour you will choose a suitable place to depot the main bulk of your provision.

As the Commanding Officer of the *Terra Nova* has been referred to the bluff Headland, shown in the photograph on page 154 *Voyage of the " Discovery,"* as the place near which you are likely to be found, it is obviously desirable that your depot should be in this vicinity.

I approve your plan to employ your time thereafter approximately as follows :

During what remains of the first fortnight of November in exploring north of Granite Harbour.

During the last fortnight in November in exploring south of Granite Harbour.

The only importance attached to the observance of this programme, apart from a consideration of the work to be done, lies in the fact that in case of an early break up of the sea ice and your inability to reach the rendezvous, the ship is directed to search the coast south of Granite Harbour.

You should act accordingly in modifying your plans.

It will certainly be wise for you to confine your movements to the regions of Granite Harbour during the second week in January.

You will carry a copy of my instructions to the Commanding Officer of the *Terra Nova*, which you are at liberty to peruse.

This should be left at your depot and the depot marked, so that the ship has a good chance of finding it in case of your absence.

You will, of course, make every effort to be at the rendezvous at the proper time, January 15, and you need not be surprised if the ship does not appear on the exact date. The Commanding Officer has been instructed in the following words :

" I wish the ship to be at Granite Harbour on or about January 15. . . . No anxiety need be felt if she is unable to reach this point within a week or so of the date named."

You are now in possession of all the information I can give you on this point, and it must be left to your discretion to act in accordance with unforeseen circumstances.

Should the ship fail to find you it is probable she will not make a protracted search before going to Cape Evans to gather further particulars and land stores ; it is to be remembered also that an extent of fast ice or pack may prevent a search of the coast at this early season.

Should the ship fail to appear within a fortnight of the date named you should prepare to retreat on Hut Point, but I am of opinion that the retreat should not be commenced until the Bays have re-frozen, probably towards the end of March. An attempt to retreat over land might involve you in difficulties, whereas you could build a stone hut provision it with seal meat, and remain in safety in any convenient station on the coast. In no case is an early retreat along the coast to be attempted without the full concurrence of the members of your party.

Should the ship embark you on or about the proper date, you will take on board your depot stores, except one week's provision. These stores should serve your travelling needs for the remainder of the season.

Whilst expressing my wishes to the Commanding Officer of the *Terra Nova*, I have given him full discretion to act according to circumstances, in carrying out the further programme of the season.

You will, of course, be under his orders and receive his instructions concerning your further movements.

In your capacity as leader of a party I cannot too strongly impress on you the necessity for caution in your movements. Although you will probably travel under good weather conditions, you must remember that violent storms occasionally sweep up the coast and that the changes of weather are quite sudden, even in summer. I urge this the more especially because I think your experiences of last year are likely to be misleading.

I am confident that it is not safe for a party in these regions to be at a great distance from its camp, and that, for instance, it would be dangerous to be without shelter in such storms as that encountered by the *Discovery* off Coulman Island early in January, 1902.

With camp equipment a party is always safe, though it is not easy to pitch tent in a high wind.

I can forsee no object before you which can justify the risk of accident to yourself or to the other members of your party.

I wish you to show these instructions to Debenham, who will take charge of the party in case you should be incapacitated.

I sincerely hope you will be able to accomplish your work without difficulty, and I am sure that Pennell will do his best to help you.

> Yours,
>
> (Signed) R. F. SCOTT.

IV.—INSTRUCTIONS FOR DOG TEAMS.

October 20.

DEAR MEARES,—In order that there may be no mistake concerning the important help which it is hoped the dog teams will give to the Southern Party, I have thought it best to set down my wishes as under :

Assuming that you carry two bags of oilcake to Hut Point, I want you to take these with five bags of forage to Corner Camp before the end of the month. This will leave two bags of forage at Hut Point.

If the motors pass Hut Point *en route* for the Barrier, I should be glad to get all possible information of their progress. About a day after they have passed if you are at Hut Point I should like you to run along their tracks for half a day with this object. The motors will pick up the two bags of forage at Hut Point—they should be placed in a convenient position for this purpose.

The general scheme of your work in your first journey over the Barrier has been thoroughly discussed, and the details are contained in Table VIII of my plan of which you should have a copy. I leave you to fix the date of your departure from Hut Point, observing that I should like you to join me at One Ton Camp, or very shortly after.

We cannot afford to wait. Look for a note from me at Corner Camp. The date of your return must be arranged according to circumstances. Under favourable conditions you should be back at Hut Point by December 19 at latest.

After sufficient rest I should like you to transport to Hut Point such emergency stores as have not yet been sent from Cape Evans. At this time you should see that the Discovery Hut is provisioned to support the Southern Party and yourself in the autumn in case the ship does not arrive.

At some time during this month or early in January you should make your second journey to One Ton Camp and leave there :

                5 units X.S. ration.
                3 cases of biscuit.
                5 gallons of oil.
        As much dog food as you can conveniently
        carry (for third journey).

This depot should be laid not later than January 19, in case of rapid return of first unit of Southern Party.

Supposing that you have returned to Hut Point by January 13, there will be nothing for you to do on the Southern road for at least three weeks. In this case, and supposing the ice conditions to be favourable, I should like you to go to Cape Evans and await the arrival of the ship.

The ship will be short-handed and may have difficulty in landing stores. I should like you to give such assistance as you can without tiring the dogs.

About the first week of February I should like you to start your third journey to the South, the object being to hasten the return of the third Southern unit and give it a chance to catch the ship.

The date of your departure must depend on news received from returning units, the extent of the depot of dog food you have been able to leave at One Ton Camp, the state of the dogs, etc.

Assuming that the ship will have to leave the Sound soon after the middle of March, it looks at present as though you should aim at meeting the returning party about March 1 in Latitude 82 or 82·30. If you are then in a position to advance a few short marches or " mark time " for five or six days on food brought, or ponies killed, you should have a good chance of affecting your object.

You will carry with you beyond One Ton Camp one X.S. ration, including biscuit and one gallon of paraffin, and of course you will not wait beyond the time when you can safely return on back depots.

You will of course understand that whilst the object of your third journey is important, that of the second is vital. At all hazards three X.S. units of provision must be got to One Ton Camp by the date named, and if the dogs are unable to perform this service, a man party must be organised.

(Signed) R. F. SCOTT.

V.—INSTRUCTIONS TO LIEUT. VICTOR CAMPBELL.

Cape Evans,
October, 1911.

MY DEAR CAMPBELL,—This letter assumes that you are landed somewhere to the north of this station and that Pennell is able to place it in your hands in the third week of February before he returns to McMurdo Sound.

From Pennell's instructions, which I have asked him to show you, you will see that there is a probability of some change in the future plans whereby some members of the Expedition remain for a second winter at Cape Evans.

You will learn the details of the situation and the history of this station from Pennell and others, and I need not go into these matters.

If things should turn out as expected, arrangements will have to be made for the *Terra Nova* to return to the Ross Sea in the open season 1912-13. Under these circumstances an opportunity offers for the continuance of useful work in all directions. I have therefore to offer you the choice of remaining in your present station for a second year or of returning in the *Terra Nova*.

I shall not expect you to stay unless :

(1) All your party are willing or can be replaced by volunteers.

(2) The work in view justifies the step.

(3) Your food supplies are adequate.

(4) Your party is in a position to be relieved with certainty on and after February 25, 1913.

(5) Levick and Priestley are willing to forgo all legal title to expeditionary salary for the second year.

I should explain that this last condition is made only because I am in ignorance of the state of the expeditionary finances.

Should you decide to stay I hope that Pennell may be able to supply all your requirements. Should you decide to return please inform Priestley that he is at liberty to stay at Cape Evans for the second winter.

The same invitation is extended to yourself should you wish to see more of this part of the continent.

We could not afford to receive more of your party.

Should you not have returned from your sledge trip in time to meet the *Terra Nova* when she bears this letter, you will understand that the choice of staying or returning is equally open to you when she returns in March.

In this case it would of course be impossible for any of your party to stay at Cape Evans.

Should you see Pennell in February and decide to return, you could remain at your station till the ship sails north in March if you think it advisable.

Being so much in the dark concerning all your movements and so doubtful as to my ability to catch the ship, I am unable to give more definite instructions, but I know that both you and Pennell will make the best of the circumstances, and always deserve my approval of your actions.

In this connection I conclude by thanking you for the work described in your report of February last. I heartily approve your decision not to winter in King Edward's Land, your courteous conduct towards Amundsen, and your forethought in returning the two ponies to this station.

I hope that all has been well with you and that you have been able to do good work. I am sure that you have done everything that circumstances permitted and shall be very eager to see your report.

With best wishes, etc.,
(Signed)   R. F. Scott.

CHAPTER XII

SOUTHERN JOURNEY—MOTOR SLEDGES ADVANCE

On October 24, 1911, the advance guard of the Southern Party, consisting of Day, Lashly, Hooper, and myself, left Cape Evans with two motor sledges as planned. We had with us three tons of stores, pony food, and petrol, carried on five 12 ft. sledges, and our own tent, etc., on a smaller sledge. The object of sending forward such a weight of stores was to save the ponies' legs over the variable sea ice, which was in some places hummocky and in others too slippery to stand on. Also the first thirty miles of Barrier was known to be bad travelling and likely to tire the ponies unnecessarily unless they marched light, so here again it was desirable to employ the motors for a heavy drag.

We had fine weather when at 10.30 a.m. we started off, with the usual concourse of well-wishers, and after one or two stops and sniffs we really got under way, and worked our loads clear of the Cape on to the smoother stretch of sea ice, which improved steadily as we proceeded. Hooper accompanied Lashly's car and I worked with Day.

A long shaft protruded 3 ft. clear each end of the motors. To the foremost end we attached the steering rope, just a set of man-harness with a long trace, and to the after end of the shaft we made fast the towing lanyard or span according to whether we hauled sledges abreast or in single line. Many doubts were expressed as to the use of the despised motors—but we heeded not the gibes of our friends who came out to speed us on our way. They knew we were doing our best to make the motors successful, and their expressed sneers covered their sincere wishes that we should manage to get our loads well on to the Barrier.

We made a mile an hour speed to begin with and stopped at Razorback Island after 3½ miles.

We had lunch at Razorback, and after that we "lumped," man-hauled, and persuaded the two motors and three tons of food and stores another mile onward. The trouble was not on account of the motors failing, but because of a smooth, blue ice surface. We camped at 10 p.m. and all slept the sleep of tired men. October 25 was ushered in with a hard wind, and it appeared in the morning as if our cars were not going to start. We had breakfast at 8 a.m. and got started on both motors at 10.45, but soon found that we were unable to move the full loads owing to the blue ice surface, so took to relaying. We advanced under three miles after ten hours' distracting work—mostly pulling the sledges ourselves, jerking, heaving, straining, and cursing—it was tug-of-war work and should have broken our hearts, but in spite of our adversity we all ended up smiling and camped close on 9 p.m.

The day turned out beautifully fine and calm, but the hard ice was absolutely spoiling the rollers of both cars.

Whilst we were preparing for bed, Simpson and Gran passed our tent and called on us. They were bound for Hut Point. I told Simpson our troubles about the surface, and he promised to telephone from Hut Point to Captain Scott.

Next day we got going with certain difficulties, and met Gran and Simpson four miles from Hut Point. They told us that a large man-hauling party was on its way out from Cape Evans to assist us. The weather was superb and we all got very sunburnt. Captain Scott and seven others came up with us at 2 p.m., but both motors were then forging ahead, so they went on to Hut Point without waiting.

Meantime we lunched, and afterwards struck a bad patch of surface which caused us frequent stops. We reached Hut Point at 8 p.m. after stopping the motors near Cape Armitage, and spent the night in the Hut there, camping with Scott's party, Meares and Dimitri.

The motor engines were certainly good in moderate temperatures, but our slow advance was due to the chains slipping on hard ice. Scott was concerned, but he made it quite clear that if we got our loads clear of the Strait between White Island and Ross Isle, he would be more than satisfied.

Meares and Bowers cooked a fine seal fry for us all, and we spent a happy evening at Hut Point. The Hut, thanks to Meares and Dimitri, was now, for these latitudes, a regular Mayfair dwelling. The blubber stove was now a bricked-in furnace, with substantial chimney, and hot plates, with cooking space sufficient for our needs, however many, were being accommodated.

On October 27 I woke the cooks at 6.30 a.m., and we breakfasted about 8 o'clock, then went up to the motors off Cape Armitage. Lashly's car got away and did about three miles with practically no stop. Our carburettor continually got cold, and we stopped a good deal. Eventually about 1 p.m. we passed Lashly's car and made our way up a gentle slope on to the Barrier, waved to the party, and went on about three-quarters of a mile.

Here we waited for Lashly and Hooper, who came up at 2.30, having had much trouble with their engine, due to overheating, we thought. When Day's car glided from the sea ice, over the tide crack and on to the Great Ice Barrier itself, Scott and his party cheered wildly, and Day acknowledged their applause with a boyish smile of triumph. As soon as Lashly got on to the Barrier, Scott took his party away and they returned to Cape Evans. It would have been a disappointment to them if they had known that we shortly afterwards heard an ominous rattle, which turned out to be the big end brass of one of the connecting rods churning up—due to a bad casting.

Luckily we had a spare, which Day and Lashly fitted, while Hooper and I went on with the 10 ft. sledge to Safety Camp.

Here we dug out our provisions according to instructions and brought them back to our camp to avoid further delay in repacking sledges. We then made Day and Lashly some tea to warm them up. They worked nobly and had the car ready by 11 p.m. We pushed on till midnight in our anxiety to acquit ourselves and our motors creditably. The thermometer showed −19·8° on camping, and temperature fell to −25° during the night.

October 28 was my birthday; all hands wished me many happy returns of the day, and I was given letters from my wife and from Forde and Keohane, who somehow remembered the date from last year—these two, with Browning and Dickason, I had brought into the Expedition from H.M.S. *Talbot,* one of my old ships. But to continue : we were all ready to start at 11 a.m. in a stiff, cold breeze, when I discovered that my personal bag had been taken off by the man-hauling party that came to assist us, so I put on ski and went to Hut Point, six miles back. I found Meares there, and he gave me a surprised but hearty welcome and wished me " Happy returns, Teddy." I explained what had happened ; it had been done of course the night before when my namesake had taken my personal bag in to Hut Point from Cape Armitage to save me the trouble of carrying it after a hard day's work with the motors. As I had had no need of it, I never noticed its presence at Hut Point, so there it was. Meares made me laugh by saying in the most friendly way, as if I was calling on him in his English home, " Stay and have lunch, won't you, Teddy ? " Of course I did, but as I was wanted by the Motor Party it was a somewhat hurried meal, fried seal liver and bacon. We were not allowed to eat bacon on account of scurvy precaution, but still, it was my birthday, and nobody let me forget it. Feeling much better and less angry after this unlooked for ski-run, I swung out to the Barrier edge, over the sea ice, up the Barrier slope, and on to the Barrier itself, where I picked up the tracks of the motors and followed them for seven miles. I remember that ski run well : I felt so very lonely all by myself on the silent Barrier, surrounded as I was by lofty white mountains, which lifted their summits to the blue peaceful heavens. I thought over the future of the Southern Party and wondered how things would be one year hence; this was indeed facing the unknown. I enjoyed the keen air, and the crisp surface was so easy to negotiate after my former Barrier visits with a heavy sledge dragging one back, but the very easiness I was enjoying made me think of Amundsen and his dogs.

If the Norwegians could glide along like this, it would be " good-bye " to our hopes of planting Queen Alexandra's flag first at the South Pole. As a matter of fact, while I was then making my way along to overtake the motors, Amundsen and his Polar party were beyond the 80th parallel, forcing their way Southward and hourly increasing their distance from us and from Captain Scott, who had not even started. Yes, Amundsen was over 150 miles farther South, and his sledge runners were slithering over the snow, casting its powdered particles aside in beautiful little clouds while I was rapidly overhauling the motors with their labouring, sorely taxed custodians, Day, Lashly, and Hooper. It seems very cruel to say this, but there's no good in shutting one's eyes to Truth, however unpleasantly clad she may be. I caught the motors late in the afternoon after running nine miles; they had only done three miles whilst I had been doing fifteen. We continued crawling along with our loads, stopping to cool the engines every few minutes, it seemed, but at 11 p.m. they overheated to such an extent that we stopped for the night. I was fairly done, but not too tired to enjoy the supper which Hooper cooked, with its many luxuries produced by him. Hooper had informed Bowers of my birthday, and obtained all kinds of good things, which we despatched huddled together in our tents, for it was about 20° below zero when we turned in well after midnight.

We intentionally lay in our bags until 8.30 next morning, but didn't get those dreadful motors to start until 10.45 a.m. Even then they only gave a few sniffs before breaking down and stopping, so that we could not advance perceptibly until 11.30. We had troubles all day, and were forced to camp on account of Day's sledge giving out at 5 p.m.—we daren't stop for lunch earlier, for once stopped one never could say when a re-start could be made.

We depoted here four big tins of petrol and two drums of filtrate to lighten load of Day's sledge. Started off at six and soon found that the big end brass on No. 2 cylinder of this sledge had given out, so dropped two more tins of petrol and a case of filtrate oils. We thereupon continued at a snail's pace, until at 9.15 the connecting rod broke through the piston. We decided to abandon this sledge, and made a depot of the spare clothing, seal meat, Xmas fare, ski belonging to Atkinson and Wright, and four heavy cases of dog biscuit. I left a note in a conspicuous position on the depot, which we finished constructing at midnight. We wasted no time in turning in.

The clouds were radiating from the S.E., a precursor of blizzard, we feared, and sure enough we got it next day, when it burst upon us whilst we were putting on our footgear after breakfast. There was nothing for it but to get back into our sleeping-bags, wherein we spent the day.

On the 31st we were out of our bags and about, soon after six, to find it still drifting but showing signs of clearing. After breakfast we dug out sledges, and Lashly and Day got the snow out of the motor, a long and rotten job. The weather cleared about 11 a.m. and we got under way at noon. It turned out very fine and we advanced our weights 7 miles 600 yards, camping at 10.40 p.m.

As will be seen, these were long days, and although he did not say it, Day must have felt the crushing disappointment of the failure of the motors—it was not his fault, it was a question of trial and experience. Nowadays we have far more knowledge of air-cooled engines and such crawling juggernauts as tanks, for it may well be argued that Scott's motor sledges were the forerunners of the tanks.

On November 1 we advanced six miles and the motor then gave out. Day and Lashly give it their undivided attention for hours, and the next day we coaxed the wretched thing to Corner Camp and ourselves dragged the loads there.

Arrived at this important depot we deposited the dog pemmican and took on three sacks of oats, but after proceeding under motor power for 1½ miles, the big end brass of No. 1 cylinder went, so we discarded the car and slogged on foot with a six weeks' food supply for one 4-man unit. Our actual weights were 185 lb. per man. We got the whole 740 lb. on to the 10 ft. sledge, but with a head wind it was rather a heavy load. We kept going at a mile an hour pace until 8 p.m.

I had left a note at the Corner Camp depot which told Scott of our trying experiences: how the engines overheated so that we had to stop, how by the time they were reasonably cooled the carburettor would refuse duty and must be warmed up with a blow lamp, what trouble Day and Lashly had had in starting the motors, and in short how we all four would heave with all our might on the spans of the towing sledges to ease the starting strain, and how the engines would give a few sniffs and then stop—but we must not omit the great point in their favour : the motors advanced the necessaries for the Southern journey 51 miles over rough, slippery, and crevassed ice and gave the ponies the chance to march light as far as Corner Camp—this is all that Oates asked for.

It was easier work now to pull our loads straight-forwardly South than to play about and expend our uttermost effort daily on those " qualified " motors.

Even Day confessed that his relief went hand in hand with his disappointment. He and Hooper stood both over six feet, neither of them had an ounce of spare flesh on them.

Lashly and I were more solid and squat, and we fixed our party up in harness so that the tall men pulled in front while the short, heavy pair dragged as " wheelers." Scott described our sledging here as " exceedingly good going," we were only just starting, that is Lashly and myself, for we two were in harness for more than three months on end.

I was very proud of the Motor Party, and deter-mined that they should not be overtaken by the ponies to become a drag on the main body. As it happened, there was never a chance of this occur-rence, for Scott purposely kept down his marches to give the weaker animals a chance.

As will be seen, we were actually out-distancing the animal transport by our average marches, for in spite of our full load we covered the distances of 15½ to 17 miles daily, until we were sure that we could not be overtaken before arriving at the appointed rendezvous in latitude 80° 30′.

Now was the time for marching though, fine weather, good surfaces, and not too cold. The best idea of our routine can be gleaned by a type specimen diary page of this stage of the journey:

" *November* 4, 1911.—Called tent at 4.50 a.m. and after building a cairn started out at 7.25. Marched up to ' Blossom ' cairn (Lat. 78° 23′ 33″ S. Long. 169° 3′ 25″ E.) where we tied a piece of black bunting to pull Crean's leg—mourning for his pony. We lunched here and then marched on till 6.55 p.m., when we camped, our day's march being 15 miles 839 yards. I built a snow cairn while supper was being prepared. Surface was very good and we could have easily marched 20 miles, but we were not record breaking, but going easy till the ponies came up. All the same we shall have to march pretty hard to keep ahead of them. Minimum temperature : – 12·7°, temperature on camping, + 5°."

We were very happy in our party, and when cooking we all sang and yarned, nobody ever seemed tired once we got quit of the motors. We built cairns at certain points to guide the returning parties. We had a light snowfall on November 6 and occasional overcast, misty weather, but in general the visibility was good, and although far out on the Barrier we got some view of the Victoria Land mountain ranges. Very beautiful they looked, too, but their very presence gave an awful feeling of loneliness.

I must admit it all had a dreadful fascination for

me, and after the others had got into their sleeping-bags I used to build up a large snow cairn, and whilst resting, now and again I gazed wonderingly at that awful country.

The Bluff stood up better than the rest, as of course it was so much nearer to us, and the green tent looked pitifully small and inadequate by itself on the Barrier, nothing else human about us. Just the sledge trail and the thrown-up snow on the tent valance, a confused whirl of sastrugi leading in no direction particularly, a glistening sparkle here, there, and everywhere when the sun was shining, and the far distant land sitting Sphinx-like on the Western horizon, with its shaded white slopes, and its bare outcrops of black basalt. Wilson in our *South Polar Times* wrote some lines entitled, " The Barrier Silence "—sometimes the silence was broken by howling blizzard, then and only then, except by the puny handful of men who have passed this way. Only in Scott's first and Shackleton's *Nimrod* Expedition had men ever come thus far.

We reached One Ton Depot on November 9, and took on four cases of biscuits and one pair of ski, which brought our loads up to 205 lb. per man. Even this extra weight permitted us to keep our marches over 12 miles, but we had the virtue of being very early risers, a sledging habit to which I owe my life.

We snatched many an hour outward and home-ward due to this.

In Latitude 80° we found an extraordinary change in the surface : so soft in fact that we found ourselves sinking in from 8 to 10 inches—this gave us a very hard day on 13th November when, with load averaging over 190 lb. per man, we hauled through it for 12 miles. Fears were expressed for the ponies at this stretch, for here they would be pulling full loads. The 14th offered no better conditions of surface, but we stuck it out for 10 hours' solid foot slogging, when we camped after hauling 12 miles.

Apart from the surface we enjoyed the weather, a wonderful calm and beautiful blue sky. On November 15, after building a guiding snow cairn, we continued southward to Lat. 80° 31' 40" S. Long. 169° 23' E., where we camped to await Scott, his party, and the ponies. I proposed to build an enormous cairn here to mark the 80½° depot, so after lunch we inspected ourselves and found nothing worse than sunburnt faces and a slight thinning down all round.

We commenced the cairn after a short rest.

November 16 passed quietly with no signs of the ponies, and on November 17 we remained in camp all day wondering rather why the ponies had not come up with us. We thought they must be doing very poor marching. To employ our time we worked hours at the cairn, which soon assumed gigantic proportions. We called it Mount Hooper after our youngest member. Day amused us very distinctly at Mount Hooper Camp.

Day, gaunt and gay, but what a lovable nature if one can apply such an adjective to him. He entertained the rest of us for a week out of *Pickwick Papers*. The proper number of hours in the forenoon were spent in building the giant depot cairn, then lunch, and then the cosy sleeping-bags and Day's reading. It was unforgettable, and I think we all watched his face, which took somehow the expression of the character he was reading about.

We put in a good deal of sleep in those days and went walks, such as they were, in a direct line away from the tent and directly back to the tent. We must surely have been the first in the world to spend a week holiday-making on that frozen Sahara, the Great Ice Barrier.

There is little enough to record during this wait at Mount Hooper. We could have eaten more than our ration, and to save fuel we occasionally had dry hoosh for supper, which means that we broke all our biscuits up and melted the pemmican over the primus, half fried the biscuit in the fat pemmican, and made a filling dish. The temperature varied between twenty below zero and a couple of degrees above.

November 20 found us growing impatient, for I find in my diary that day :

" Once again we find no signs of the ponies : we all say D —— and look forward to the next meal. Day reads more Pickwick to us and keeps us out of mischief. I got sights for error and rate of chronometer watches, but these are not satisfactory with so short an epoch as our stay at Mount Hooper, when change in altitude is so slow. Beyond working out the sights I did really nothing. Temperature at 8 p.m. +7°, Wind South-West 3 – 4. Cirrus clouds radiating from S.W. Minimum temperature – 14°."

But at last relief from our inactivity came to us. On 21st November, just before 5 a.m., Lashly woke me and said the ponies had arrived. Out we all popped to find Atkinson with poor old " Jehu," Wright with " Chinaman," and Keohane with my old friend " James Pigg."

They looked tired, the ponies' leaders, and we looked as though we had come out of a bull fight in a barn, with our hair grown long and full of the loose reindeer hairs from the sleeping-bags, all mixed with our beards and jerseys. After hallos and handshakes, smiles and grunts, we asked for news, and were gratified to find that all was well with men and beasts alike. What delay there was was due to blizzards and to the marches being purposely kept down to give the weaker animals a chance. Day facetiously remarked, " We haven't seen anything of Amundsen "—seeing that the valiant Norseman was in Latitude 85° 30′ S. nearly eleven thousand feet up above the altitude of the Barrier at this date one is not surprised.

For all our peace of mind it was well we did not know it.

We yarned away about ourselves and our experiences, then got our cooker under way to have breakfast and to await the arrival of Captain Scott and the seven lustier ponies. They arrived before our breakfast was ready ; more greetings and much joy in the motor party. Scott expressed his satisfaction at our share in the advance, hurriedly gave us further instructions, and then proceeded, leaving us to join at their camp 3½ miles farther south. Accordingly we deposited a unit of provisions at the cairn, put up a bamboo with a large black flag on it, left two of the boxes of biscuit from One Ton Depot and three tins of paraffin, and then set out.

We came up to the Main Camp at 10 o'clock in the forenoon, pitched our tent, had a conference with Captain Scott, cadged some biscuits, and then cooked lunch and got into our sleeping-bags to await the hour of 6 p.m. before commencing our southward march as pioneers and trail breakers.

Scott had with him the following, leading ponies : Wilson, Oates, Bowers, Cherry-Garrard, Edgar Evans, and Crean, besides the aforesaid three with the " crocks."

Meares and Dimitri drove dog teams and every one was in good health and sparkling spirits. Our leader ordered the motor party, or man-hauling party, as we were now termed, to go forward and advance 15 miles daily, and to erect cairns at certain prearranged distances, surveying, navigating, and selecting the camping site. The ponies were to march by night and rest when the sun was high and the air warmer. Meares's dogs were to bring up the rear—and start some hours after the ponies since their speed was so much greater.

So we started away at 8.15 p.m., marched 7 miles and a bittock to lunch, putting up a " top-hat " cairn at 4 miles, two cairns at the lunch camp, one cairn three miles beyond, and so on according to plan.

Atkinson's tent gave us some biscuit, cheese, and seal liver, so that day we lived high. After lunch we continued until the prescribed distance had been fully covered.

We noticed that there were ice crystals like spikes, with no glide about them, and the surface continued thus until 3 a.m. when there was a sudden change for the better.

Quite substantial pony walls were built by the horsemen when they camped—all these marks ensuring a homeward marching route like a buoyed channel.

CHAPTER XIII

THE BARRIER STAGE

DEPOTS were made every 65 miles: they were
marked by big black flags flying from bamboos, and
we saw one of them, Mount Hooper, nine miles
away. Each depot contained one week's rations
for every returning unit.

That outward Barrier march will long be remembered, it was so full of life, health, and hope
—our only sad days came when the ponies were
killed, one by one. But hunger soon defeated
sentiment, and we grew to relish our pony-meat
cooked in the pemmican " hoosh."

On November 24 Oates slew poor old " Jehu "
by a pistol shot in Latitude 81° 15'—this being the
first pony to go. The dogs had a fine feed from the
poor animal's carcass, and Meares was very glad,
likewise Dimitri.

Incidentally, the dogs were not the only ones
who feasted on " Jehu's " flesh. Pony-meat cooks
very well, and it was a rare delicacy to us, the
man-haulers.

As will be gathered, Scott proposed to kill pony
after pony as a readjustment to full load became
possible with the food and fodder consumption.
The travelling now was a vastly different matter
from the work of the autumn. The weather was fine
and the going easy. Every day made sledging more

pleasant, for the ponies had got into their swing, and the sun's rays shed appreciable warmth.

Although we spoke of day and night still, it must be remembered that there was really no longer night, for the sun merely travelled round our heavens throughout the twenty-four hours. Its altitude at midnight would be about 12 or 13 degrees, whilst at noon it would have risen to 28 or 29.

Some of the days of travel were without incident almost, the men leading their ponies in monotonous file across the great white waste. The ponies gave little trouble ; Meares's dogs, with more dash, contained their drivers' attention always.

Day and Hooper turned back in Latitude 81° 15′ at " Jehu's " grave, and Atkinson, his erstwhile leader, joined the man-haulers. The two who now made their way homeward found considerable difficulty in hauling the sledge, so they bisected it and packed all their gear on a half sledge. They were accompanied by two invalid dogs, Cigane and Stareek, and their adventures homeward bound were more amusing than dangerous—the dogs were rogues and did their best to rob the sledge during the sleeping hours. In due course Day and Hooper reached Cape Evans none the worse for their Barrier trudge.

Wright's pony, Chinaman, was shot on November 28, and the Canadian joined the man-haulers. We were glad of his company and his extra weight.

On November 29 we passed Scott's farthest South (82° 17′), and near this date had light snow and thick weather.

On November 30 we had a very hard pull, the

Barrier surface being covered with prismatic crystals—without any glide we felt we might as well be hauling the sledges over ground glass, but diversion in the shape of Land-oh : I think I sighted Mount Hope refracted up, and pointed it out to Captain Scott.

On December 1 we began to converge the coast rapidly, and we were only thirty miles from the nearest land. The view magnificent, though lonely and awful in its silence.

One would very soon go mad without company down here.

December 1 saw the end of " Christopher," but as the soldier fired his pistol at him the pony threw up his head and the bullet failed to kill, although passing through the beast's forehead. Christopher ran to the lines bleeding profusely, but Keohane and I kept him from the other ponies, and Oates shortly after put another bullet into the wretched animal, which dropped him. Christopher was no loss, as he gave endless trouble on the Barrier march. However, he was tender enough, as we found when Meares cut him up for the dogs and brought our tent a fine piece of undercut.

On December 2 we had a trying time, starting off in a perfectly poisonous light, which strained our eyes and made them very painful. It snowed almost incessantly throughout the day. Nevertheless we had a dim, sickly sun visible which helped the steering. As the pony food was running short the pony " Victor " was shot on camping.

I visited Meares and Dimitri in the dog-tent, and they gave me some " overs " in the shape of cocoa and biscuit, for which I was truly grateful, as I had been hungry for a month.

A blizzard started on December 4, which delayed us for some hours. Our party found it had a surplus of 27 whole biscuits—no one could account for this ; we told Bowers, however, and he did not seem surprised, so I think he shoved in a few biscuits here and there. He told me that some tins carried 2 lb. more than was marked on them. We covered about 13 miles despite the bad weather beginning the day.

On December 4 we arrived within 12 miles of Shackleton's gap or Southern Gateway : we could see the outflow of the Beardmore Glacier stretching away to our left like a series of huge tumbling waves. As we advanced southwards hopes ran high, for we still had the dogs and five ponies to help us. Scott expected to camp on the Beardmore itself after the next march, but bad luck, alas, was against us. The land visible extended from S.S.W. through S. to N.W. More wonderful peaks or wedge-shaped spines of snow-capped rock. The first and least exciting stage of our journey was practically complete. A fifth pony was sacrificed to the hungry dogs—" Michael," of whom Cherry-Garrard had only good words to say—but then the altruistic Cherry only spoke good words. We did over 17 miles on December 4, heading for the little tributary glacier which Shackleton named the Gap ; it bore S. 9° E. fifteen miles distant when we put up our tent.

Whilst marching well ahead of the pony party we unconsciously dropped into a hollow of an undulation, and foolishly did not spot it when we paused to build a cairn. Continuing our march we looked back to find no cairn. This first indicated to us the existence of undulations in the neighbourhood, and we frequently lost the ponies to view.

We appreciated that we were outdistancing them, however, and camped at 8 p.m.

It being my cooking week, and, as we fondly imagined, our penultimate day on the Great Ice Barrier, combined with a very good march and a very bright outlook, we had an extra fine hoosh; it contained the full allowance of pemmican, a pannikin full of pony flesh cut in little slices, about 1½ pints of crushed biscuit from our surplus, and some four ounces of cornflour with pepper and salt.

I also had the pleasure of issuing four biscuits each, or twice the ration, Meares and Dimitri having given us eight whole biscuits which they spared from their supply.

The dog drivers were not so ravenous as the man-hauling party, which was natural, but still it was uncommonly generous of them to give us part of their ration for nothing.

I made an extra strong whack of cocoa, as we still had some of my private tea left, so could save cocoa. I brought tea in lieu of tobacco in my personal bag. At least that night the man-hauling party turned in on full stomachs.

We were all tired out and asleep in no time, confident and expectant, but before enjoying the comfort and warmth of our sleeping-bags had an admiring look at the land stretched out before us, and particular application of the eye to the Gap or Southern Gateway, which seemed to say " Come on."

So far on the journey I have not mentioned the word " blizzard " seriously, for we had not hitherto been hampered severely. The 5th December was in truth a Black Day for all. Once more the demon of bad luck held the trump cards against us. Another blizzard started, which tore our chances of any great success to ribbons—it was the biggest knock-down blow that Scott sustained in the whole history of his expedition to date. Here he was, a day's march from the Beardmore Glacier, with fourteen men, in health and high fettle, with dogs, ponies, food, and everything requisite for a great advance, but it was not to be, our progress was barred for four whole days, and during that period we had essentially to be kept on full ration, for it would have availed us nothing to lose strength in view of what we must yet face in the way of physical effort and hardship —we were but one day's march from Mount Hope, our ponies had to be fed, the dogs had to be fed, but they could do no work for their food. There was nothing for it but cheerful resignation. Our tent breakfasted at the aristocratic hour of 10.15 a.m., and Atkinson and I went out to fill the cooker afterwards—the drift was terrible and the snow not fine as usual, but in big flakes driving in a hard wind from S.S.E. It was not very cold, perhaps it would have helped things later if it had been. Our tents quickly snowed up for nearly three feet to leeward. In the camp we could only sleep and eat, the tent space became more and more congested, and those lying closest to the walls of the tents were cramped by the weight of snow which bore down on the canvas. The blizzard on the second day pursued its course with unabated violence, the temperature increased, however, and we experienced driving sleet. The tent floor cloths had pools of water on them, and water dripped on our faces as we lay in our sleeping-bags. Outside the scene was miserable enough, the poor ponies cowering behind their snow walls the picture of misery. Their more fortunate companions, the dogs, lay curled in snug balls covered in snow and apparently oblivious to the inclemency of the weather. Our lunch at 5.30 broke the monotony of the day.

We had supper somewhere near 9 p.m. and then slept again.

December 6 found still greater discomfort, for we had sleet and actually rain alternating. The wind continued and ploughed and furrowed the surface into a mash. Our tents became so drifted up that we had hardly room to lie down in our bags. I fancied the man-haulers were better off than the other tents through having made a better spread, but no doubt each tent company was sorrier for the others than for itself. We occasionally got out of our bags to clear up as far as we were able, but we couldn't sit around and look foolish, so when not cooking and eating we spent our time in the now saturated bags. The temperature rose above freezing point, and the Barrier surface was 18 inches deep in slush. Water percolated everywhere, trickling down the tent poles and dripping constantly at the tent door.

We caught this water in the aluminium tray of our cooker.

The ponies arrived at the state of having to be dug out every now and again. They were wretchedness itself, standing heads down, feet together, knees bent, the picture of despair. Hard and cruel as it may seem, it was planned that we should keep them alive, ekeing out their fodder until December 9, when it was proposed that we should use them to drag our loads for 12 miles and shoot them, the last pound of work extracted from the wretched little creatures.

I am ashamed to say I was guilty of an unuttered complaint after visiting the ponies, for I wrote in my diary for December 6 concerning the five remaining Siberian ponies:

" I think it would be fairer to shoot them now, for what is a possible 12 miles' help ? We could now, pulling 200 lb. per man, start off with the proper man-hauling parties and our total weights, so why keep these wretched animals starving and shivering in the blizzard on a mere chance of their being able to give us a little drag ? Why, our party have never been out of harness for nearly 400 miles, so why should not the other eight men buckle to and do some dragging instead of saving work in halfpenny numbers ? "

Still, it is worthy of mention that on the day the ponies did their last march every man amongst their leaders gave half his biscuit ration to his little animal.

This dreadful blizzard was a terrific blow to Oates. He of all men set himself to better the ponies' state during the bad weather. The animals lost condition with a rapidity that was horrible to observe. The cutting wind whirling the sleet round the ponies gave them a very sorry time, but whenever one peeped out of the tent door there was Oates, wet to the skin, trying to keep life in his charges. I think the poor soldier suffered as much as the ponies. He had felt that every time he re-entered his tent (which was also Captain

Scott's) that he took in more wet snow and helped to increase the general discomfort. This being the case when he went out to the ponies, he stopped out, and kept his vigil crouching behind a drifted up pony-wall. We others could not help laughing at him, after the blizzard, when he wrung the icy water out of his clothing. His personal bag was in a fearful state, his sodden tobacco had discoloured everything, and as he squeezed his spare socks and gloves a stream of nicotine-stained water flowed out. I am unable to reproduce his observations on the subject—they were dry, picturesque, and to the point, and even our bluejackets, who were none too particular about language, looked at Oates with undisguised astonishment at the length and variety of his emergency vocabulary.

December 7 showed no change : the blizzard was continuous, food our only comfort. Personally I read Atkinson's copy of *Little Dorrit*, for it sufficed nothing to despair ; we could not move, and one had to be patient.

Next day we had less wind, but it snowed most of the day. We did, all the same, get glimpses of the sun and one of the land. Dug out all sledges and hauled them clear, then tried the surface, and to Scott's and our own surprise my party hauling on ski dragged the sledge with four big men sitting on it over the surface as much as we chose.

I had thought it beyond our power, it is true. We then returned to camp. Without ski one sank more than knee deep in the snow. The horses were quite unable to progress, sinking to their bellies, so no start was made.

We shifted our tent and re-spread it on new snow well trampled down. This brief respite from our sleeping-bags freed our cramped limbs. Weather improved and we did not find it necessary after all to get back into our bags, for it was still warm and quite pleasant sitting in the tent.

What a sight the camp had presented before we started digging out. The ponies like drowned rats, their manes and tails dank and dripping, a saturated blotting-paper look about their green horse cloths, eyes half closed, mouths flabby and wet, each animal half buried in this Antarctic morass, the old snow walls like sand dunes after a storm.

The green tents just peeping through the snow, mottled and beaten in, as it were, all sledges well under, except for here and there a red paraffin oil tin and the corner of an instrument box peeping out. Our ski-sticks and ski alone stood up above it all, and those sleeping-bags, ugh—rightly the place was christened " Shambles Camp."

On December 9 the blizzard was really over ; we completed the digging out of sledges and stores and wallowed sometimes thigh-deep whilst getting the ponies out of their snow-drifted shelters. Then we faced probably the hardest physical test we had had since the bailing out in the great gale a year ago. We had breakfast and got away somewhere about 8 a.m. My party helped the pony sledges to get away for a mile or two ; the poor brutes had a fearful struggle, and so did we in the man-hauling team. We panted and sweated alongside the sledges, and when at last Captain Scott sent us back to bring up our own sledge and tent we were quite done. Arrived at the Shambles Camp we cooked a little tea, and then wearily hauled our sledge for hour after hour until we came up with the Boss, dead cooked—we had struggled and wallowed for nearly 15 hours. The others had certainly an easier time but a far sadder time, for they had to coax the exhausted ponies along and watch their sufferings, knowing that they must kill the little creatures on halting.

Oh, Lord—what a day we had of it. Fortunately we man-haulers missed the " slaughter of the innocents," as some one termed the pony killing. When we got to the stopping place all five ponies had been shot and cut up for dog and man food.

This concluded our Barrier march : the last act was tragic enough in its disappointment, but one felt proud to be included in such a party, and none of us survivors can forget the splendid efforts of the last five ponies.

Meantime Roald Amundsen had a gale in Lat. 87 —88° on December 5, with falling and drifting snow, yet not too bad to stop his party travelling : he was 11,000 feet above our level at this time and covering 25 miles a day. He also experienced thick weather but light wind on the 7th December and on the day of our sorrowful march he was scuttling along beyond Shackleton's farthest South, indeed close upon the 89th Parallel. It is just as well we did not know it too.

CHAPTER XIV

ON THE BEARDMORE GLACIER AND BEYOND

PROBABLY no part of the Southern Journey was enjoyed more thoroughly than that stage which embraced the ascent of the Beardmore Glacier. Those who survive it can only have refreshing reminiscences of this bright chapter in our great sledge excursion. Scientifically it was by far the most interesting portion travelled over, and to the non-scientific it presented something interesting every day, if only in the shape, colour, and size of the fringing rocks and mountains—a vast relief from the monotony of the Barrier travel.

First we had Mount Hope at the lower end of the Glacier. Mount Hope is a nunatak of granite, about 2800 feet in height, of which the summit is strewn with erratics, giving evidence of former glaciation of far greater extent.

This was the first land we had passed close to since leaving Hut Point six weeks previously, and now we had roughly 150 miles of travelling, with something to look at, some relief for the eyes to rest on in place of that dazzling white expanse of Barrier ice, with its glitter and sparkle, so tiring to the eyes. We knew that we must expect crevasses now, hidden and bare, and we also knew that we must every day rise our camps until we reached the plateau summit in 10,000 feet. The Beardmore itself is about 120 miles in length and from 10 to 30 miles wide. We had no geologist with us, but specimens have been collected by Shackleton's people, and our own members, particularly Scott's Polar sledge party, which are sufficient to give a history of this part of Antarctica.

December 10 showed our party on to the Glacier, but we were not " out of the wood " by this date. For we had some hard graft marching up the steep incline called by Shackleton the Southern Gateway. We had made a depot of three ten-foot sledges in good condition to be used for the homeward journey over the Barrier by each returning unit —realising that the descent of the Glacier would knock our sledges about and most likely break them up to some extent.

We were now organised into three teams of four, pulling 170 lb. per man, and in this formation we made the advance up the Glacier.

The teams were as follows :

1.—Scott.	2.—Evans	3.—Bowers.
Wilson.	(Lieut.).	Cherry-
Oates.	Atkinson.	Garrad
Evans	Wright.	Crean.
(Seaman).	Lashly.	Keohane.

With us we kept the dog teams pulling 600 lb. of our own weights and the 200 lb. gross for placing in the Lower Glacier Depot.

Soft snow made the dragging very heavy, and in the afternoon, working on ski, I am sorry to say my party dropped astern and got into camp an hour late—it could not be helped, we had borne the brunt of the hard work ; Lashly and I had man-hauled daily for five weeks, and Atkinson and Wright for some time also. I had a long talk next morning after breakfast with Captain Scott. He was disappointed with our inability to keep up with the speed of the main party, but I pointed out that we could not expect to do the same as fresh men—the other eight had only put on the sledge harness for the first time on December 10 : Scott agreed, but seemed worried and fretful. However that may be, we got into the lunch camp first of the three sledges, to have our short-lived triumph turned to disaster by a very poor show after the meal—Scott was much disappointed and dissatisfied : he appeared to think Atkinson was done ; Wilson said Wright was played out and Lashly tired. They both seemed to think I was all right, but all the same I felt that my unit had been called on to do more than its share and was suffering as a natural consequence. The depot was built in a conspicuous position, and this done, Meares's work ended. He and Dimitri came along with us for a while and then turned back for a long, lonely run over the inhospitable Barrier.

To help us Meares and the Russian dog-boy had travelled farther South than their return rations allowed for, and for the 450 mile Northward march to Cape Evans the two of them went short one meal a day rather than deplete the depots. It is a dreadful thing on an Antarctic sledge journey to forfeit a whole meal daily, and Meares's generosity should not be forgotten.

The advance of Scott's men up the Beardmore was retarded considerably by the deep, wet snow which had accumulated in the lower reaches of the Glacier.

Panting and sweating we could only make 4 mile marches until the 13th December, and even then the soft snow was 18 inches deep. On the 14th we made a good 9 miles, but only by dint of our utmost efforts—we worked on ski, and I tremble to think what we should have done here without them. The aneroids gave us a rise of about 500 feet a day. Things were improving now, and on December 15 we passed the 84° parallel—about this time we succeeded in covering 9 to 10 miles daily, and to do this we marched that same number of hours. A good deal of snow covering the mountain ranges, but some remarkable outcrops of rock to vary the scenery. The temperature was very high, and we were punished severely on this account, for the snow was like beef dripping, and we flopped about in it and hove our sledges along with no glide whatever to help us move forward. Such panting, puffing, and sweating, but all in good humour and bent on doing our best. Snowing hard in the latter part of the afternoon just as the surface was improving—we were forced to camp before the proper time on this account. On camping we calculated that we were 2500 feet above the Barrier, the surface promising better things, for there was hard blue ice six inches from the surface, and the snow itself was fairly close-packed and good for ski.

On December 16 we were out of our sleeping-bags at 5 and we were under way by 7 a.m., marching till noon, when we lunched and took sights and angles. The surface remained fairly good until 2 p.m., when it took an unaccountable turn for the worse. We covered 12 miles.

Several of us dropped a leg down crevasses here and there, nothing alarming. We reached 3000 feet altitude, and the day ended in the most perfect weather. For the first time since leaving Corner Camp we felt that our ration was sufficient ; we had now commenced the " Summit ration," which contained considerable extra fats. Snow-blindness caused trouble here and there, due principally to our removing our goggles when they clouded up—due to sweating so much in the high temperature. The goggles, which Wilson was responsible for, served excellently. Yellow and orange glasses were popular, but some preferred green. As we progressed and our eyes had to be used for long periods without glasses for clearing crevasses, etc., we found that a double glass acted best, and used this whenever the going was easy and goggles could be used.

The contrast between the goggled and the ungoggled state was extraordinary—when one lifted one's orange-tinted snow glasses it was to find a blaze of light that could scarcely be endured. Snow-blindness gave one much the same sensations as those experienced by standing over a smoking bonfire keeping eyes open.

Sunday, December 17, differed from the preceding days, for we got into huge pressure ridges— we hauled our sledges up these and tobogganed down the other sides, progressing half the forenoon thus. We wore our excellent crampons and made lighter work of our loads than we had done since facing the Beardmore, and now that the summer season was well advanced the surface snow on the Glacier had mostly disappeared through the effects of the all day sun added to the early summer winds. The clouding of our goggles made the crevasses more difficult to spot, and one or other of the party got legs or feet down pretty often.

This and the following day were precursors to good marches and easy times. We made the Mid-Glacier Depot in Latitude 84° 33′ 6″ S., Longitude 169° 22′ 2″ E., and set therein one half-week's provision. We marked the depot cairn with bamboo and red flag to show up against the ice as well as to contrast with the land. Hitherto only black flags had been employed to mark depots.

The weather and surface were both in our favour at last. It was sunny, warm, and clear now, and there was nothing to impede us. Wilson did a large amount of sketching on the Beardmore—his sketches, besides being wonderful works of art, helped us very much in our surveys.

Fringing the great glittering river of ice were dark granite and dolerite hills, some were snow-clad and some quite bare, for their steepness resisted the white cloak of this freezing clime. The new hills were surveyed, headlands plotted, and names bestowed where Shackleton had not already done so. Of course we had Shackleton's charts, diaries, and experience to help us. We often discussed Shackleton's journey, and were amazed at his fine performance. We always had full rations, which Shackleton's party never enjoyed at this stage. After December 17 our marches worked up from 13 to 23 miles a day.

Shackleton bestowed the name of Queen Alexandra Range on the huge mountains to the westward of the Beardmore.

The most conspicuous is the "Cloudmaker," which he gives as 9.971—I like the 1 foot when heights are so hard to determine hereabouts! To the three secondary ranges, on the S.W. extreme of the Beardmore, nearly in 85°, he gave the names

Adams, Marshall, and Wild, after his three companions on the farthest South march. To get into one's head what we had to look at on the upper half of the Beardmore, imagine a moderate straight slope : this is the Glacier like a giant road, white except where the sun has melted the snow and bared the blue ice. Looking up the Glacier an overhang of ice-falls and disturbances, with three nunataks or mountains sticking through the ice-sheet like islands—the disturbance is mostly to the left (Eastwards) of these, and the road here looks cruelly steep even where it is not broken up. Down the Glacier the great white way is broken here and there where tributary glaciers join it, and above the Cloudmaker the glacier is cut up badly in several places, how badly we were not to know until the middle of January, 1912—but of that more anon. To the left (S.E.) a great broad river of ice, the Mill Glacier, and so on.

The land is extraordinary—gigantic snow drifts like huge waves breaking against a stone pier beset the lower cliff faces and steeper slopes, then dark red-brown rock carved by glaciers long since vanished, and above this rocky bands of limestone, sandstone, and dolerite. Some rocky talus showing through the big snow drifts, and in some cases talus alone.

From my letter to be taken by the next homeward party in case I missed the ship :

" The Wild range is extraordinary in its curious stratification, and one feels when gazing at it something of a wish to scramble along the crests, if only to feel land underfoot instead of ice, ice, ice.

" The prevailing colours here are blacks, grays,

reds, like the cliffs at Teignmouth and Exmouth, and another more chocolate red. Then the whites in all kind of shade—fancy different shades of white, but there are here any amount of them, and a certain sparkle of blue ice down the Glacier where the sun is shining on it that reminds one of a tropical sea. Except when marching we don't spend much time out of our tents, but I take a breather now and again when surveying, and then I sit on a sledge-box and wonder what is in store for us and where all this will lead us. Amundsen has certainly not come this way, although dogs could work here easily enough."

On December 20 Scott came into our tent after supper and told us that the first return party would be Atkinson (in charge), Wright, Cherry-Garrard, and Keohane, and that they would turn back after the next day's march.

We were all very sad, but each one thus detailed loyally abided by the decision of our chief. I worked till nearly midnight getting out copy of route and bearings for Wright to navigate back on.

Here is a specimen page of my diary :

" *December* 21.
" Out at 5.45 a.m. and away at 8. Had a very heavy pull up steep slope close to S.E. point of Buckley Island. Passed over many crevasses and dropped into some. Once I fell right down in a bottomless chasm to the length of my harness. I was pulled out by the others, Bowers and Cherry helping with their Alpine rope. Not hurt but amused. All of us dropped often to our waists and Atkinson completely disappeared once, but we

got him out. We got into a very bad place at noon, and a fog coming on had to stop and lunch as one could not see far. This has been our worst day for crevasses up to now, some of them are 100 feet across, but well bridged.

" It was very cold, with a sharp southerly wind when we started, but later on got quite warm. We rose 1130 feet in the forenoon and made 5 miles 1565 yards up to lunch. We started again at 3 o'clock, and the fog lifting, we made a good march for the day : 11 miles 200 yards geographical (Stat. 12 miles 1388 yards). In the afternoon we had a very heavy drag and did not camp till 7.30 p.m., about 4 miles S. 30° W. of Mount Darwin (summit), Latitude 85° 7' S., Longitude 163° 4' E.

" Our height above the Barrier is 7750 feet by aneroid.

" Had a fine hoosh with a full pannikin of pony meat added to celebrate our ' De-tenting,' which takes place to-morrow morning. We make a depot here with half a week's provision for two parties."

We repacked the sledges after breakfast. This place was called the Upper Glacier Depot—and it marked the commencement of the third and final stage of the Poleward Journey. We said good-bye to Atkinson's party, and they started down the Glacier after depositing the foodstuffs they had sledged up the Beardmore for the Polar Party and the last supporting party. Atkinson and his tent-mates now had to face a homeward march of 584 miles. They spent Christmas Day collecting geological specimens, and reached Cape Evans on January 28. They had some sickness in the shape

H

of enteritis and slight scurvy, but Dr. Atkinson's care and medical knowledge brought them through safely.

Captain Scott with his two sledge teams now pushed forward, keeping an average speed of 15 miles per day, with full loads of 190 lb. a man.

When we started off we were :

Scott.	Self.
Wilson.	Bowers.
Oates.	Crean.
Seaman Evans.	Lashly.

We steered S.W. to begin with to avoid the great pressure ridges and ice falls which barred our way to the South. We began to rise very perceptibly, and, looking back after our march, realised what enormous frozen falls stretch across the top of the Beardmore. I noted that these, with Scott's consent' should be called " The Shackleton Ice Falls," according to *his* track he went *up* them. When we looked back on starting our march we could see the depot cairn with a black flag tied to a pair of 10 foot sledge runners for quite three miles—it promised well for picking up. Next day we were away early, marching 8½ miles to lunch camp, and getting amongst crevasses as big as Regent Street, all snow bridged.

We rushed these and had no serious falls ; the dangerous part is at the edge of the snow bridge, and we frequently fell through up to our armpits just stepping on to or leaving the bridge. We began now to experience the same tingling wind that Shackleton speaks of, and men's noses were frequently frost-bitten. On Christmas Eve we were 8000 feet above the Barrier, and we imagined we were clear of crevasses and pressure ridges. We now felt the cold far more when marching than we had done on the Beardmore.

The wind all the time turned our breath into cakes of ice on our beards. Taking sights when we stopped was a bitterly cold job : fingers had to be bared to work the little theodolite screws, and in the biting wind one's finger-tips soon went. Over 16 miles were laid behind us on Christmas Eve when we reached Latitude 85° 35′ S., Longitude 159° 8′ E. I obtained the variation of the compass here—179° 35′ E., so that we were between the Magnetic and Geographical Poles.

The temperature down to 10° below zero made observing unpleasant, when one had cooled down and lost vitality at the end of the day's march.

Christmas Day, 1911, found our two tiny green tents pitched on the King Edward VII. Plateau—the only objects that broke the monotony of the great white glittering waste that stretches from the Beardmore Glacier Head to the South Pole. A light wind was blowing from the South, and little whirls of fine snow, as fine as dust, would occasionally sweep round the tents and along the sides of the sledge runners, streaming away almost like smoke to the Northward. Inside the tents breathing heavily were our eight sleeping figures—in these little canvas shelters soon after 4 a.m. the sleepers became restless and occasionally one would wake, glance at one's watch, and doze again. Exactly at 5 a.m. our leader shouted " Evans," and both of us of that name replied, " Right-o, sir."

Immediately all was bustle, we scrambled out of our sleeping-bags, only the cook remaining in each tent. The others with frantic haste filled the aluminium cookers with the gritty snow that here lay hard and windswept. The cookers filled and passed in, we gathered socks, finnesko, and putties off the clothes lines which we had rigged between the ski which struck upright in the snow to save them from being drifted over in the night. The indefatigable Bowers swung his thermometer in the shade until it refused to register any lower, glanced at the clouds, made a note or two in his miniature meteorological log book, and then blew on his tingling fingers, noted the direction of the wind, and ran to our tent. Inside all had lashed up their bags and converted them into seats, the primus stove burnt with a curious low roar, and peculiar smell of paraffin permeated the tent. By the time we had changed our footgear the savoury smell of the pemmican proclaimed that breakfast was ready. The meal was eaten with the same haste that had already made itself apparent.

A very short smoke sufficed, and Captain Scott gave the signal to strike camp. Out went everything through the little round door, down came both tents, all was packed in a jiffy on the two 12-foot sledges, each team endeavouring to be first, and in an incredibly short space of time both teams swung Southward, keeping step, and with every appearance of perfect health. But a close observer, a man trained to watch over men's health, over athletes training, perhaps, would have seem something amiss.

The two teams, in spite of the Christmas spirit, and the " Happy Christmas " greetings they exchanged to begin with, soon lost their springy step, the sledges dragged more slowly, and we gazed ahead almost wistfully.

Yes, the strain was beginning to tell, though none of us would have confessed it. Lashly and I had already pulled a sledge of varying weight—but mostly a loaded one—over 600 miles, and all had marched this distance.

During the forenoon something was seen ahead like the tide race over a rocky ledge—it was another ice fall stretching from East to West, and it had to be crossed, there could be no more deviation, for since Atkinson's party turned we had been five points West of our course at times. Alas, more wear for the runners of the sledge, which meant more labour to the eight of us, so keen to succeed in our enterprise—soon we are in the thick of it ; first one slips and is thrown violently down, then a sledge runs over the slope of a great ice wave.

The man trying to hold it back is relentlessly thrown, and the bow of the sledge crashes on to the heel of the hindermost of those hauling ahead with a thud that means " pain." But the victim utters no sound, just smiles in answer to the anxious questioning gaze of his comrades.

Something happened in the last half of that Christmas forenoon. Lashly, whose 44th birthday it was, celebrated the occasion by falling into a crevasse 8 feet wide.

Our sledge just bridged the chasm with very little to spare each end, and poor Lashly was suspended below, spinning round at the full length of his harness, with 80 feet of clear space beneath him. We had great difficulty in hauling him up on account of his being directly under the sledge. We got him to the surface by using the Alpine rope. Lashly was none the worse for his fall, and one of my party wished him a " Happy Christmas," and another " Many Happy Returns of the Day," when he had regained safety. Lashly's reply was unprintable.

Soon after this accident we topped the ice fall or ridge, and halted for lunch—we had risen over 250 feet, according to aneroid ; it seemed funny enough to find the barometer standing at 21 inches instead of 30.

Lunch camp, what a change. The primus stove fiercely roaring, the men light up their pipes and talk Christmas—dear, cheery souls, how proud Scott must have been of them ; no reference to the discomforts of the forenoon march, just brightness and the nicest thoughts for one another, and for "those," as poor Wilson unconsciously describes them, by humming : " Keep our loved ones, now far absent, 'neath Thy care." After a mug of warming tea and two biscuits we strike camp, and are soon slogging on. But the crevasses and icefalls have been overcome, the travelling is better, and with nothing but the hard, white horizon before us, thoughts wander away to the homeland—sweet little houses with well-kept gardens, glowing fires on bright hearths, clean, snowy tablecloths and polished silver, and then the dimpled, smiling faces of those we are winning our spurs for. Next Christmas may we hope for it ? Yes, it must be.

But with the exception of Lashly and Crean that daydream never came true, for alas, those whose dearest lived for that Christmas *never* came home, and the one other spared lost his wife, besides his five companions.

The two teams struggled on until after 8 p.m., when at last Scott signalled to camp. How tired we were—almost cross. But no sooner were the tents up than eyes looked out gladly from our dirty, bearded faces. Once again the cooker boiled, and for that night we had a really good square meal— more than enough of everything—pemmican with pieces of pony meat in it, a chocolate biscuit, " ragout " raisins, caramels, ginger, cocoa, butter, and a double ration of biscuits. How we watched Bowers cook that extra thick pemmican. Had he put too much pepper in ? Would he upset it ? How many pieces of pony meat would we get each ? But the careful little Bowers neither burnt nor upset the hoosh : it was up to our wildest expectations. No one could have eaten more.

After the meal we gasped, we felt so comfortable.

But we had such yarns of home, such plans were made for next Christmas, and after all we got down our fur sleeping-bags, and for a change we were quite warm owing to the full amount of food which we so sorely needed.

After the others in my tent were asleep, little Birdie Bowers, bidding me " Good-night," said, " Teddy, if all is well next Christmas we will get hold of all the poor children we can and just stuff them full of nice things, won't we ? "

It was unthinkable then that five out of the eight of us would soon be lying frozen on the Great Ice Barrier, their lives forfeited by a series of crushing defeats brought about by Nature, who alone metes out success or failure to win back for those who venture into the heart of that ice-bound continent.

Our Latitude was now 85° 50′ S., we were 8000 feet above the Barrier. Temperature −8°, with a fresh southerly wind, but we didn't care that night how hard it blew or whether it was Christmas or

Easter. We had done 17 miles distance and success lay within our grasp apparently.

On the following day we were up at six and marched a good 15 miles south with no opposition from crevasses or pressure ridges. The march over the Plateau continued without incident—excepting that on December 28 my team had a great struggle to keep up with Captain Scott's.

The surface was awfully soft, and though we discarded our outer garments we sweated tremendously. At about 11 a.m. Scott and I changed places. I found his sledge simply glided along whereas he found no such thing. The difference was considerable. After lunch we changed sledges and left Scott's team behind with ease. We stopped at the appointed time, and after supper Captain Scott came into our tent and told us that we had distorted our sledge by bad strapping or bad loading. This was, I think, correct, because Oates had dropped his sleeping-bag off a few days back through erring in the other direction and not strapping securely—we meant to have no recurrence and probably racked our sledge by heaving too hard on the straps.

The 29th was another day of very hard pulling. We were more than 9000 feet up—very nearly at the " summit of the summit." Quoting my diary I find set down for December 30 and 31 as follows :

" Saturday, *December* 30.

" Away at 8 a.m. Had a hell of a day's hauling. We worked independently of the other sledge, camping for lunch at 1 p.m. about half a mile astern of them. Then off again, and hauled till 7.15 p.m., when we reached Captain Scott's camp, he being then stopped $\frac{3}{4}$-hour. The surface was frightful and they had a heavy drag. Our distance to-day was 12 miles 1200 yards statute. We all turned in after our welcome hoosh, too tired to write up diaries even.

" Bill came in and had a yarn while we drank our cocoa.

" We are now about 9200 feet above the Barrier, temperature falls to about −15° now. Position 86° 49′ 9″ S., 162° 50′ E."

" *December* 31.

" Out at 5.45, and then after a yarn with Captain Scott and our welcome pemmican, tea and biscuit. we in our tent depoted our ski, Alpine rope, and ski shoes, saving a considerable weight. We then started off a few minutes ahead of Captain Scott, and his team never got near us, in fact they actually lost ground. We marched for 5½ hours solid, and had a good heavy drag, but not enough to distress us. We stopped at 1.30 p.m., having done 8 miles 116 yards statute. After our lunch we made a depot and put two weekly units in the snow cairn, which we built and marked with a black flag. The seamen (Evans and Crean) and Lashly spent the afternoon converting the 12 foot sledges to 10 foot with the spare runners, while the remainder of us fore-gathered in Captain Scott's tent, which Evans fitted with a lining to-day, making it beautifully warm. We sat in the tents with the door open and the sun shining in—doing odd jobs. I worked out sights and wrote up this diary, which was a few days adrift. Temperature −10°.

" We are now past Shackleton's position for December 31, and it does look as if Captain Scott were bound to reach the Pole. Position 86° 55′ 47″ S., 175° 40′ E.

" At 7 p.m. Captain Scott cooked tea for all hands.

" At 8 p.m. the first sledge was finished and the men went straight on with the second. This was finished by midnight, and, having seen the New Year in, we had a fine pemmican hoosh and went to bed."

New Year's Day found us in Latitude 87° 7′ S. Height, 9300 feet above Barrier—a southerly wind, with temperature 14° below zero.

On 2nd January I found the variation to be exactly 180°. A skua gull appeared from the south and hovered round the sledges during the afternoon, then it settled on the snow once or twice and we tried to catch it.

Did 15 miles with ease, but we were now only pulling 130 lb. per man.

On January 3 Scott came into my tent before we began the day's march and informed me that he was taking his own team to the Pole. He also asked me to spare Bowers from mine if I thought I could make the return journey of 750 miles short-handed —this, of course, I consented to do, and so little Bowers left us to join the Polar party. Captain Scott said he felt that I was the only person capable of piloting the last supporting party back without a sledge meter. I felt very sorry for him having to break the news to us, although I had foreseen it— for Lashly and I knew we could never hope to be in the Polar party after our long drag out from Cape Evans itself.

We could not all go to the Pole—food would not

allow this. Briefly then it was a disappointment, but not too great to bear ; it would have been an unbearable blow to us had we known that almost in sight were Amundsen's tracks, and that all our dragging and straining at the trace had been in vain.

On 4th January we took four days' provision for three men and handed over the rest of our load to Scott.

Then we three, Lashly, Crean, and myself, marched south to Latitude 87° 34' S. with the Polar party, and, seeing that they were travelling rapidly yet easily, halted, shook hands all round, and said good-bye, and since no traces of the successful Norwegian had been found so far, we fondly imagined that our flag would be the first to fly at the South Pole. We gave three huge cheers for the Southern party, as they stepped off, and then turned our sledge and commenced our homeward march of between 750 and 800 statute miles. We frequently looked back until we saw the last of Captain Scott and his four companions—a tiny black speck on the horizon, and little did we think that we would be the last to see them alive, that our three cheers on that bleak and lonely plateau summit would be the last appreciation they would ever know.

This day the excitement was intense, for it was obvious that with five fit men—the Pole being only 146 geographical miles away—the achievement was merely a matter of 10 or 11 days' good sledging.

Oates's last remark was cheerful : " I'm afraid, Teddy, you won't have much of a ' slope ' going back, but old Christopher is waiting to be eaten on the Barrier when you get there."

CHAPTER XV

RETURN OF THE LAST SUPPORTING PARTY

SCOTT had already made a great geographical journey in spite of adverse weather conditions, which had severely handicapped him throughout, but he was nevertheless behindhand in his expectations, and although the attainment of the Pole was practically within his grasp, the long 900 mile march homeward from that spot had to be considered. It was principally on this account that Captain Scott changed his marching organisation and took Bowers from the last supporting party.

After the first day's homeward march I realised that the nine hours' marching day was insufficient. We had to make average daily marches of 17 miles in order to remain on full provisions whilst returning over that featureless snow-capped plateau.

Although the first day northward bound was radiantly fine and the travelling surface all that could be desired, we were compelled to push on until quite late to ensure covering the prescribed distance—for a short march on the first day would have augured a gloomy future for us.

Reluctant as I was to confess it to myself, I soon realised that the ceding of one man from my party had been too great a sacrifice, but there was no denying it, and I was eventually compelled to explain the situation to Lashly and Crean and lay bare the naked truth. No man was ever better served than I was by these two ; they cheerfully accepted the inevitable, and throughout our homeward march the three of us literally stole minutes and seconds from each day in order to add to our marches, but it was a fight for life. The rarified air made our breathing more difficult, and we suffered from shortness of breath whenever the inequalities of the surface became severe, and sudden jerks conveyed themselves to our tired bodies through the medium of the rope traces.

Day after day we fought our way northward over the high Polar tableland. The silence now that we had no other party with us was ghastly, for beyond the sound of our own voices and the groaning of the sledge runners when the surface was bad there was no sound whatever to remind us of the outer world. As mile after mile was covered our thoughts wandered from the Expedition to those in our homeland, and thought succeeded thought while the march progressed until the satisfying effect of the last meal had vanished and life became one vast yearning for food.

Three days after leaving Captain Scott we encountered a blizzard and were forced to continue our marches although faced with navigational difficulties which made it impossible for us to maintain more than a very rough northward direction. Muffled up tightly in our wind-proof clothing, we did all in our power to prevent the dust-fine snowflakes which whirled around from penetrating into the tiniest opening in our clothes. The blizzard blinded and baffled us, forcing us always to turn our faces from it. The stinging wind cut and slashed our cheeks like the constant jab of a thousand frozen needle points.

This first blizzard which fell upon us lasted for three whole days, and at the end of that time we found ourselves considerably wide of our course.

On the 7th January, in spite of a temperature of 22° below zero, a fresh southerly wind and driving snow, Lashly, Crean, and myself laid 19 miles behind us. On the 8th we again covered this distance, although the weather was so bad that we entirely lost the track, and on the following day, when the blizzard was at its worst, we fought our way forward for over 16 miles. When the blizzard eventually abated we had hazy weather, but got an occasional glimpse of the sun, with which we corrected our course, and on the 13th January my party found itself right above the Shackleton Icefalls, and gazed down upon the more regular surface of the Beardmore Glacier hundreds of feet below us.

To reach the glacier we were faced with two alternatives : either to march right round the ice-falls, as we had done coming south, and thus waste three whole days, or to take our lives in our hands and attempt to get the sledge slap over the falls. This would mean facing tremendous drops, which might end in a catastrophe. The discussion was very short-lived, and with rather a sinking feeling the descent of the great ice falls was commenced. We packed our ski on the sledge, attached spiked crampons to our finnesko, and guided the sledge through the maze of hummocks and crevasses.

The travelling surface was wind-swept and consequently too easy, for the sledge would charge down a slippery slope of blue ice and capsize time after time. In places the way became so steep that our united efforts were needed to avoid the yawning

chasms which beset our path. We were compelled to
remain attached to the sledge by our harness, for
otherwise there was always the danger of our slipping into one of the very crevasses that we were
keeping the sledge clear of, and in this manner, with
the jumping and jolting of that awful descent,
frequent cases of over-running occurred, the sledge
fouling our traces and whisking us off our feet.
We encountered fall after fall, bruises, cuts, and
abrasions were sustained, but we vied with one
another in bringing all our grit and patience to
bear ; scarcely a complaint was heard, although
one or other of us would be driven almost sick
with pain as the sledge cannoned into this or that
man's heel with a thud that made the victim clench
his teeth to avoid crying out.

The whole forenoon we worked down towards
the more even surface of the great glacier itself, but
the actual descent of the steep part of the Shackleton Icefalls was accomplished in half an hour.
We came down many hundred feet in that time.

None of us can ever forget that exciting descent.
The speed of the sledge at one point must have been
60 miles an hour. We glissaded down a steep blue
ice slope ; to brake was impossible, for the sledge
had taken charge. One or other of us may have
attempted to check the sledge with his foot, but to
stop it in any way would have meant a broken leg.
We held on for our lives, lying face downwards on
the sledge. Suddenly it seemed to spring into the
air, we had left the ice and shot over one yawning
crevasse before we had known of its existence almost
—I do not imagine we were more than a second in
the air, but in that brief space of time I looked at
Crean, who raised his eyebrows as if to say, " What

next ! " Then we crashed on to the ice ridge beyond this crevasse, the sledge capsized and rolled over and over, dragging us three with it until it came to a standstill.

How we ever escaped entirely uninjured is beyond me to explain. When we had recovered our breath we examined ourselves and our sledge. One of my ski-sticks had caught on a piece of ice during our headlong flight and torn itself from the sledge. It rolled into the great blue-black chasm over which we had come, and its fate made me feel quite cold when I thought of what might have happened to us. When my heart had stopped beating so rapidly from fright, and I had recovered enough to look round, I realised that we were practically back on the Beardmore again, and that our bold escapade had saved us three days' solid foot slogging and that amount of food. So we pitched our little tent, had a good filling meal, and then, delighted with our progress, we marched on until 8 p.m. That night in our sleeping-bags we felt like three bruised pears, but being in pretty hard condition in those days, our bruises and slight cuts in no way kept us from hours of perfect, contented slumber.

I see in my diary for January 13, 1912, I have noted that we came down 2000 feet, but I doubt if it really was as much—we then had no means of measuring.

January 14 found us up at 5.45 (really only 4.45, because in order not to make my seamen companions anxious I handicapped my watch after the first day's homeward march, putting the hands on one hour each morning before rising, and back when I got the chance, so that we marched from 10 to 12 hours a day). We hauled our sledge for six hours until we reached the Upper Glacier Depot under Mount Darwin. Here we took 3½ days' stores as arranged, and after sorting up and repacking the depot had lunch and away down the Glacier, camping at 7.30 p.m. off Buckley Island, fairly close to the land. Temperature rose above zero that night.

Next day we were away at 8 a.m. with our crampons on, we came down several steep ice slopes, blue ice like glass, Lashly hauling ahead and Crean and I holding on to the sledge. We bumped a lot, and occasionally the sledge capsized. But we made good nearly 22 miles. We covered between 18 and 20 miles on January 16, and were in high glee at our progress. We camped, however, in amongst pressure ridges and huge crevasses, 14 miles from the Cloudmaker or mid-glacier depot. We hoped next day to reach this depot. January 16 was a pleasant day, its ending peaceful, with a sufficiency of excellent sledging rations and the promise of a similar day to succeed it. On this day hopes had run high ; our clothes were dry, the weather mild and promising, besides which, we were camped in the full satisfaction of having a good many miles in hand. We cheerfully discussed our arrival at the next depot, after which we knew that no anxieties need be felt, given even moderately good luck and weather, that did not include too great a proportion of blizzard days. The musical roar of the primus and the welcome smell of the cooking pemmican whetted our appetites deliciously, and as the three of us sat around the cooker on our rolled up fur bags, the contented expression on our dirty brown faces made our bearded ugliness almost handsome. We built

wonderful castles in the air as to what luxuries
Lashly, who was a famous cook, should prepare
on our return to winter quarters. There we had
still some of the New Zealand beef and mutton
stored in my glacier cave, and one thing I had set
my heart on was a steak and kidney pudding which
my friend Lashly swore to make me.

After the meal we unrolled our sleeping-bags and
luxuriantly got into them, for the recent fine
weather had given us a chance to dry thoroughly
the fur and get the bags clear of that uncomfortable
clamminess due to the moisture from our bodies
freezing until the sleeping-bags afforded but little
comfort. The weather looked glorious, there was
not a cloud in the sky, and towards 10 o'clock the
sun was still visible to the S.S.W. We could see it
through the thin, green canvas tent wall as we
turned in, still in broad daylight, and the warmth
derived from it made sleep come to us quite easily.

I woke at five the next morning, and, rousing my
companions, we were up and about in a minute.
The primus stove and cooking apparatus were
brought into the tent once more ; our sleeping footgear was changed for our marching finneskoe and
good steel-spiked crampons fixed to the soft fur
boots to give us grip in places where the ice was blue
and slippery. By 6 a.m. the little green tent was
struck, the sledge securely packed, and the three of
us commenced a day's march, the details of which,
although it occurred over nine years ago, are so
fresh in my memory that I have not even to refer
to my sledging diary.

We commenced the day unluckily, for a low
stratus cloud had spread like a tablecloth over the
Beardmore and filled up the glacier with mist. This

added tremendously to our difficulties in steering, for we had no landmarks by which to set our course, although I knew the approximate direction of descent and could make this by means of a somewhat inadequate compass. The refinements in steering were not sufficient to keep us on the good blue ice surface down which we could have threaded our way had we commanded a full view of the glacier. Our route led us over rougher ice than we should normally have chosen, and the outlook was distinctly displeasing. The air was thick with countless myriads of tiny floating ice crystals, and the great hummocks of ice stood weirdly shapen as they loomed through the frozen mist. I appreciated that we were getting into trouble, but hoped that the fog would disperse as the sun increased its altitude. We fell about a good deal, and to my consternation the surface became worse and worse. We were, however, covering distance in an approximately northward direction, and our team achieved with stubborn purpose what would have appeared impossible to us when we first visited this great, white, silent continent.

It was no good going back, and we could not tell whether the good track was to the right or the left of our line of advance. As new and more troublesome obstacles presented themselves, the more valiantly did my companions set themselves to win through. Crean and Lashly had the hearts of lions. The uncertain light of the mist worried us all three, and we were forced to take off our goggles to see to advance at all.

We continued until midday, when to my great relief the mist showed signs of dispersing, and the sun, a sickly yellow orb, eventually showed through.

It was surrounded by a halo which was reflected in
rainbow colouring in the minute floating ice crystals.
I looked round for a spot suitable for camping, for
we were pretty well exhausted, and it was worth
while waiting for the mist to disperse. No time
would be wasted since the halt would do for our
lunch. With the greatest difficulty we found
amongst the hummocky ice a place to set up our
tent. A space was found somehow, and rather
gloomily the three of us made a cooker full of tea.
We munched our biscuit in silence, for we were too
tired to talk. From time to time I went outside
the tent, and certainly the atmosphere was clearer.
Odd shapes to the east and west showed themselves
to be the fringing mountains which so few eyes
had ever rested on. Gradually they took form and
I was able more or less to identify our whereabouts.
We finished our lunch, Crean had a smoke, and
then we got under way.

A little discussion, a lot of support, and a wealth
of whole-hearted good-fellowship from my companions gave me the encouragement which made
leading these two men so easy.

Warmed by the tea, cheered by the meal, and
rested by the halt, we pushed on once more,
although to go forward was uncertain and to work
back impossible since we were too exhausted to do
such pulling upward as would be necessary to reach
a place from whence a new start could be made, even
if we succeeded in re-discovering our night camp
of yesterday.

For hours we fought on, sometimes overcoming
crevasses by bridging them with the sledge where
its length enabled this to be done. The summer sun
had cleared the snow from this part of the glacier,

laying bare the great blue, black cracks, and they were horrible to behold. If the breadth of a crevasse was too large to be crossed we worked along the bank until an ice bridge presented itself along which we could go. As the sun's rays grew more powerful, the visibility became perfect, and I must confess we were disappointed to see before us the most disheartening wilderness of pressure ridges and disturbances. We were in the heart of the Great Ice Fall which is to be found half-way down the Beardmore Glacier. We struggled along, for there is no other expression which aptly describes our case. Had we not been in superb physical training and in really hard condition all three of us must have collapsed. We literally carried the sledge, which weighed nearly four hundred pounds.

When the afternoon march had already extended for hours we found ourselves travelling mile after mile across the line of our intended route to circumvent the crevasses. They seemed to grow bigger and bigger. At about 8 p.m. we were travelling on a ridge between two stupendous open gulfs, and we found a connecting bridge which stretched obliquely across. I saw that it was necessary to move round or across a number of these wide open chasms to reach the undulations which we knew from our ice experience must terminate this broken up part of the glacier. In vain I told myself that these undulations could not be so far away.

To cross by the connecting bridge which I have just spoken about was, to say the least of it, a precarious proceeding. But it would save us a mile or two, and in our tired state this was worth considering. After a minute's rest we placed the sledge

on this ice bridge, and, as Crean described it afterwards, " We went along the crossbar to the H of
Hell." It was not all misnamed either, for Lashly,
who went ahead, dared not walk upright. He
actually sat astride the bridge and was paid out
at the end of our Alpine rope. He shuffled his way
across, fearful to look down into the inky blue
chasm below, but he fixed his eyes on the opposite
wall of ice and hoped the rope would be long
enough to allow him to reach it and climb up, for
he never would have dared to come back. The
cord *was* sufficient in length, and he contrived
finally to make his way on to the top of the ridge
before him. He then turned round and looked
scaredly at Crean and myself. I think all of us
felt the tension of the moment, but we wasted no
time in commencing the passage. The method of
procedure was this. The sledge rested on the narrow
bridge which was indeed so shaped that the crest
only admitted of the runners resting one on each
side of it ; the slope away was like an inverted " V "
and while Lashly sat gingerly on the opposite ridge,
hauling carefully but not too strongly on the rope,
Crean and I, facing one another, held on to the
sledge sides, balancing the whole concern. It was
one of the most exciting moments of our lives.
We launched the sled across foot by foot as I
shouted " One, Two, Three—Heave." Each time
the signal was obeyed we got nearer to the opposite
ice slope. The balance was preserved, of course,
by Crean and myself, and we had to exercise a most
careful judgment. Neither of us spoke, except for
the launching signal, but each looked steadfastly
into the other's eyes—nor did we two look down.
A false movement might have precipitated the whole

gang and the sledge itself into the blue-black space of awful depth beneath. The danger was very real, but this crossing was necessary to our final safety. As in other cases of peril, the tense quiet of the moment left its mark on the memories of our party for ever. Little absurd details attracted all our attention, for instance, I noticed the ruts in the cheeks of my grimy *vis-à-vis*, for Crean had recently clipped his beard and whiskers. My gaze was also riveted on a cut, or rather open crack caused in one of his lips by the combined sun and wind. Thousands of little fleeting thoughts chased one another through our brains, as we afterwards found by comparison, and finally we were so close to Lashly that he could touch the sledge. He reached down, for the bridge was depressed somewhat where it met the slope on which he sat.

He held on tight, and somehow Crean and I wriggled off the bridge, sticking our crampons firmly into the ice and crawling up to where Lashly was. We all three held on to the Alpine line, and in some extraordinary fashion got to the top of the ridge, where we anchored ourselved and prepared to haul up the sledge. As I said before, it weighed about 400 lb., and to three exhausted men the strain which came upon us when we hauled the sledge off the bridge tested us to the limit of our strength. The wretched thing slipped sideways and capsized on the slope, nearly dragging us down into that icy chasm, but our combined efforts saved us, and once again the perils of the moment were forgotten as we got into our sledge harness and started to make the best of our way to the depot.

By now we were exhausted, rudely shaken, and

our eyes were smarting with the glare and the glint of the sun's reflections from that awful maze of ice falls. I felt my heart would burst from the sustained effort of launching that sledge, which now seemed to weigh a ton. There seemed no way out of this confused mass of pressure ridges and crevasses. We were "all out," and come what may I had to change our tactics, accordingly I ordered a halt. No room could be found to pitch our tent and I could not see any possibility of saving my party. We could stagger on no farther with the dreadfully heavy sledge. The prospect was hopeless and our food was nearly gone. Some rest must be obtained to give us strength for this absolute battle for life. The great strain of the day's efforts had thoroughly exhausted us, and it took me back to the last day of the December blizzard which caused the eventual loss of the Polar Party and the ruin of Captain Scott's so excellently laid plans. I remembered the poor ponies after their fourteen hours' march, their flanks heaving, their black eyes dull, shrivelled and wasted. The poor beasts had stood, with their legs stuck out in strange attitudes, mere wrecks of the beautiful little animals that we took away from New Zealand, and I could not help likening our condition to theirs on that painful day. The three of us sat on the sledge—hollow-eyed and gaunt looking. We were done, our throats were dry, and we could scarcely speak. There was no wind, the atmosphere was perfectly still, and the sun slowly crept towards the southern meridian, clear cut in the steel blue sky. It gave us all the sympathy it could, for it shed warm rays upon us as it silently moved on its way like a great eye from

Heaven, looking but unable to help. We should have gone mad with another day like this, and there were times when we came perilously close to being insane. Something had to be done. I got up from the sledge, cast my harness adrift, and said, " I am going to look for a way out ; we can't go on." My companions at first persuaded me not to go, but I pointed out that we could not continue in our exhausted condition. If only we could find a camping place, and we could rest, perhaps we should be able to make a final effort to get clear.

I moved along a series of ice bridges, and the excitement gave me strength once more. I was surprised at myself for not being more giddy when I walked along the narrow ice spines, but the crampons attached to my finneskoe were like cat's claws, and without the weight of the sledge I seemed to develop a panther-like tenacity, for I negotiated the dangerous parts with the utmost ease. After some twenty minutes hunting round I came to a great ice hollow.

Down into it I went and up the other side. This hollow was free from crevasses, and when I got to the top of the ice mound opposite I saw yet another hollow. Turning round I gazed back towards where I had left our sledge. Two tiny, disconsolate figures were silhouetted against the sunlight—my two companions on our great homeward march, one sitting and one standing, probably looking for my reappearance as I vanished and was sighted again from time to time. I felt a tremendous love for those two men that day. They had trusted me so implicitly and believed in my ability to win through. I turned northward again, stepped down into the next hollow and stopped. I was in an enormous depression but not a crevasse to be seen, for the sides of the depression met quite firmly at the bottom in smooth, blue, solid ice.

In a flash I called to mind the view of the Ice Fall from the glacier on our outward journey with Captain Scott, I remembered the huge frozen waves, and hoped with all my optimistic nature that this might be the end of the great disturbance. I stood still and surveyed the wonderful valley of ice, and then fell on my knees and prayed to God that a way out would be shown me.

Then I sprang to my feet, and hurried on boldly. Clambering up the opposite slope of ice, I found a smooth, round crest over which I ran into a similar valley beyond.

Frozen waves here followed in succession, and hollow followed hollow, each less in magnitude than its forerunner.

Suddenly I saw before me the smooth, shining bed of the glacier itself, and away to the north-west was the curious reddish rock under which the Mid Glacier Depot had been placed. My feelings hardly bear setting down. I was overcome with emotion, but my prayer was answered and we were saved.

I had considerable difficulty in working back to the party amongst the labyrinth of ice bridges, but I fortunately found a patch of hard snow whereon my crampons had made their mark. From here I easily traced my footmarks back, and was soon in company with my friends. They were truly relieved at my news. On consulting my watch I found that I had been away one hour. It took us actually three times as long to work our sledge out into the smooth ice of the glacier, but this reached, we camped and made some tea before marching on to the depot, which lay but a few miles from us.

We ate the last of our biscuits at this camp and finished everything but tea and sugar, then, new men, we struck our little camp, harnessed up and swept down over the smooth ice with scarcely an effort needed to move the sledge along. When we reached the depot we had another meal and slept through the night and well on into the next day.

Consulting my old Antarctic diary I see that the last sentence written on the 17th January says, " I had to keep my goggles off all day as it was a matter of life or death with us, and snow blindness must be risked after . . ." (a gap follows here until 29th January). The next day I had an awful attack of snow blindness, but the way down the glacier was so easy that it did not matter. I forgot whether Lashly or Crean led then, but I marched alongside, keeping in touch with the trace by hitching the lanyard of my sundial on to it and holding this in my hand. I usually carried the sundial slung round my neck, so that it was easy to pick it up and consult it. That day I was in awful pain, and although we had some dope for putting on our eyes when so smitten, I found that the greatest relief of all was obtained by bandaging my eyes with a poultice made of tea leaves after use—quaint places, quaint practices but the tip is worth considering for future generations of explorers and alpine climbers.

Our homeward march continued for day after day with no very exciting incidents. We met no more crevasses that were more than a foot or so wide, and we worked our way down on to the Great Ice Barrier with comparatively easy marches, although the distances we covered were surprising to us all—seventeen miles a day we averaged.

On the 30th January Lashly and I had been fourteen weeks out, and we had exhausted practically every topic of conversation beyond food, distances made good, temperatures, and the weather. Crean, as already set down, had started with the Main Southern Party a week after Lashly and I had first set out as the pioneers with those wretched failures, the motor sledges. By this time I had made the unpleasant discovery that I was suffering from scurvy. It came on with a stiffening of the knee joints, then I could not straighten my legs, and finally they were horrible to behold, swollen, bruised, and green. As day followed day my condition became worse: my gums were ulcerated and my teeth loose. Then finally I got hæmorrhage. Crean and Lashly were dreadfully concerned on my behalf, and how they nursed me and helped me along no words of mine can properly describe. What men they were. Those awful days—I trudged on with them for hundreds of miles, and each step hurt me more. I had done too much on the outward journey, for what with building all the depot cairns ahead of the pony party, and what with the effects of the spring sledge journey, too much had been asked of me. I had never been out of harness from the day I left Hut Point, for even with the motor sledges we practically pulled them along. Crean had had an easier time, for he had led a pony up to the foot of the Beardmore Glacier, and Lashly had not done the spring sledging journey, which took a certain amount out of me with its temperatures falling to 73° below zero. The disappointment of not being included in the Polar Party had not helped me much, and I must admit that my prospects of winning through became duller day by day. I suffered absolute agonies in forcing my way along, and eventually I could only push myself by means of a ski-stick, for I could not step out properly. I somehow waddled on ski until one day I fainted when striving to start a march. Crean and Lashly picked me up, and Crean thought I was dead. His hot tears fell on my face, and as I came to I gave a weak kind of laugh.

They rigged the camp up once more and put me in my bag, and then those two gallant fellows held a short council of war. I endeavoured to get them to leave me when they came in with their suggestions, but it was useless to argue with them, and I now felt that I had shot my bolt. I vainly tried to persuade them to leave me in my sleeping-bag with what food they could spare, but they put me on the sledge, bag and all, and strapped me as comfortably as they could with their own sleeping-bags spread under me to make for greater ease.

How weary their marches must have been—ten miles of foot slogging each day. I could see them from the sledge by raising my head—how slowly their legs seemed to move—wearily but nobly they fought on until one day a blizzard came and completely spoilt the surface. The two men had been marching nearly 1500 miles, their strength was spent, and great though their hearts were, they had now to give up. In vain they tried to move the sledge with my wasted weight upon it—it was hopeless.

Very seriously and sadly they re-erected our tent and put me once again inside. I thought I was being put into my grave. Outside I heard them talking, low notes of sadness, but with a certain thread of determination running through what they said. They were discussing which should go and which should stay. Crean had done, if anything, the lighter share of the work, as already explained, and he therefore set out to march thirty-five miles with no food but a few biscuits and a little stick of chocolate.

He hoped to find relief at Hut Point. Failing this, he would go on if possible to Cape Evans.

Crean came in to say good-bye to me. I thanked him for what he was doing in a weak, broken sort of way, and Lashly held open the little round tent door to let me see the last of him. He strode out nobly and finely—I wondered if I should ever see him again. Then Lashly came in to me, shut the tent door, and made me a little porridge out of some oatmeal we got from the last depot we had passed.

After I had eaten it he made me comfortable by laying me on Crean's sleeping-bag, which made my own seem softer, for I was very, very sore after being dragged a hundred miles on a jolting, jumping sledge. Then I slept and awoke to find Lashly's kind face looking down at me. There were very few wounded men in the Great War nursed as I was by him.

A couple of days passed, and every now and then Lashly would open up the tent door, go out and search the horizon for some possible sign of relief. The end had nearly come, and I was past caring ; we had no food, except a few paraffin saturated biscuits, and Lashly in his weakened state without food could never have marched in. He took it all very quietly—a noble, steel true man—but relief

did come at the end of that day when everything
looked its blackest.

We heard the baying of the dogs, first once, then
again. Lashly, who was lying down by my side
quietly talking, sprang to his feet, looked out, and
saw !

They galloped right up to the tent door, and the
leader, a beautiful gray dog named Krisravitsa,
seemed to understand the situation, for he came
right into the tent and licked my hands and face.
I put my poor weak hands up and gripped his
furry ears. Perhaps to hide my feelings I kissed
his old hairy, Siberian face with the kiss that was
meant for Lashly. We were both dreadfully
affected at our rescue.

Atkinson and the Russian dog-boy, Dimitri, had
come out hot-foot to save us, and of all men in the
Expedition none could have been better chosen than
" Little Aitch," our clever naval doctor. After
resting his dogs and feeding me with carefully
prepared foodstuffs, he got me on one sledge and
Lashly on the other, the dogs were given their
head, and in little more than three hours we covered
the thirty-five miles into Hut Point, where I was
glad to see Crean's face once more and to hear first
hand about his march. It had taken him eighteen
hours' plodding through those awful snows from
our camp to Hut Point, where fortunately he met
Atkinson and Dimitri and told them of my condition.

After the Expedition was over the King gave
Lashly and Crean the Albert Medal for their
bravery in helping me win through.

It is little enough tribute that I have dedicated
this book to these two gallant fellows.

CHAPTER XVI

THE POLE ATTAINED—SCOTT'S LAST MARCHES

THE details of Scott's final march to the Pole, and the heartrending account of his homeward journey, of Evans's sad death, of Oates's noble sacrifice, and of the martyr-like end of Wilson, Bowers, and Scott himself have been published throughout the length and breadth of the civilised world. In *Scott's Last Expedition*—Vol. I. the great explorer's journals are practically reproduced in their entirety. Mr. Leonard Huxley, who arranged them in 1913, had had to do with Scott's first work, *The Voyage of the " Discovery,"* and, as Mr. Huxley has said, these two works needed but little editing. Scott's last fine book was written as he went along, and those of us who have survived the Expedition and the Great War, and we are few, are more than proud to count ourselves among the company he chose.

A synopsis of his march from 87° 35′ to the South Pole, and a recapitulation of the events which marked the homeward march must certainly find their way into this book, which is after all only the husk of the real story.

However much the story is retold—and it has been retold by members of the Expedition as well as by others—the re-telling will never approach the story as told by Scott himself : for the kernel one must turn to Volume I. of *Scott's Last Expedition* : However, perhaps I can give something of interest ;

here is what little Bowers says in extracts from his diary, given me by his mother :

"*January* 4.—Packed up sledge with four weeks and three days' food for five men, five sleeping-bags, etc. I had my farewell breakfast with Teddy Evans, Crean and Lashly. Teddy was frightfully cut up at not going to the Pole, he had set his heart on it so.

" I am afraid it was a very great disappointment to him, and I felt very sorry about it. Poor Teddy, I am sure it was for his wife's sake he wanted to go. He gave me a little silk flag she had given him to fly on the Pole. After so little sleep the previous night I rather dreaded the march.

" We gave our various notes, messages, and letters to the returning party and started off. They accompanied us for about a mile before turning, to see that all was going on well.

" Our party was on ski with the exception of myself. I first made fast to the central span, but afterwards connected up to the bow of the sledge, pulling in the centre between the inner ends of Captain Scott's and Dr. Wilson's traces.

" This was found to be the best place, as I had to go my own step. Teddy and party gave us three cheers and Crean was half in tears. They had a featherweight sledge to go back with, of course, and ought to run down their distance easily.

" We found we could manage our load easily, and did 6·3 miles before lunch, completing 12·5. by 7·15 p.m. Our marching hours are nine per day. It is a long slog with a well-loaded sledge, and more tiring for me than the others as I have no ski. However, as long as I can do my share all day and keep fit, it does not matter much one way or the other.

I

" We had our first north wind on the Plateau to-day, and a deposit of snow crystals made the surface like sand latterly on the march. The sledge dragged like lead. In the evening it fell calm, and although the temperature was 16° it was positively pleasant to stand about outside the tent and bask in the sun's rays. It was our first calm since we reached the summit too. Our socks and other damp articles which we hang out to dry at night became immediately covered with long feathery crystals exactly like plumes.

" Socks, mitts, and finneskoe dry splendidly up here during the night. We have little trouble with them compared with spring and winter journeys. I generally spread my bag out in the sun during the $1\frac{1}{2}$ hours of lunch time, which gives the reindeer hair a chance to get rid of the damage done by the deposit of breath and any perspiration during the night. . . ."

He seemed to have made no entry for some days after this, but he is interesting to quote later.

The Polar Party covered the 145 geographical miles that remained in a fortnight ; on the 7th January they reached apparently the summit of the Plateau, 10,570 ft. in Latitude 88° 18' 70" S. Longitude 157° 21' E., but their marches fell short of expectations due to the bad surfaces met with.

Scott kept copious notes in his diary of everything that mattered. He was delighted with his final selection, and as usual pithy and to the point when describing. Here, for example, is something of what he wrote of his companions :

(From *Scott's Last Expedition*, Vol. I.)

" WILSON.—Quick, careful and dexterous, ever thinking of some fresh expedient to help the camp life ; tough as steel on the traces, never wavering from start to finish.

" PETTY OFFICER EVANS.—A giant worker, with a really remarkable headpiece—he is responsible for every sledge, every sledge-fitting, tents, sleeping-bags, harness, and when one cannot recall a single expression of dissatisfaction with any one of these items, it shows what an invaluable assistant he has been. . . .

" BOWERS.—Little Bowers remains a marvel—he is thoroughly enjoying himself. I leave all the provision arrangements in his hands, and at all times he knows exactly how we stand . . . Nothing comes amiss to him, and no work is too hard. . . .

" OATES.—Each is invaluable. Oates had his invaluable period with the ponies : now he is a foot slogger and goes hard the whole time, does his share of camp work and stands the hardships as well as any of us. I would not like to be without him either. So our five people are perhaps as happily selected as it is possible to imagine."

Certainly no living man could have taken Scott's place effectively as leader of our Expedition—there was none other like him. He was the Heart, Brain, and Master.

On January 11 just the slightest descent had been made, the height up being now 10,540 ft., but it will be noticed that they were then getting temperatures as low as 26° below zero : my party on that date got 10° higher thermometer readings. Surface troubles continued to waylay them, and their distances, even with five men, were disappointing, due undoubtedly to this.

On 13th both Bowers and Scott write of a surface like sand, and of tugging and straining when they ought to be moving easily. On 14th some members began to feel the cold unmistakably, and on the following day the whole party were quite done on camping.

The saddest note on the outward march is struck on January 16 when Bowers sighted a cairn of snow and a black speck, which turned out to be a black flag tied to a sledge runner, near the remains of a camp—this after such a hopeful day on the 15th, when a depot of nine days' food was made only 27 miles from the Pole—and Scott wrote in his diary:

" . . . It ought to be a certain thing now, and the only appalling possibility the sight of the Norwegian Flag forestalling ours. . . ."

Still, there it was, dog tracks, many of them, were picked up and followed to the Polar Area. Scott, Wilson, Oates, Bowers, and Seaman Evans reached the South Pole on 17th January, 1912, a horrible day, temperature 22° below zero. The party fixed the exact spot by means of one of our little four-inch theodolites, and the result of their careful observations located the Pole at a point which only differed from Amundsen's " fix " by half a mile, as shown by his flag.

This difference actually meant that the British and Norwegian observers differed by *one scale division on the theodolite*, which was graduated to half a minute of arc.

Experts in navigation and surveying will always look on this splendidly accurate determination as a fine piece of work by our own people as well as by the Norwegian Expedition.

Lady Scott has remarked on the magnificent spirit shown by her husband and his four specially-selected tent-mates when they knew that Queen Alexandra's little silk Union Jack had been anticipated by the flag of another nation. Scott and his companions had done their best, and never from one of them came an uncharitable remark.

In our Expedition Committee Minute Book it is recorded that the following were found at the Pole :

A letter from Captain Amundsen to Captain Scott :

> " Poleheim,
> 15*th* December, 1911.

" DEAR CAPTAIN SCOTT, As you probably are the first to reach this area after us, I will ask you kindly to forward this letter to King Haakon VII. If you can use any of the articles left in the tent please do not hesitate to do so. The sledge left outside may be of use to you. With kind regards I wish you a safe return.

> " Yours truly,
> ROALD AMUNDSEN."

Also another note :

" The Norwegian Home, Poleheim, is situated in 89° 58′ S. Lat. S.E. by E. compass 8 miles.

> (Signed)   ROALD AMUNDSEN.

" 15*th* December, 1911."

The Norwegian Explorers' names recorded at Poleheim were : Roald Amundsen, Olaf Bjaaland, Helmer Hanssen, Oskar Wisting, Sverre Hassel.

Scott left a note in the Norwegian tent with the names of himself and his companions, and in his diary he agreed that the Norwegian explorers had made thoroughly sure of their work and fully carried out their programme.

Scott considered the Pole to be 9500 feet above the Barrier—1000 feet lower than the Plateau altitude in 88°.

Bowers took the sights to fix the South Pole.

On the 19th January the northward march was commenced : the party had before them then a distance of over 900 miles (statute). Bowers writes on this date quite nonchalantly :

" . . . A splendid clear morning, with fine S.W'ly wind blowing—during breakfast time I sewed a flap attachment on to my green hat so as to prevent the wind from blowing down my neck on the march. We got up the mast and sail on the sledge and headed North, picking up Amundsen's cairn and our outgoing tracks shortly afterwards. Along this we travelled until we struck the other cairn and finally the Black Flag where we had made our sixth (?) outward camp. We then with much relief left all traces of the Norwegian behind, and I headed on my own track till lunch camp, when we had come 8.1 miles. In the afternoon we passed No. 2 Cairn of the British route, and fairly slithered along with a fresh breeze. It was heavy travelling for me, not being on ski, but one does not mind being tired if a good march is made. We did 16 altogether for the day, and so should pick up our last depot to-morrow afternoon. The weather became fairly thick soon after noon, and at the end of the afternoon there was considerable drift with a mist caused by ice crystals and parhelion.

"*January* 20.—Good sailing breeze again this morning ; it is a great pleasure to have one's back to the wind instead of having to face it. It came on thicker later, but we sighted the last depot soon after 1 p.m. and reached it at 1-15 p.m. The red flag on the bamboo pole was blowing out merrily to welcome us back from the Pole, with its supply of the necessaries of life below. We are absolutely dependent on our depots to get off the Plateau alive, and so welcome the lovely little cairns gladly. At this one, called the ' Last Depot,' we picked up four days' food, a can of oil, some methylated spirit (for lighting purposes), and some personal gear we had left there. The bamboo was bent on to the floor-cloth as a yard for our sail instead of a broken sledge runner of Amundsen's, which we had found at the Pole and made a temporary yard of. As we had marched extra long in the forenoon in order to reach the depot, our afternoon march was shorter than usual. The wind increased to a moderate gale, with heavy gusts and considerable drift. We would have had a bad time had we been facing it. After an hour I had to shift my harness aft so as to control the motions of the sledge.

"Unfortunately the surface got very sandy latterly, but we finished up with 16.1 miles to our credit and camped in a stiff breeze, which rendered itself into a blizzard a few hours later. I was glad we had our depot safe.

"*January* 21.—Wind increased to force 8 during night, with heavy drift ; in the morning it was blizzing like blazes, and marching was out of the question. The wind would have been of great assistance to us, but the drift was so thick that steering a course would have been next to impossible, so we decided to await developments and get under way as soon as it showed any signs of clearing. Fortunately it was short lived, and instead of lasting the regulation two days it went off in the afternoon, and 2.45 found us off with our sail full. It was good running on ski, but soft plodding for me on foot. I shall be jolly glad to pick up my dear old ski. They are nearly 200 miles away yet, however. The breeze fell altogether latterly, and I shifted up into my old place, a middle number of the five. Our distance completed was 5.52 miles when camp was made again. Our old cairns are of great assistance, also the tracks, which are obliterated in places by heavy drift and hard sastrugi, but can be followed easily.

"*January* 22.—We came across Evans's sheep-skin boots this evening. They were almost covered after their long spell since they fell off the sledge. The breeze was in from the S.S.W., but got bright and light. At lunch camp we had completed 8.2 miles. In the afternoon the breeze fell altogether and the surface acted on by the sun became perfect sand-dust. The light sledge pulled by five men came along like a drag without a particle of slide or go in it. We were all glad to camp soon after 7 p.m. I think we were all pretty tired out. We did altogether 19.5 miles for the day. We are now only 30 miles from the 1½° depot and should reach it in two marches with any luck.

" *January* 23.—Started off with a bit of a breeze which helped us a little. After the first two hours it increased to force 4 S.S.W., and filling the sail we sped along merrily, doing 8¾ miles before lunch. In the afternoon it was even stronger. I had to go back in the sledge and act as guide and brakesman. We had to lower the sail a bit, but even then she ran like a bird. We are picking up our old cairns famously. Evans got his nose frost-bitten, not an unusual thing with him, and as we were all getting pretty cold latterly, we stopped at a quarter to seven, having done 15½ miles. We camped with considerable difficulty owing to the force of the wind.

" *January* 24.—Evans got his fingers all blistered with frostbites, otherwise we are all well, but thinning, and in spite of our good rations getting hungrier daily.

" I sometimes spend much thought on the march with plans for making a pig of myself on the first opportunity. As this will be after a farther walk of 700 miles they will be a bit premature. It was blowing a gale when we started, and it increased in force. Finally, with the sail half down, one man detached tracking ahead, and Titus and I breaking back, we could not always keep the sledge from over-running. The blizzard got worse and worse, till having done only 7 miles we had to camp soon after 12 o'clock. We had a most difficult job camping, and it has been blowing like blazes all the afternoon. I think it is moderating now— 9 p.m.

" We are only 7 miles from our depot and the delay is exasperating.

" *January* 25.—It was no use turning out at our

usual time (5.45 a.m.) as the blizzard was as furious as ever.

" We therefore decided on a late breakfast and no lunch unless able to march. We have only three days' food with us and shall be in Queer Street if we miss the depot.

" Our bags are getting steadily wetter, so are our clothes.

" It shows a tendency to clear off now (breakfast time), so, D.V., we may march after all. I am in tribulation as regards meals now, as we have run out of salt, one of my favourite commodities. It was owing to Atkinson's party taking back an extra tin by mistake from the Upper Glacier Depot.

" Fortunately we have some depoted there, so I will only have to endure another two weeks without it.

" 10 p.m.—We have got in a march after all, thank the Lord.

" Assisted by the wind we made an excellent run down to our $1\frac{1}{2}$ Depot, where the big red flag was blowing out of driving drift. Here we picked up $1\frac{1}{4}$ cans of oil, and one week's food for five men, together with some personal gear depoted.

" We left the bamboo and the flag on the cairn. I was much relieved to pick up this depot ; now we have only one other source of anxiety in the endless snow summit, viz., the third depot in Latitude 86° 56′ S. In the afternoon we did 5.2 miles. It was a miserable march, blizzard all the time and our sledge either sticking on sastrugi or overrunning the traces. We had to lower the sail half down, and Titus and I hung on to her—it was most strenuous work as well as much colder than pulling ahead. Most of the time we had to brake back with all our strength to keep the sledge from overrunning. Bill got a bad go of sun-glare from following the track without goggles on.

" *January 26.*—This day last year we started the depot journey. I did not think so short a time would turn me into an old hand at Polar travelling, neither did I imagine all the time that I would be returning from the Pole.

" *January 29.*—Our record march to-day. With a good breeze and improving surface we were soon in amongst the double tracks where the supporting party left us. Then we picked up the memorable camp where I transferred to the advance party. How glad I was to change over. The camp was much drifted up, and immense sastrugi . . . etc."

Day's marches, temperatures, and so on, then his diary commences missing days out and only contains two line entries in short, sharp notes such as :

" *January 31.*—Picked up depot 11.20 a.m. Picked up my ski 6.15 p.m. No wind latterly— heavy surface. 13½ —Bill's leg—Evans's fingers— extra biscuits, etc." ; and

" *February 11.*—Very heavy surface—ice crystals —movement of upper currents—Evans cook— finer weather—lower temperature— sastrugi. Run 11.1."

It was probably the beginning of the end.

February brought little to the party but bad luck and reverses. Wilson had strained a tendon in his leg. Evans's fingers were in a bad state through frostbite, and on the first of the month Scott himself had fallen and shaken himself badly. Temperatures low, too low for any good surface.

February 4 found the party amongst crevasses, both Scott and Evans falling into them. Notwithstanding all their troubles they made a fine pace over the ice-capped plateau and down the Beardmore. Evans's fall on February 4 crocked him up a good deal, and he suffered from facial frostbites. His condition all the time now was causing the gravest anxiety. The summit journey ended on February 7. On the 8th valuable geological specimens were collected and brought along, and then the descent of the Great Glacier commenced. The Beardmore temperatures to begin with were rather high, and Scott seems to have considered this a disadvantage, for he says it made the party feel slack. Evans was rested half-way down the Beardmore, Oates looking after him, while the other made a halt for geological investigation by the Cloudmaker depot.

But poor Evans had sustained a severe concussion through falling and hitting his head on the 4th, and the party on his account was so delayed that the surplus foodstuffs rapidly diminished, and the outlook became serious. Bad weather was again encountered, and on February 17, near the foot of the Glacier, Seaman Evans died. Wilson expressed the opinion that Evans must have injured his brain by the fall. It was a great surprise to all of us to hear of Evans failing so early, as he was known to be a man of enormous strength, and a tried sledger. He was also a veteran in Antarctic experience, having made some wonderful journeys under Scott in the *Discovery* days.

After reaching the Lower Glacier Depot on the 17th the bereaved little band pushed Northward with fine perseverance, although they must have known by their gradually shortening marches that little hope of reaching their winter quarters remained. Their best march on the Barrier was only 12 miles, and in the later stages their marches dropped to 4. The depots were, as stated, some 65 miles apart, but 'the temperatures fell as they advanced, instead of rising, as expected, and we find them recording − 46.2° one night. Surfaces were terrible—" like pulling over desert sand, not the least glide in the world."

Poor Oates's feet and hands were badly frostbitten—he constantly appealed to Wilson for advice. What should he do, what could he do ? Poor, gallant soldier, we thought such worlds of him. Wilson could only answer " slog on, just slog on." On March 17, which was Oates's birthday, he walked out to his death in a noble endeavour to save his three companions beset with hardships, and as Captain Scott himself wrote, " It was the act of a brave man and an English gentleman—we all hope to meet the end with a similar spirit, and assuredly the end is not far."

Scott, Wilson, and Bowers fought on until March 21, only doing about 20 miles in the four days, and then they were forced to camp 11 miles south of One Ton Depot. They were kept in camp by a blizzard which was too violent to permit them to move, and on March 25 Captain Scott wrote his great message to the public :

MESSAGE TO THE PUBLIC

The causes of the disaster are not due to faulty organisation, but to misfortune in all risks which had to be undertaken.

1.—The loss of pony transport in March, 1911, obliged me to start later than I had intended, and obliged the limits of stuff transported to be narrowed.

2. The weather throughout the outward journey, and especially the long gale in 83° S., stopped us.

3. The soft snow in lower reaches of glacier again reduced pace.

We fought these untoward events with a will and conquered, but it cut into our provision reserve.

Every detail of our food supplies, clothing, and depots made on the interior ice sheet and over that long stretch of 700 miles to the Pole and back worked out to perfection. The advance party would have returned to the glacier in fine form and with surplus of food, but for the astonishing failure of the man whom we had least expected to fail. Edgar Evans was thought the strongest man of the party.

The Beardmore Glacier is not difficult in fine weather, but on our return we did not get a single completely fine day ; this with a sick companion enormously increased our anxieties.

As I have said elsewhere we got into frightfully rough ice, and Edgar Evans received a concussion of the brain—he died a natural death, but left us a shaken party, with the season unduly advanced.

But all the facts above enumerated were as nothing to the surprise which awaited us on the Barrier. I maintain that our arrangements for returning were quite adequate, and that no one in the world would have expected the temperatures and surfaces which we encountered at this time of the year. On the summit in Latitude 85° 86° we had - 20° - 30°. On the Barrier in Latitude 82°,

10,000 feet lower, we had $-30°$ in the day, $-47°$ at night pretty regularly, with continuous head wind during our day marches. It is clear that these circumstances come on very suddenly, and our wreck is certainly due to this sudden advent of severe weather, which does not seem to have any satisfactory cause. I do not think human beings ever came through such a month as we have come through, and we should have got through in spite of the weather but for the sickening of a second companion, Captain Oates, and a shortage of fuel in our depots, for which I cannot account, and finally, but for the storm which has fallen on us within 11 miles of the depot at which we hoped to secure our final supplies. Surely misfortune could scarcely have exceeded this last blow. We arrived within 11 miles of our old One Ton Camp with fuel for one last meal and food for two days. For four days we have been unable to leave the tent—the gale howling about us. We are weak, writing is difficult, but for my own sake I do not regret this journey, which has shown that Englishmen can endure hardships, help one another, and meet death with as great a fortitude as ever in the past. We took risks, we knew we took them ; things have come out against us, and therefore we have no cause for complaint, but bow to the will of Providence, determined still to do our best to the last. But if we have been willing to give our lives to this enterprise, which is for the honour of our country, I appeal to our countrymen to see that those who depend on us are properly cared for.

Had we lived, I should have had a tale to tell of the hardihood, endurance, and courage of my companions which would have stirred the heart of every

Englishman. These rough notes and our dead bodies must tell the tale, but surely, surely a great rich country like ours will see that those who are dependent on us are properly provided for.

(Signed)   R. SCOTT.

This chapter would be incomplete without Wilson's own beautiful lines from the *South Polar Times* :

THE BARRIER SILENCE

The Silence was deep with a breath like sleep
   As our sledge runner slid on the snow,
And the fateful fall of our fur-clad feet
   Struck mute like a silent blow.
On a questioning " hush," as the settling crust
   Shrank shivering over the floe ;
And the sledge in its track sent a whisper back
   Which was lost in a white-fog bow.
And this was the thought that the Silence wrought
   As it scorched and froze us through,
Though secrets hidden are all forbidden
   Till God means man to know.
We might be the men God meant should know
   The heart of the Barrier snow,
   In the heat of the sun, and the glow
   And the glare from the glistening floe,
As it scorched and froze us through and through
   With the bite of the drifting snow.

CHAPTER XVII

THE SECOND WINTER—FINDING OF THE POLAR PARTY

THE foregoing story of triumph and disaster going hand in hand to Scott dwarfed the remaining chapters of the Expedition's history into insignificance. I venture, however, to give a *résumé* of what was happening elsewhere in this region at the time.

The Norwegian explorers commenced their trip homeward to Framheim in the Bay of Whales, a distance of 870 English miles, on December 17, 1911, and made the amazing marching average of 22½ miles a day for this distance.

On January 25, 1912, at 4 a.m., Amundsen's men regained the shelter of their winter quarters, when poor Scott was still only 30 miles from the Pole on his return journey.

This undoubtedly establishes the superiority of dogs in great numbers for Polar sledge travelling, for Scott delayed his start on account of the inability of his ponies to face the severity of the Barrier weather conditions before November 1. Peary in the North had already with dogs achieved what Amundsen did in the South. Captain Amundsen has always expressed his wonder at our performance—and in his modest way he told me he himself could never have manhauled as Scott's men did.

Concerning the attempts to support the Southern party, Scott's instructions were quite clear, and they were certainly obeyed. As a matter of fact there was never any anxiety felt for the Southern party until after March 10. They themselves never imagined they would reach Hut Point before that time, and as the last supporting party had won through short-handed, and after pulling in harness for 1500 miles, it was not considered likely that the Southern party would fail—unless overtaken by scurvy.

What actually happened was this. Stores were landed by those at the base station on the re-arrival of the *Terra Nova*, and Atkinson, who was the senior member of those not now returning in her to civilisation, took over the dogs according to Scott's directions. He proceeded to Hut Point with Dimitri and the two dog teams on 13th February, and was kept in camp by bad weather until 19th, when Crean reached the Hut and brought in the news of my breakdown and collapse at Corner Camp. A blizzard precluded a start for the purpose of relieving me, but this expedition was undertaken immediately the weather abated. It was only during a temporary clear that Lashly and I were rescued.

Considering my condition, Atkinson judged that if help could be obtained from Cape Evans, his duty was to stay with me and save my life if possible, and to depute Cherry-Garrard or Wright to take the dog-teams out to One Ton Camp with Dimitri.

Scott would have preferred Wright to remain at Cape Evans, because he had now relieved Simpson as physicist—Simpson being recalled by the Indian Government.

So it was decided that Cherry-Garrard should take out the teams, which he did, with twenty-four days' food for his own unit and two weeks' surplus stores for the Southern party, with all kinds of special delicacies.

The real object of this trip was to hasten the Southern party's return rather than to succour them.

Cherry-Garrard and Dimitri had a tough time of it. They, however, reached One Ton Camp on March, and were held there by blizzard weather, which made travelling impossible. Temperatures of 40° below zero and lower were experienced, the dogs were suffering acutely, and Cherry-Garrard had to decide on the better course—to remain at One Ton Camp, which Scott would surely make, if thus far north, with two competent navigators in his team, or to scout and risk missing the party, whilst using up the dogs' remaining strength. He very properly remained at One Ton Camp and made his depot on 10th March, and after satisfying himself that over a month's travelling rations were in the depot, Cherry-Garrard started homeward, but he had by no means a sinecure in this journey back— his dogs went wild at the start, smashed the sledge-meter adrift, fought, and would keep no definite direction, thick weather set in, and they had a fearful time marching northwards.

The season was rapidly closing, and without the practice in fog navigation which the naval officers had, the situation of the unit was alarming. The two men got into severe pressure and found great open crevasses—this with their dogs ravenous and out of hand. Dimitri practically collapsed, and being unable to express himself properly in English, one can picture what Cherry-Garrard had to contend with. Late on March 16 they won through to Hut Point in exceedingly bad condition. Atkinson was seriously alarmed, and had two more sick men to nurse back to strength.

The dogs were frost-bitten, gaunt, and quite unfit for further work that season. Meantime during the absence of the dog teams, before there was anxiety on Scott's account, Pennell, responding to Atkinson's letter for help, brought the *Terra Nova* up towards Hut Point, and a party under Rennick conveyed me in pitiful state to the ship in my sleeping-bag.

I was placed in the Captain's cabin, and given Drake and Day as nurses. I owe them a great debt too. Atkinson had still to remain at my side, for I was even then at death's door—and it is only due to Atkinson's unremitting care that I am alive to-day. He came up therefore in the ship and participated in the search for Campbell in the vicinity of Evans's Coves, but after several unsuccessful attempts the *Terra Nova* temporarily abandoned her objective and returned to Cape Evans on March 4. Here Keohane was picked up and taken with Atkinson to Hut Point—Pennell relieved Atkinson of further responsibility on my account and then landed him with Keohane here. It was impressed on Atkinson that there was very little chance of relieving Campbell with ice conditions as they were. They laid up a store of seal meat and blubber against the return of Scott's company, while the ship made another fruitless attempt to relieve Campbell. She did not return South after this on account of the sea freezing and her own coal shortage, but proceeded back to New

Zealand, in accordance with her Commanding Officer's instructions. Pennell was not justified in keeping the *Terra Nova* any later in the McMurdo Sound.

Now let us consider poor Atkinson. He had Dimitri and Cherry-Garrard at Hut Point in a state of collapse—he had on 16th March the knowledge that the Polar Party were still on the Barrier with a season closing in and a certainty of low temperature —there was no communication with Cape Evans, for the ice had gone out and left open water between the two positions. After discussing the situation fully, Atkinson and Keohane started out alone to succour Scott's party. It was on March 26 that Atkinson and Keohane set out, this being later in the year than we had sledged in 1911, when it will be remembered we gave up depot-laying on account of the hardship entailed, although we were fresh men and had not undergone the severe test of a long season's sledge work. Atkinson could only manage about nine miles daily, he and Keohane got practically no sleep owing to the cold, and they turned homeward after depositing a week's food supply at Corner Camp, in case it could be made use of. Atkinson was morally certain that the Polar Party had perished by this time, and, as he states in his record of proceedings ("The last year at Cape Evans, *Scott's Last Expedition*, Vol. II."), Scott's last diary entry was made before he and Keohane reached Corner Camp. Atkinson arrived back at Hut Point on April 1, 1912, utterly worn out, and in great concern on Campbell's account, for the Northern party were known to be somewhere on the coast. He could do nothing without assistance from Cape Evans, and he awaited, therefore, the opportunity of reaching the base station as we all had done when stranded at Hut Point twelve months previously. On April 10, leaving Cherry-Garrard to tend the dogs, Atkinson, Keohane, and Dimitri made their way to Cape Evans via the Castle Rock, Glacier Tongue route, as described in the earlier part of this narrative, but, as it happens, under almost unparalleled conditions, for they sailed over the ice, riding on their sledge, such was the excellence of the sea-ice surface.

The indefatigable Atkinson called the members together to discuss plans and decide as to future relief work. The idea of making a farther journey on to the Ice Barrier to succour Scott was rejected as useless—for there was no hope whatever for the Southern party, and Atkinson himself knew what the Barrier travelling was like. There was, however, a chance of relieving Campbell and his five companions, known to have been set ashore in the neighbourhood of Terra Nova Bay, and with this end in view, Atkinson, Wright, Keohane, Williamson, Gran, and Dimitri set off on April 13.

The last two were left at Hut Point whilst Atkinson and the other three worked round the Southern end of McMurdo Sound on the sea-ice and up the coast to Butter Point. It was a dangerous proceeding, but Atkinson was undaunted by the perils of the sea ice breaking up, and he carried out a tip-and-run sort of journey with great pluck and endurance, establishing a depot of a fortnight's foodstuffs at Butter Point. On April 20 the ice was seen to break up and drift seawards from Butter Point, thus finally putting a stop to any further search or relief work. A somewhat hazardous return journey landed Atkinson's team at Hut Point, and his whole party was re-collected at the Cape Evans Base by May 1 with the dogs.

Here Lashly was looking after the seven mules presented by the Indian Government, which the ship had brought down to enable Scott to explore further the extent of the Victoria Land Coast, S.E. of the Beardmore.

Everything at Cape Evans in the scientific line was carried on as in the preceding winter, and although the staff was reduced the records and observations were continued as heretofore.

The Second Winter Party consisted of:

Officers—Atkinson, Wright, Debenham, Nelson, Cherry-Garrard, Gran. *Men*—Archer, Williamson, Crean, Lashly, Keohane, Dimitri, Hooper.

Mr. Archer, our capable chief cook and steward, replaced Clissold, and Williamson exchanged with Forde. The winter work of the Hut was re-organised by Atkinson, so that every one was detailed to do that for which he was best suited. Considering what the party had faced already, that they were living in the shadow of a great disaster, and that Campbell's fate was in doubt, one must feel that in a way they had the hardest time of all in the Expedition. They had to sit down, as it were, and wait in uncertainty for the winter to pass, then go out in search to ascertain the fate of their leader, and probably that of Campbell.

I can only give a brief summary of the second winter, taken from Atkinson's and Gran's accounts: the weather was probably exceptional from the persistency of the early winter blizzards. There was a great dearth of seal-meat, due to the ice blowing out from the North Bay and to the lack of ice everywhere in May month.

Debenham gave great joy to the company after examining the geological specimens brought by Atkinson's supporting party from the Beardmore. Fossils of plants and small marine animals were found amongst them.

Ice formed at the end of May, but again blew out in June—close on to midwinter, when the sea was seen to be phosphorescent, and Atkinson writes: "We had a wonderful show of phosphorescence—we saw a seal chasing a school of fish, the fish outlined with phosphorescence, and the seal with a glowing snout and all his body bright in hot pursuit."

On midwinter day, after the attendant festivities, Atkinson called the members together and outlined his plans for the coming season.

He says, "Two alternatives lay before us. One was to go South and try to discover the fate of Captain Scott's party. I thought it most likely that they had been lost in a crevasse on the Beardmore Glacier. Whether their bodies could be found or not, it was highly desirable to go even as far as the Upper Glacier Depot, nearly 600 miles from the Base, in the hope of finding a note left in some depot which could tell whether they had fulfilled their task or turned back before reaching the Pole. On general grounds it was of great importance not to leave the record of the Expedition incomplete, with one of its most striking chapters a blank.

"The other alternative was to go West and North to relieve Campbell and his party, always supposing they had survived the winter. If they had come through the winter every day of advancing summer would improve their chances of living on in Terra Nova Bay. At the same time there was good prospect of their ultimately being relieved by the ship, if indeed she had not taken them off in the autumn. As for ourselves, it seemed most improbable that we could journey up the coast owing to the abnormal state of the ice. Instead of being frozen for the winter, the whole Sound to the north and west of Inaccessible Island was open water during July ; the ice was driven out by the exceptionally strong and frequent winds, and there was little chance of a firm road forming for the spring. Under these conditions officers and men unanimously supported the decision to go South."

An important fact is noted by Atkinson which is worth including for the guidance of future expeditions. Six new sledges came down per *Terra Nova* from Messrs. Hagen of Christiania, with tapered runners—the breadth of the runner in front being 4 inches, diminishing to $2\frac{1}{2}$ on the after part of the sledge. Compared with our original 12-foot pattern the new sledges contrasted to great advantage over the old. The idea seems to be that the broad iron portion should run over and smooth the track for the after tapered portion.

The sun returned after its four months' absence on August 23 and found the little party in excellent health and cheerful spirits. The mules and dogs had been carefully exercised to be ready and fit for the new journey South. A depot was laid 12 miles south of Corner Camp in mid-October, and another by the dogs soon after. On October 29 Wright, Nelson, Gran, Lashly, Crean, Williamson, Keohane, and Hooper left with six mules, sledges, and a considerable provision store to search for Captain Scott and the Polar Party. Atkinson followed with Cherry-Garrard and Dimitri on 1st November, taking the best available dogs in two teams. Without any great trouble they reached One Ton Camp on November 10, having joined forces with the mule party. Atkinson notes that here he found, as we had done before, an oil shortage from paraffin tins in the depot leaking, although there was no hole discernible. Some stores had been spoilt in consequence. On the morning of 12th November the party found what they sought—Scott's tent, snowed up and presenting a cairn-like appearance.

From Gran's diary the following is taken :

" It has happened—horrible, ugly fate, only 11 miles from One Ton Depot, Scott, Wilson, and Birdie. All ghastly. I will never forget it as long as I live : a terrible nightmare could not have shown more horror than this ' Campo Santo.' In a tent, snow covered to above the door, we found the three bodies. Scott in the middle, half out of his bag, Birdie on his right, and Uncle Bill on the left, lying head towards the door. . . . Bowers and Wilson seem to have passed away in a kind of sleep. . . . Concerning our unlucky Polar Party we learned that Petty Officer Evans died at the Lower Glacier Depot ; he was done, and had fallen coming down the Glacier : death was the result of a concussion of the brain. On the Barrier they met with extreme low temperatures. Down to − 50° in the night time for weeks, also head wind.

" ' Soldier ' had got his feet frost-bitten badly and suffered enormously. He understood that the salvation of the party depended on his death—but as death would not relieve him he went out of the tent in a blizzard to meet it. The three others arrived here at this camp March 21 with food for two days and fuel for one meal. A terrible blizzard prevented them from getting in, and on March 29 all was finished.

" Scott writes in his diary : ' There is no more hope, and so God look after our people. . . .' All this only a day's march from plenty. . . . We buried them this morning, a solemn undertaking. How strange it was to see men bareheaded whilst the wind blew with the thermometer at −20°. We are now going to look for ' Soldier ' and then return to look for Campbell. I must say our Expedition is not given much luck . . . the sun is shining beautifully in this place of death : over the Bluff this morning stood a distinct cross in clouds."

It continues : " November 12, Lunch time :

" We have built a cairn—a 12-foot cairn—and put a cross made of a pair of skis on it. . . ." Gran says later, and it is worth quoting : " When I saw those three poor souls the other day, I just felt that I envied them. They died having done something great. How hard death must be for those who meet it having done nothing."

Atkinson in his account says :

" We recovered all their gear and dug out the sledge with their belongings on it. Amongst these were 35 lb. of very important geological specimens which had been collected on the moraines of the Beardmore Glacier : at Doctor Wilson's request they had stuck to these up to the very end, even when disaster stared them in the face and they knew that the specimens were so much weight added to what they had to pull. . . ."

The following record was left :

"November 12, 1912, Latitude 79 degrees, 50 minutes, South. This cross and cairn are erected over the bodies of Captain Scott, C.V.O., R.N., Doctor E. A. Wilson, M.B., B.C., Cantab., and Lieutenant H. R. Bowers, Royal Indian Marine— a slight token to perpetuate their successful and gallant attempt to reach the Pole. This they did on January 17, 1912, after the Norwegian Expedition had already done so. Inclement weather with lack of fuel was the cause of their death. Also to commemorate their two gallant comrades, Captain L. E. G. Oates of the Inniskilling Dragoons, who walked to his death in a blizzard to save his comrades, about eighteen miles south of this position ; also of Seaman Edgar Evans, who died at the foot of the Beardmore Glacier. " The Lord gave and the Lord taketh away ; blessed be the name of the Lord.' "

This was signed by all the members of the party.

" I decided then to march twenty miles south with the whole of the Expedition and try to find the body of Captain Oates. For half the day we proceeded south, as far as possible along the line of the previous season's march. On one of the old pony walls, which was simply marked by a ridge of the surface of the snow, we found Oates's sleeping-bag, which they had brought along with them after he had left.

" The next day we proceeded thirteen miles more south, hoping and searching to find his body. When we arrived at the place where he had left them, we saw that there was no chance of doing so. The kindly snow had covered his body, giving him a fitting burial. Here, again, as near to the site of the death as we could judge, we built another cairn to his memory, and placed thereon a small cross and the following record: " Hereabouts died a very gallant gentleman, Captain L. E. G. Oates of the Inniskilling Dragoons. In March, 1912, returning from the Pole, he walked willingly to his death in a blizzard, to try and save his comrades, beset by hardships. This note is left by the Relief Expedition of 1912.' "

Atkinson writes also, and it should be inserted most certainly here, referring to their return after hunting for poor Oates's body :

" On the second day we came again to the resting place of the three and bade them there a final farewell. There alone in their greatness they will lie without change or bodily decay, with the most fitting tomb in the world above them."

Atkinson could not have expressed himself more beautifully. My book should end here, but there is an epilogue to it : it is the illuminating story of Campbell and his northern party, with a short indication of what was done elsewhere by the Expedition's men.

The homeward journey was made in sorrow and doubt, for Atkinson's little band of brothers had to shoulder another responsibility—the determination of Campbell's fate.

On November 27, 1912, Gran's diary gives as follows :

" Great news again—great, good news. Campbell here and his party safe at Cape Evans. They just missed us going out. They lived a winter *à la* Eskimo, Igloo and so on, and have been quite comfortable, so they say. Campbell is looking very well. He is now in command, and intends to do only small trips—Erebus and so on. . . ."

Atkinson now handed over to Campbell, and whilst mentioning this it is just as well to call attention to the splendid services of Dr. Atkinson. Grit and loyalty were his outstanding qualities. He was later on specially promoted to Surgeon Commander for his work in the Expedition.

CHAPTER XVIII

ADVENTURES OF THE NORTHERN PARTY

To set forth concisely the adventurous story of Campbell's Northern Party in a single chapter is no light task. Raymond Priestley has written it in book form already, just as Griffith-Taylor has published his particular narrative of the Western Journey in *The Silver Lining*. Both books are of absorbing interest to those who are fond of Polar literature.

I have, I hope, made clear the reason of Campbell's landing at Cape Adare. Mr. Borchgrevink in his *Southern Cross* Antarctic Expedition used this position as his winter quarters, and found, just as Campbell did, that it was not a suitable part of the Antarctic continent for making extensive sledge journeys from. Still, King Edward's Land was denied him. Amundsen was established before him in the Bay of Whales, and in spite of diligent search the Cape Adare choice was the only one left to Victor Campbell and his five companions. Scott's instructions have already been reproduced in this volume : he mentioned Robertson Bay, and Cape Adare is at the N.E. extreme of the Promontory bounding the Bay to the East-ward.

Campbell was by no means satisfied with his landing place, but coal was short in the *Terra*

Nova and the season drawing in. He had vainly searched for a more profitable wintering place, and it was not until February 17 that he got his chance of landing here even.

The party and their stores were put ashore on the beach which the *Southern Cross* Expedition had chosen, for want of a better spot where their stuff could be set safely on land. Loose ice and surf hampered operations, for owing to shallow water, boats had to convey hut, gear, and equipment from the ship instead of sledges taking it over fast ice, as was the case at Cape Evans. It was truly a case of bundling Campbell and Co. out of the ship, and only their great optimism and *bonhomie* kept this party from despair. As it turned out they had some of the best of the Expedition game, since neither disaster nor terrific disappointment dogged their steps as in Scott's case, for up till the very last they were in blissful ignorance of our dreadful plight in the main party.

The old huts left by Borchgrevink in 1900 were much dilapidated : one snowed up inside, and the other roofless and full of penguin guano. The snow was all removed from the snow-choked hut, and this shack used as a temporary shelter during the building of the Château Campbell. The work of landing stores from the *Terra Nova* was accomplished in two days, and the ship, after tooting a farewell to the little party on her siren, steamed away and left them to their own devices.

The Cape Adare locality is a famous penguin rookery, and Campbell's men might for all the world have been erecting their hut on Hampstead Heath during a Bank Holiday, for the penguins gathered in their thousands around them in a cawing, squawking crowd.

Penguins are the true inhabitants of Antarctica, and have flourished for countless ages in these parts. Surgeon Levick, Campbell's doctor, has written a splendid little book entitled *Antarctic Penguins* (Heinemann), which tells all about the little beggars in popular language. The members landed with Lieutenant Victor Campbell were :

Levick	.	.	.	Surgeon and Zoologist.
Priestley	.	.	Geologist.
Abbott	.	.	.	Seaman.
Browning	.	.	Seaman.
Dickason	.	.	Seaman.

The three seamen were chosen by Campbell after careful observation on the outward voyage.

The Northern Party Hut was completed and first inhabited by March 5. An ice house for the storage of fresh meat was constructed, or rather hollowed out of an iceberg grounded close to. Unfortunately, this had to be evacuated owing to a surf causing the berg to disintegrate, and as Campbell puts it, " we had only just time to rescue the forty penguins with which we had stocked it, and carry the little corpses to a near ice-house built of empty cases filled with ice."

To appreciate best the surrounding hereabouts one may as well give a brief description of the Cape Adare and Robertson Bay environment. The place on which the hut was built is a small triangular beach cut off from the mainland by inaccessible cliffs. A fine bay, containing an area of perhaps nine hundred square miles, lies to the westward, and south and behind this the Admiralty Range of Mountains rises in snowy splendour to heights of

K

10,000 feet or more ; other ranges are visible far to the westward, whilst black basalt rocks overhang the station.

Several wall-faced glaciers are visible, but according to Campbell none are possible to climb on to, nor do they lead up to the inland plateau. On this account the party were unable to accomplish any serious sledging whilst landed here. Other things were undertaken, and the members did excellent meteorological, geological, and magnetic work, while Campbell himself made some good surveys. Priestley has added greatly to our geological knowledge, and he, with his previous Antarctic experience, made himself invaluable to his chief. The Aurora observations show much more variegated results than we got at Cape Evans, where, as pointed out, there was a great absence of colour beyond pale yellow in the displays.

The principal drawback of the beach here was its covering of guano and manure dust from the myriads of penguins and their predecessors. I had gone ashore at Cape Adare as a sub-lieutenant on January 8, 1903, to leave a record, and I remember that we had literally to trample on the penguins to get across the beach to Borchgrevink's hut—how interesting it all was, my first landing on this inhospitable continent : my impressions left a wonderful memory of mouse-coloured, woolly little young of the Adelie penguin—I even remember taking one away and trying unsuccessfully to bring it up. It must have taken Campbell's crew a long time to get accustomed to the pungent odour thereabouts. Levick dressed the ground with bleaching powder to help dispel that dreadful

odour of guano before Campbell's men put down
their hut floor.

There is little to be set down concerning the
Cape Adare winter—the routine much resembled
our own winter routine at Cape Evans ; it was
much warmer, however, and being six degrees
farther north the sun left the party nearly a month
later and returned the same amount earlier ; they
had little more than two months with the sun
below the horizon in fact.

There is a certain amount of quiet humour about
Campbell's record ; for instance, he states that they
used their " pram " or Norwegian skiff and tried
trawling for biological specimens on March 27—
" our total catch was one sea-louse, one sea-slug,
and one spider."

It is very interesting to note that in March they
had Aurora in which " an arc of yellow stretched
from N.W. to N.E., while a green and red
curtain extended from the N.W. horizon to the
zenith."

The " pram " was Campbell's gift to the Expedition. He was always alive in the matter of small
boats and their uses, and he was the first to use
" kayaks " by making canvas boats to fit round the
sledges ; these were light enough and might have
well been used by us in the Main Party. Had poor
Mackintosh possessed one in Shackleton's last
expedition he and his companions would probably
have saved themselves—if they had carried a canvas
cover on a sledge with them—however it is always
easy to be wise after the event.

Levick's medical duties were very light indeed :
they included the stopping of one of Campbell's
teeth, and the latter says, " As he had been flensing

a seal a few days before, his fingers tasted strongly of blubber."

Priestly took charge of the meteorology for this station in addition to his own special subjects.

Abbott was the carpenter, Browning the acetylene gas-man, and Dickason the cook and baker. With these ends in view Mr. Archer had had Dickason in the galley on board during the outward voyage.

This hut of theirs was stayed down with wire hawser on account of the gales recorded by the *Southern Cross* Expedition.

The company's alarm clock, an invention of Browning's, deserves the description taken from Campbell's diary : " We have felt the want of an alarm clock, as in such a small party it seems undesirable that any one should have to remain awake the whole night to take the 2–4 a.m. observations, but Browning has come to the rescue with a wonderful contrivance. It consists of a bamboo spring held back by a piece of cotton rove through a candle which is marked off in hours. The other end of the cotton is attached to the trigger of the gramophone, and whoever takes the midnight observations winds the gramophone, ' sets ' the cotton, lights the candle, and turns the trumpet towards Priestley, who has to turn out for the 2 a.m. At ten minutes to two the candle burns the thread and releases the bamboo spring, which being attached to the trigger, starts the gramophone in the sleeper's ear, and he turns out and stops the tune ; this arrangement works beautifully and can be timed to five minutes."

Curiously enough Campbell's men sustained far more frostbites than we at Cape Evans did : in all

my four Antarctic voyages I have never been frost-
bitten beyond a touch here and there on the finger-
tips working instruments, yet I occasionally now get
chilblains in an ordinary English winter.

A short expedition was made by Campbell,
Priestley, and Abbott on July 29, to determine
the travelling condition and find out what sort
of surface would be met with for coastwise sledging
to come when the season opened. Speed worked
out at little over seven miles a day on the outward
trip to Duke of York Island. The salt-flecked,
smooth ice was heavier going than much rougher
stuff where pressure obtained.

On August 8 a small two-day geological expedition was undertaken, and prepared to start on a
more extensive journey westward ; the party were
disappointed to find the ice had all blown out and
left them water-girdled ; a blizzard of unusual
violence followed the exit of ice, and the storehouse
roof was torn away.

It must have been a severe blow to the energetic
Campbell that he was denied serious sledging while
quartered at Cape Adare. Minor expeditions were
undertaken and some useful information gleaned,
but unsafe ice and unsatisfactory conditions all
round prevented any of the really long journeys
Campbell would otherwise have made.

The *Terra Nova* was sighted on January 4, and in
two days Campbell, his party and belongings were
safely on board and proceeding along the coast eager
to try their fortunes farther South, Evans Coves in
Latitude 75° being the next objective. The ship
was placed alongside the Piedmont here on January
8, near a big moraine close north of the Coves.
A depot of provisions was established, and an

arrangement was come to between Pennell and Campbell that the latter should be picked up on February 18. A map of Victoria Land should be referred to in order to see where Campbell was working.

It was proposed to sledge round Mount Melbourne to Wood Bay, and examine the neighbourhood geologically and geographically. The sledge team found some remarkable ice structures and new and interesting glaciers. They had a crop of small adventures, and found sandstone rock containing fossil wood and many other excellent fossils, garnets, etc., besides which Campbell did good work surveying. A new glacier was named after Priestley and another after Campbell.

More fossils were discovered on February 1, and a quantity of lichens, shells, worm casts, and sponge spicules were discovered in the locality of Evans Coves, to which the party returned. On February 17 they began to look for the *Terra Nova*, but as time went on and she did not put in an appearance Campbell prepared to winter. Pennell as we know had met with ice conditions that were insuperable, and he never got the ship within 30 miles of the coast. Pennell, Rennick, and Bruce did all that men could do to work the *Terra Nova* through, but communication was impossible that season, and the Northern Party was left to face the rigours of a Polar winter with nothing more than four weeks' sledging ration and 270 lb. of biscuits extra. His companions could not have been better chosen to help Campbell through this ordeal. The leader knew his men absolutely, and they themselves were lucky in having such a resourceful and determined officer in charge.

On March 1 Victor Campbell selected a hard snow slope for the winter home, and into this he and his men cut and burrowed until they had constructed an igloo or snow house, 13 feet by 9. They insulated this with blocks of snow and seaweed. A trench roofed with sealskins and snow formed the entrance, and at the sides of this passage they had their store rooms and larder.

All the time this house was under construction a party was employed killing penguins and seals, for which they kept a constant lookout. By March 15 their larder contained 120 penguins and 11 seals. After this date gale succeeded gale and the winter set in with a long run of bad weather. Campbell and his companions led a very primitive existence here for six and a half months.

They only had their light summer sledging clothes to wear, and these soon became saturated with blubber : their hair and beards grew, and they were soon recognisable only by their voices. Some idea of their discomforts will be gleaned by a description of their diet. Owing to their prospective journey to Cape Evans, Campbell had first to reduce the biscuit supply from eight to two biscuits a day, and then to one.

Generally their diet consisted of one mug of " pemmican and seal hoosh " and a biscuit for breakfast, *nothing* for lunch, a mug and a half of seal, one biscuit and three-quarters of a pint of thin cocoa for supper. On Sundays weak tea was substituted for cocoa, this they re-boiled for Mondays' supper, and the dried leaves were used for tobacco on Tuesdays.

Their only luxuries were a piece of chocolate and twelve lumps of sugar weekly, and twenty-five raisins apiece were kept for birthdays. One lucky find was thirty-six fish in the stomach of a seal, which fried in blubber proved excellent. The biscuit ration had to be stopped entirely from July to September. The six men cooked their food in sea-water as they had no salt, and seaweed was used as a vegetable. Priestley is reported to have disliked it, and no wonder, for it has probably rotted in the sun for years, and the penguins have trampled it all down, apart from anything worse.

Campbell kept a wonderful discipline in his party, and as they were sometimes confined to the igloo for days, Swedish drill was introduced to keep them healthy. A glance at their weather record shows how necessary this was. We find one day snowing hard, next day blowing hard, and the third day blowing and snowing hard, nearly all through the winter. But there was never a complaint.

On Sunday divine service was performed, which consisted of Campbell reading a chapter of the Bible, followed by hymns. They had no hymn book, but Priestley remembered several, while Abbott, Browning and Dickason had all been at some time or other in a choir.

To add to their discomfort, owing to the state of their clothing and meagre food supply, they were very susceptible to frostbites, and Jack Frost made havoc with feet, fingers, and faces.

We should here give a little thought to the dark dreariness of their surroundings. This party was not so very far north of Cape Evans, and their winter was only about three weeks shorter if measured by the sun's absence below the horizon —the contrast between the " palace " at Cape

Evans and the ice-cave at Campbell's position is ridiculous, and to think that the little crew remained cheerful and in harmony under such troglodyte conditions, it makes one wonder more and more at the manner of the men. They had none of the comfort, entertainment, and good feeling of their co-explorers at the base, the very dimensions of their habitation explains for itself the cramped nature of their existence, and yet no complaints, and nothing but unswerving loyalty to their boss. Weaker minded men would have broken down mentally under the strain of living through that winter.

The sunlight went at the beginning of May, gradually leaving them with those peculiar drawn-out half lights, which we all grew to know so well—the whimpering purple clouds, the sad-looking hills, and the desolate ice slopes and snow drifts—the six men were imprisoned with sullen hills and unassailable mountains for jailers, until they had undergone their sentence, the sea their chief jailer, for the sea had set them there and it was for the sea to decide on the time of their release.

Boots had long since given out, and they had to guard against ruining their finneskoe or it would have been good-bye to any sledging round to Cape Evans when the sea did freeze. Seal blubber was utilised for cooking, and whenever seals were killed the chunks of this greasy stuff had to be carried to the igloo on the men's backs—this meant that their clothes soon smelt very badly, which circumstance added to the misery of their living conditions.

On May 6 Campbell's party sustained a severe disappointment, for they saw what appeared to be four men coming towards them. Immediately they jumped to the conclusion that the ship had been frozen in and that this was a search party. The four figures turned out to be Emperor penguins, and although disappointing in one way they served to replenish the larder, and so had their use.

Here are three specimen diary pages extracted from Campbell's journey:

April 9.—Warmer to-day. We saw a small seal on a floe but were unable to reach him. The bay remains open still. On the still days a thin film of ice forms, but blows out as soon as the wind comes up. In these early days, before we had perfected our cooking and messing arrangements, a great part of our day was taken up with cooking and preparing the food, but later on we got used to the ways of a blubber stove, and things went more smoothly. We had landed all our spare paraffin from the ship, and this gave us enough oil to use the primus for breakfast, provided we melted the ice over the blubber fire the day before. The blubber stove was made of an old oil tin cut down. In this we put some old seal bones taken from the carcasses we found on the beach.

" A piece of blubber skewered on to a marline-spike and held over the flame dripped oil on the bones and fed the fire. In this way we could cook hoosh nearly as quickly as we could on the primus. Of course the stove took several weeks of experimenting before it reached this satisfactory state. With certain winds we were nearly choked with a black, oily smoke that hurt our eyes and brought on much the same symptoms as accompany snow-blindness.

" We take it in turns to be cook and messman,

working in pairs : Abbott and I, Levick and Browning, Priestley and Dickason, and thus each has one day on in three. The duties of the cooks are to turn out at 7 and cook and serve out the breakfast, the others remaining in their bags for the meal. Then we all have a siesta till 10.30, when we turn out for the day's work. The cook starts the blubber stove and melts blubber for the lamps. The messman takes an ice-axe and chips frozen seal-meat in the passage by the light of a blubber lamp. A cold job this and trying to the temper, as scraps of meat fly in all directions and have to be carefully collected afterwards. The remainder carry up the meat and blubber, or look for seals. By 5 p.m. all except the cooks are in their bags, and we have supper. After supper the cooks melt ice for the morning, prepare breakfast, and clear up."

" *May* 7.—A blizzard with heavy drift has been blowing all day, so it was a good job we got the penguins. We have got the roof on the shaft now, but in these blizzards the entrance is buried in snow, and we have a job to keep the shaft clear. Priestley has found his last year's journal, and reads some to us every evening.

" From now till the end of the month strong gales again reduced our outside work to a minimum, and most of our energies were directed to improving our domestic routine.

" We have now a much better method for cutting up the meat for the hoosh. Until now we had to take the frozen joints and hack them in pieces with an ice-axe. We have now fixed up an empty biscuit tin on a bamboo tripod over the blubber fire. The small pieces of meat we put in this to thaw : the larger joints hang from the bamboo. In this way they thaw sufficiently in the twenty-four hours to cut up with a knife, and we find this cleaner and more economical.

" We celebrated two special occasions on this month, my wedding day on the 10th, and the anniversary, to use a paradox, of the commissioning of the hut on the 17th, and each time the commissariat officer relaxed his hold to the extent of ten raisins each.

" Levick is saving his biscuit to see how it feels to go without cereals for a week. He also wants to have one real good feed at the end of the week. His idea is that by eating more blubber he will not feel the want of the biscuit very much."

" *July* 4.—Southerly wind, with snow, noise of pressure at sea and the ice in the Bay breaking up. Evidently there is wind coming, and the sea ice which has recently formed will go out again like the rest. It is getting rather a serious question as to whether there will be any sea ice for us to get down the coast on. I only hope that to the South of the Drygalski ice tongue, where the south-easterlies are the prevailing winds, we shall find the ice has held. Otherwise it will mean that we shall have to go over the plateau, climbing up by Mount Larsen, and coming down the Ferrar Glacier, and if so we cannot start until November, and the food will be a problem.

" We made a terrible discovery in a hoosh to-night : a penguin's flipper. Abbott and I prepared the hoosh. I can remember using a flipper to clean the pot with, and in the dark Abbott cannot have seen it when he filled the pot. However, I assured

every one it was a fairly clean flipper, and certainly
the hoosh was a good one."

In this diary are some remarkable entries.
Attempts were made to vary the flavour of the
" Hooshes "—one entry is very queer reading : it
related how after trying one or two other ex-
pedients Levick used a mustard plaster in the
pemmican and seal stew. The unanimous decision
was that it must have been a linseed poultice, for
mustard could not be tasted at all, yet the flavour
of linseed was most distinct.

Campbell says that Midwinter Day gave them
seasonable weather, pitch dark, with wind and a
smothering drift outside. The men awoke early
and were so eager and impatient for their full
ration on this special occasion that they could not
remain in their sleeping-bags, but turned out to
cook a " full hoosh breakfast " for the first time
for many weeks that evening they repeated the
hoosh and augmented it by cocoa with sugar in it,
then four citric acid and two ginger tabloids. The
day concluded with a smoke and a sing-song, a
little tobacco having been put by for the
event.

Soon after Midwinter Day a heavy snowstorm
blocked the igloo entrance completely ; in consequence the air became so bad that the primus stove
went out and the lights would not burn. The
inmates had to dig their way out to avoid being
suffocated. This impoverishment of air had already
happened through the same cause on other occasions, so the flickering and going out of the lamps
warned immediately of danger, and a watch was
set. Normally the chimney would have served,

but this itself was buried under the snow until built up afresh.

The winter passed in dismal hardship, and even when the rare spells of fine weather occurred the party dare not venture far afield in their meagre, oil-saturated clothing—severe frostbite would have spelt disaster.

What the place must have looked like by moonlight I hate to think ; by daylight with sunshine it looked bad enough, but from Levick's description it looked, when the moon was shining through storm cloud, like an inferno, with its lugubrious ridges, its inky shadows, and wicked ice-gleams.

The odd figures of the blubber-smeared, grimy men added the Dante touch.

The sun came back at last, and with it the party's spirits rose considerably ; they indulged in bets and jokes at one another's expense. Browning and Dickason were undoubtedly the wittiest, and " the fish supper bet " is worth inclusion. Short said these two started an argument on the name of a certain public-house situate on Portsmouth Hard. One said one name, one argued another, until Dr. Levick was invited to settle the dispute by arbitration, the loser to stand the winner a fish supper. Eventually Browning was adjudged to be correct, and Dickason in a fit of generosity shouted, " All right, old man, and for every fish you eat I'll stand you a quart of beer." " Right-o, the only fish I cares for is whitebait," replied Browning.

Towards the end of the winter, owing to the unusual diet, sickness set in in the shape of enteritis. Browning suffered dreadfully, but always remained cheerful. The ravages of the illness weakened the party sadly, and details are too horrible to write

about—suffice it that the party lost control of their
organs, a circumstance that rendered existence in
their wintering place a nightmare of privations.

Preparations were made for the party's departure
in the spring and the sledges overhauled. A depot
of geological specimens was established and marked
by a bamboo.

A curious ailment developed itself, which was
named " Igloo Back," from constant bending in the
low-roofed igloo. It was due to the stretching of
the ligaments around the spine and was a painful
thing for the " cave-dwellers."

Campbell and his companions started for Cape
Evans on September 30. Progress was slow and
the party weak, but thanks to their grit and to
Campbell's splendid leadership, the Northern Party
all got through to the winter quarters alive.
Browning had to be carried on the sledge part of
the way, but fortunately they picked up one of
Griffith-Taylor's depots, and the biscuit found here
quite altered Browning's condition

Poor Campbell was glad to get his party out of
the dirt and dark of the igloo, but they were so
weak that they could only march a mile from the
first day, however the sledging ration contained
good foodstuff compared to what they had eaten
for weeks previously ; and, oh, wise precaution !
Campbell had deposited a small store of spare
wind clothing and woollen underclothes against
the journey over the sea to Cape Evans. This he
issued on leaving that awful " Igloo," and the
luxury of getting into dry, clean clothing after
the greasy rags they discarded was indescribable.
For nine months had they worn those dirty garments without change.

The second day homeward at most gave five miles, but although tired out the party were in good spirits " at leaving the dirt and squalor of the hut behind." They were making their way south along the coast, sledging over the " Piedmont." Shortly after starting, the company were faced with an enormous crevasse, but this was safely negotiated by means of a snow bridge " 175 paces across." Pace gradually lengthened and strengthened, and on 12th October 11 miles was covered, and on camping Erebus and Mount Melbourne were both in sight.

I do not propose to write a description of this journey back, it was not so dangerous as others had been, because seals and Emperor penguins were met with along the route, and so they ran no risk of starving ; but they ran a great risk of losing Browning, who caused the doctor the gravest concern. They laboured home, however, and the leader's diary for one Red Letter, and Two Black Letter days must be included here, for they explain themselves :

" *October* 29.—Turned out at 4.30 a.m. A fine day, but a bank of cloud to the south and a cold westerly wind. A two hours' march brought us to Cape Roberts, where I saw through my glasses a bamboo stuck on the top of the cape. Leaving the sledges, Priestley and I climbed the cape, when we found a record left by the Western Party last year before they were picked up, and giving their movements, while near by was a depot of provisions they had left behind. We gave such a yell the others ran up the slope at once. It seemed almost too good to be true.

" We found two tins of biscuits, one slightly broached, and a small bag each of raisins, tea, cocoa, butter, and lard.

" There were also clothes, diaries, and specimens from Granite Harbour. I decided to camp here and have a day off.

" Dividing the provisions between the two tents, we soon had hoosh going and such a feed of biscuit, butter, and lard as we had not had for nine months, and we followed this up with sweet, thick cocoa. After this we killed and cut up a seal, as we are getting short of meat and there is every prospect of a blizzard coming on.

" Levick and Abbott saw a desperate fight between two bull seals to-day. They gashed each other right through skin and blubber till they were bleeding badly.

" We had another hoosh and more biscuit and lard in the evening ; then we turned into our bags and, quite torpid with food, discussed our plans on arriving at Cape Evans. We had quite decided we should find no one there, for we believed the whole party had been blown north in the ship while trying to reach us. Still discussing plans we fell asleep.

" What with news from the main party and food (although both were a year old), it was the happiest day since we last saw the ship. I awoke in the night, finished my share of the butter and most of my lard, then dozed off again."

" *November* 6.—Another fine day. We marched till 1 p.m., when our sledge broke down, the whole runner coming off. As we were only one mile from Hut Point I camped. Priestley, Dickason, and I walked in to look for news and get another sledge, as I was sure some would be there.

"As we neared the Point we noticed fresh tracks of mule and dogs. I pointed them out to Priestley, and said, 'I hope there is nothing wrong with the Pole Party, as I do not like the look of these.' He said, 'No more do I.' We ran up to the hut and found a letter from Atkinson to the 'Commanding Officer, *Terra Nova.*' I opened this and learnt the sad news of the loss of the Polar Party. The names of the party were not given, and finding Atkinson in charge of the search party which had started, I was afraid 2 units, or 8 men, were lost. Finding a sledge only slightly damaged, I took that back to the camp, getting back there about 5 p.m.

"We were all rather tired, so instead of starting straight on to Cape Evans, we had supper and went to sleep. Before turning in we made a depot of the broken sledge, all rock specimens, clothes and food, so as to travel light to Cape Evans. I was very anxious to get there as soon as possible, as I thought there was a chance that there might be one or two mules or enough dogs to enable me to follow the search party. It had been a great disappointment for us to have missed them by a week, as we were all anxious to join in the search."

"*November 7.*—4 a.m. A lovely morning. After a hasty breakfast we were off, arriving at Cape Evans at 5 p.m. We found no one at home, but a letter on the door of the hut gave us all the news and the names of the lost party. Very soon Debenham and Archer returned, giving us a most hearty welcome, and no one can realise what it meant to us to see new faces and to be home after our long winter.

" Our clothes, letters, etc., had been landed from the ship, and we were able to read our home letters, which we had only time to glance at in the ship in February. Archer provided a sumptuous dinner that night, and we sailed into it in a way that made Debenham hold his breath. A bath and change of clothes completed the transformation."

CHAPTER XIX

NARRATIVE OF THE " TERRA NOVA "

THE second ascent of Mount Erebus was carried out in December, 1912, by a party under Raymond Priestley, and although it cannot be described in a little volume like this a really fine scientific journey was made by Griffith-Taylor, Debenham, Gran, and Petty Officer Forde. They had the best time of the lot, for they carried out their explorations in blissful ignorance of the tribulations of Scott, Campbell, Atkinson and myself, whose stories I have tried to summarise.

For breezy reading and real bright narrative commend me to Griffith-Taylor. Volume II. of *Scott's Last Expedition* contains the story of the " Western Journeys " as written by him, and they give quite truly the Silver Lining to the Cloud which formed about the rest of our Expedition.

For lightheartedness and good fellowship our Australian geologists should be given first prize.

It is of little use writing about distances covered and dangers overcome in this connection, but if one considers that the Western Geological Party surveyed, examined, charted, photographed, and to some extent plodded over a mountainous, heavily glaciated land lying in an area of the entire acreage of Kent, Sussex, Hants, Dorset, Devon, and Cornwell, one gets a fair idea of what " Griff " and Co. were playing at.

Taylor was the first professional physiographer to visit the Antarctic Continent, and besides being an all round man of science he was an admirable fellow, with the widest outlook on life of any man amongst us.

I cannot pretend to write on geology ; Taylor, Debenham, and Priestley are still drawing up reports on Antarctic physiography and glacial geology on our fossils collected, on the Barrier Movement, and the retreating ice of that Frozen Wonderland. Some day another expedition, more up to date than ours, will force its way into the Heart of that Frigid Zone. If this expedition sets out soon. I hope I may command it when I am still fresh and fit—if that great good fortune comes my way I shall telegraph to Griff and ask him to be my " Uncle Bill," and to help me as Wilson helped Scott.

As this is only a popular version of the last Scott Antarctic Expedition I have not collected any scientific appendices, and I have tried not to throw any bouquets at one member more than another if I have failed I have done it accidentally, for one has no favourites after nearly ten years. My especial friends in the Expedition were the lieutenants, Campbell, Pennell, Rennick, Bowers, and Bruce, and of the scientists I was most fond of Nelson.

The concluding part of this narrative is concerned with our little ship, for which we had such affection.

To connect the story up one must go back to the time when on March 3, 1912, the *Terra Nova* made her last call for the year at Cape Evans—here she embarked those members returning home, who for various causes had not been collected before. Then it will be remembered that Keohane was taken to Hut Point and landed with Atkinson, and afterwards, owing to the thickening up of the ice in McMurdo Sound, the ship's head was turned Northward. The ice conditions off the Bay where Campbell was landed were terrific, and the little whaler had a tough time forcing her way out into the Ross Sea once more after failure to relieve him.

She arrived in New Zealand on April 1, to learn of Amundsen's success, and I went home a physical wreck with Francis Drake, the secretary, to carry out Scott's wishes in the matter of finance. It was many months before I could get about in comfort, but my wife nursed me back to health. Several scientific and other members dispersed to their respective duties in civil life. Pennell temporarily paid off the seamen who had joined in New Zealand, and took the ship away to survey Admiralty Bay in the Sounds according to arrangements made with the New Zealand Government. During this operation we had the great misfortune to lose by drowning Stoker Petty Officer Robert Brissenden.

Finally the little *Terra Nova* filled up with coal and left for the South to pick up Scott and his expedition. She was once more under my command as her original Captain, Pennell very gracefully and unselfishly standing down to the position of second in command.

The programme included an extensive sounding cruise, guided to some degree by what Professor David of Sydney University wished for, to throw further light on the great earth folds. The voyage was like its predecessors, except that we purposely kept in Longitude 165 W. to sound over new portions of the ocean, every opportunity being taken to gain fresh information and fulfil the requirements of the biological programme too. We had hardly our share of gales this voyage, and although we expected to meet with the pack in about 66 S. Latitude, it was not reached until we had attained the 69th parallel—two degrees farther South than we had found it in the *Terra Nova's* first two voyages.

The only other expedition that had explored the Eastern part of the Ross Sea so far was that under Ross in the *Erebus* and *Terror*. We did not gain anything by forcing the pack so far East, however, for we encountered a heavy belt of ice through which we fought our way for 400 miles.

The weather mostly served us well, and great credit is due to Rennick, Lillie, and Pennell for their sounding, biological, and magnetic work respectively—they were indefatigable, and even though it blew hard on occasions, thanks to Rennick's expert handling of the Lucas machine we obtained several soundings in 3000 fathoms when less ardent hydrographers would have surrendered to the bad weather.

January 15 found us passing through loose pack —sometimes the ship was in large open leads—we stopped on one of these and sounded. To our surprise we found 368 fathoms, volcanic rock—in 72° 0′ S., 168° 17′ W. we found the depth 2322 fathoms, so we had struck the continental shelf right enough in Latitude 73°. By 8 p.m. we were in even shallower water—in fact we discovered a shoal in only 158 fathoms—it was a great discovery for us, and Lillie immediately put over the Agassiz trawl. After dragging it along the bottom for half an hour we hauled in and found the net full of stuff. Big-mouthed fish, worms, spiders, anemones, sea-cucumbers, polyzoa, prawns, little fish like sardines, one spiky fish like nothing on earth, starfish and octopus, limpets with jointed shells, sponges, ascidians, isopods, and all kinds of sea lice. Enough to keep Lillie busy for weeks.

The evening before we finally broke through into open water was beautifully still, and a low cloud settled down in the form of a thick fog—it was a change from the fine, clear weather—frost rime settled everywhere, and for a time we had to stop. There was a weird stillness over all, and whenever the ship was moved amongst the ice-floes a curious hiss was heard ; this sound is well known to all ice navigators : it is the sear of the floe against the greenheart sheathing which protects the little ship, and it is to the ice-master what the strange smell of the China Seas is to the far Eastern navigator, what the Mediterranean " cheesy odours " and the Eucalyptus scents of Australia are to the P. and O. officers, and what the pungent peat smoke of Ireland is to the North Atlantic seaman. I suppose the memory of the pack ice hissing around a wooden ship is one of the little voices that call—and they sometimes call as the memory of " a tall ship and a star to steer her by " calls John Masefield's seamen " down to the sea again." I sometimes feel a mute fool at race meetings, society dinner parties, and dances, the lure of the little voices I know then at its strongest. It is felt by the Polar explorer in peace times and in the hey-day of prosperity, and it is surely that which called Scott away, when he had everything that man wants, and made him write as he lay nobly dying out there in the snowy wild :

" How much better has it been than lounging in too great comfort at home."

But this is yielding dream to my narrative, and I must apologise and continue with the closing chapter.

After this fog, which held us up awhile, we got into one more lot of pack varying in thickness and containing some fine long water lanes, and then we made for Cape Bird, which we rounded on January 18, to find open water right up to Cape Evans.

A tremendous feast was prepared, the table in the wardroom decked with little flags and silk ribbons. Letters were done up in neat packets for each member, and even champagne was got up from the store : chocolates, cigarettes, cigars, and all manner of luxury placed in readiness.

The ship was specially scrubbed and cleaned, yards were squared, ropes hauled taut and neatly coiled down, and our best Jacks and Ensigns hoisted in gala fashion to meet and acclaim our leader and our comrades. Glasses were levelled on the beach, and soon we discerned little men running hither and thither in wild excitement ; a lump stuck in my throat at the idea of greeting the Polar Party with the knowledge that Amundsen had anticipated us, it was something like having to congratulate a dear friend on winning second prize in a great hard won race—which is exactly what it was. But it was not even to be that : the ship rapidly closed the beach, engines were stopped, and a thrill of excitement ran through us. The shore party gave three cheers, which we on board replied to, and espying Campbell I was overjoyed, for I feared more on his behalf than on the others, owing to the small amount of provisions he had left him at Evans Coves. I shouted out, " Campbell, is every one well," and after a moment's hesitation he replied, " The Southern Party reached the South Pole on the 17th January, last year, but were all lost on the return journey—we have their records." It was a moment of hush and overwhelming sorrow—a great stillness ran through the ship's little company and through the party on shore.

I have been reminded of it particularly on the anniversaries of Armistice Day.

The great silence was broken by the order to let the anchor fall : the splash which followed and the rattle of the chain gave us relief, and then Campbell and Atkinson came off in a boat to tell us in detail how misfortune after misfortune had befallen our leader and his four brave comrades. Slowly and with infinite sadness the flags were lowered from the mastheads and Scott's little *Terra Nova* stood bareheaded at the Gate of the Great Ice Barrier.

From the bridge one heard the occasional clatter of plates and cutlery, for the steward was busy removing the table dressings and putting away the things that we had no heart for any longer. The undelivered letters were taken out of the bunks, which had been spread with white clean linen for our chief and the Polar team, and Drake sealed them up for return to the wives and mothers who had given up so much in order that their men might achieve.

A great cross was now carved of Australian jarrah, on which was carved by Davis :

In
Memoriam
CAPT. R. F. SCOTT, R.N.,
DR. E. A. WILSON, CAPT. L. E. G. OATES, INS. DRGS.
LT. H. R. BOWERS, R.I.M.,
PETTY OFFICER E. EVANS, R.N.,
Who Died on their
Return from the
Pole—March,
1912.
To Strive, To Seek,
To Find,
And Not To
Yield.

This cross was borne on a sledge over the frozen
sea to Hut Point, and thence carried by Atkinson,
and those who had taken part in the search for
Captain Scott, to the top of Observation Hill,
which is in full view of Cape Evans, and also of
Captain Scott's original winter quarters in the
Discovery Expedition. The cross overlooks also
his resting place : The Great Ice Barrier.

As there is nothing to cause this wooden cross to
rot, it will remain standing for an indefinite time.

We left a year's stores for a dozen people at
Cape Evans and re-embarked the remainder of our
possessions.

The collections and specimens were carefully
stowed in our holds, and then we took the ship to
Cape Royds and Granite Harbour, where geological
depots had been made by Priestley, Taylor, and
Debenham.

Finally we revisited Evans Coves, and secured
the ship to a natural wharf of very hard sea ice,

which stretches out some distance from the Piedmont.

Priestley here secured his party's geological dump, and while he was away the remainder of the expedition in little relays visited the igloo where Campbell and his party spent the previous winter. Concerning the igloo, the following are my impressions, taken from my diary :

" Never in my life have I experienced such sensations as I did on this occasion. The visit to the igloo explained in itself a story of hardship that brought home to us what Campbell never would have told. There was only one corner of it where a short man could stand upright. In odd corners were discarded clothes, saturated in blubber and absolutely black with smoke ; the weight of these garments was extraordinary, and how Campbell's party ever lived through what they did I don't know.

" Although the igloo was once white inside, blubber stoves had blackened it throughout. No cell prisoners ever had such discomforts. (Campbell's simple narrative I read aloud to Bruce from Campbell's diary. It was a tale of altruism and grit, so simply told, full of disappointments and privations, all of which they accepted with fortitude and never a complaint. I had to stop reading it as it brought tears to my eyes and made my voice thick—ditto old Bruce.) After spending half an hour at the igloo, and after Pennell had done some magnetic work, picked up our ice anchors and steamed away."

On 27th January, 1913, after breakfast, I called

the staff together in the wardroom and read out my plans for the future, officially assumed the command and control of the Expedition.

I then appointed Lieuts. Campbell, Pennell, Bruce, Surgeon E. L. Atkinson, and Mr. Francis Drake as an executive committee, with myself as president, to assist me in satisfactorily terminating the Expedition. I asked every member of the staff publicly if he had any questions to put, and also if he could suggest any better combination for the committee. As all were unanimous in the fairness of the selection, it stands. The minutes of the proceedings were taken down and my remarks placed verbatim among the records of the Expedition.

We left a depot of provisions at the head of the Bay, its position being marked by a bamboo and flag.

This depot contains enough foodstuffs to enable a party of five or six men to make their way to Butter Point, where another large depot exists.

Early on 26th January we left these inhospitable coasts, and those who were on deck watched the familiar rocky, snow-capped shores fast disappearing from view. We had been happy there before disaster overtook our Expedition, but now we were glad to leave, and some of us must have realised that these ice-girt rocks and mountains were not meant for human beings to associate their lives with. For centuries, perhaps for all time, no other human being will set foot upon the Beardmore, and it is doubtful if ever the great inland plateau will be re-visited, except perhaps by aeroplane.

When we left it was a " good-night " scene for most of us. The great white plateau and peaks were grimly awaiting winter, and they seemed to mock our departing exploring ship as though glad to be left in their loneland Silence.